JUST PLAIN MURDER

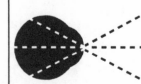

This Large Print Book carries the
Seal of Approval of N.A.V.H.

AN AMISH MYSTERY

JUST PLAIN MURDER

LAURA BRADFORD

THORNDIKE PRESS
A part of Gale, a Cengage Company

Farmington Hills, Mich • San Francisco • New York • Waterville, Maine
Meriden, Conn • Mason, Ohio • Chicago

LIBRARY OF CONGRESS CIP DATA ON FILE.
CATALOGUING IN PUBLICATION FOR THIS BOOK
IS AVAILABLE FROM THE LIBRARY OF CONGRESS

ISBN-13: 978-1-4328-5775-2 (hardcover)

Published in 2019 by arrangement with Berkley, an imprint of Penguin Publishing Group, a division of Penguin Random House LLC

Printed in Mexico
1 2 3 4 5 6 7 23 22 21 20 19

For Mom.
I love you.

ACKNOWLEDGMENTS

I can't tell you what a thrill it was to write another installment in this series. Claire, Jakob, Esther, Eli, Aunt Diane, Annie, and Ben hold a special place in my heart. And based on the emails I get on my website on a near daily basis, they do for many of you, as well. Thank you for that.

One of my favorite parts of being an author (aside from the writing part) is getting to meet my readers at book signings and reader events. One such reader event, Murder on the Menu in Wetumka, AL, had reader Lauri Biegler winning the opportunity to have her name used for a character of my choosing in my Amish Mysteries. Lauri, I hope you enjoy your turn in the literary spotlight!

A big shout-out is in order for my editor, Michelle Vega, and my agent, Jessica Faust. Their unwavering belief in me and my ability is invaluable. Thanks you, ladies!

And finally, if you have a moment, be sure to visit laurabradford.com to learn more about this series, as well as my new Amish-based women's fiction novel, *Portrait of a Sister.*

CHAPTER 1

She was on the porch when he drove up, the sight of his car, followed by his full-face smile as he spotted her, eliciting a dreamy sigh she was pretty sure hadn't come from her own mouth. A glance at the wicker chair to her right simply confirmed that observation.

"I heard that, you know." Claire Weatherly smoothed her hand over the simple late-summer dress she'd almost forgotten she owned and abandoned the porch swing. "And while I probably should say something about you being every bit as incorrigible as Grandma ever was, I'm just going to say I feel exactly the same way when I see him. Times a hundred."

Diane Weatherly stilled her knitting needles. "I wasn't looking at Detective Fisher, dear."

Claire darted her own attention back to the parking lot just long enough to confirm

Jakob had exited his car but was still just out of earshot. "You weren't?"

"No. I was looking at *you,* dear." Tucking her needles into the multicolored ball of yarn wedged between her knees, the sixty-two-year-old woman tilted her head down just enough to afford an uninhibited view of Claire across the top of her reading glasses. "One day, when you have a child of your own, you'll understand."

"That's mighty cryptic, Aunt Diane."

"It's just the best defense I can offer." Diane's thinning lips twitched with a grin just before her eyes led Claire's back to the handsome man now no more than three strides away from the porch steps. "Now, go give him a proper greeting so I can sigh in peace."

Claire tried to nibble back a laugh but it was no use. Instead, she closed the gap between them, kissed the top of her aunt's head, and then turned back toward the steps as a still-smiling Jakob reached the top. "You look mighty happy this morning. Is it from seeing me or knowing that *she* " — Claire hooked her thumb at first Diane and then the waiting picnic basket on the floor beneath the swing — "can't help but toss in a few extra goodies earmarked especially for you?"

"That depends. What are these *extra goodies* of which you speak?" Then, pulling her toward him before her answering gasp could gain much momentum, he stemmed the rest with a sweet kiss. "Mmmm . . . You taste good."

Bracing her hand against his chest, she stepped back just enough to ensure a front-row view of the dimple sighting she knew was near. "That's because those extra goodies that were *supposed* to be for you were really, really, *really* delicious . . ."

"Claire!"

"What?" She peeked back at her aunt. "Don't tell me he didn't have that coming."

"I *did* have that coming . . ." Jakob stepped around Claire, greeted Diane with a kiss on the cheek, and then claimed a spot on the porch swing. "That said, you were kidding, right?"

She joined him on the floral cushion. "I was if you were."

"Phew . . ." He rested his right arm along the back of the swing and found the perfect amount of sway with a practiced foot. "So, Diane . . . Guess who called me last night to say he's back in town for a few days?"

"Who?"

"Russ Granger."

A quick clap hijacked Claire's attention

11

back to the wicker chair and the woman whose smile rivaled the late-September sun. "Oh, Jakob, that's wonderful! I bet Callie and the children are positively thrilled!"

"Callie Davidson?" At her aunt's nod, Claire moved on, tidbits of information she'd managed to glean during her past eighteen-plus months in Heavenly falling into place a piece at a time. "That's the redhead that lives over by the playground, isn't it? The one with the three little tow-heads that couldn't be any cuter if they tried?"

Diane nodded. "That's right. And Russ is her father. He retired down to Florida close to ten years ago after —"

"Serving as chief of the Heavenly Police Department," Claire finished as she turned her focus back on her swing mate. "Oh, Jakob, no wonder you were smiling like that when you walked up! Your mentor is back in town!"

He nuzzled his chin against the side of her head and then leaned back to look out over the same fields that had served as a backdrop for his Amish childhood. "Trust me, Claire, that smile was all about you. Still, I'm pretty excited to see Russ again, too. It's been a long time. He wanted me to come out and meet him at Murphy's on

Route 65 when he called, but I was already in bed and I didn't want to take a chance of missing my alarm when it went off this morning."

"We could have rescheduled our picnic!" Claire protested. "Especially for something like seeing an old friend."

"I know that. But I didn't *want* to reschedule."

"Do you two keep in touch on the phone?" Diane asked as she transferred the yarn from her lap to the small table at her elbow.

"We try. And sometimes we go through spurts where we do pretty well with that. But more often than not, I'm busy, he's busy . . . You know how it is."

Hiking her calf onto the swing, Claire turned so her back was flush against the armrest and her view was of Jakob and her aunt. "Isn't Russ retired?"

"On paper, yes. But once a cop, always a cop."

"Meaning?" she prodded.

"Russ has police work in his blood. Which means he got himself hired on at the station in his new town inside the first month of being down there."

"But not as a chief," Diane interjected.

Jakob nodded. "Right. Not as a chief. According to him, he fiddles around at the front desk. Said it kept his finger on the pulse and him out of Amelia's hair."

"I take it Amelia is his wife?" At Diane's slow nod and downtrodden expression, Claire sighed. "And I take it she's since passed?"

"She did. About five years ago, I believe." At Diane's nod, Jakob continued. "He retreated for a while after that. Didn't return my calls, didn't acknowledge the notes I sent, et cetera. But eventually he got his feet back under him and he'd send me an occasional text to see how I was doing. When I told him I was considering coming back here if I could get a job, he pulled some strings and, well, here I am."

"Remind me to thank him." Claire rested her cheek against his hand, watching him as he appeared to drift away in thought. After a few moments of silence, though, he caught her looking at him and smiled. "So?" she asked. "When and where are you going to get to meet up with him again?"

"Tonight. At Heavenly Brews. Eight o'clock. And I'm kind of hoping you'll be with me when I do."

She drew back, surprised. "But you haven't seen him in what? Two years, at least?"

"Actually, it's been almost eight."

"Then you don't need me tagging along, Jakob," she protested. "Go. Spend time with him. Talk cop stuff, tell him all the great things you've done since you've been here in Heavenly — the cases you've solved. You can introduce us a different day, before he heads back home."

"I want him to meet you *now*, Claire. Besides, there's nothing Russ and I need to talk about that we can't talk about with you sitting at the table, too." Toeing the swing to a stop, he pushed his fingers through his sandy blond hair and laughed. "I'm telling you, Russ is quite a character. He sees everything and forgets nothing. It's one of the reasons he made a heckuva cop and chief."

She waited for his hand to return to his lap and then captured it inside her own. "So what you're telling me is he'll probably have some cute stories to share about you from your Rumspringa days?"

"Oh, no doubt. Stories I've long forgotten but he hasn't, I'm quite sure. Some that go back even before my Rumspringa, too."

"Before? But how? You weren't able to hang around the station until you were on Rumspringa, right?"

"True. But that doesn't mean I wasn't intrigued by men in uniform before that . . .

15

And Russ being Russ noticed, of course. He made sure to wave whenever he caught me peeking out at him from the back of Dat's buggy on the way through town." Jakob turned his hand inside hers so they could intertwine their fingers and then nudged his chin toward the Amish countryside in the distance. "Some of my fascination was simply because they looked different. I saw English from the back of Dat's buggy often, but police officers? Not so much. But it wasn't just about the uniforms and the shiny things hanging off them. It was the way they held themselves, the way they'd get down to eye level with English children we'd pass in town, and the way the English children looked back at them — like they were something special, something to be respected.

"I remember this time, when I was no more than six, maybe seven, and we were coming back from a horse auction or something. Dat was driving, of course, and I was sitting in the back of the buggy with Martha. We were heading down Lighted Way, which was nothing like it is today in terms of the number of stores. Anyway, this guy comes running out of a shop. And by running, I mean *running*. Anyway, a few seconds later, the shopkeeper comes out and starts yelling that this guy stole something from his store. Russ, who must have been sitting by an open window in the station house or something, comes running out, takes no more than a split second to get his bearings, and takes off after this guy. Before Dat's horse had all four feet on the gravelly part of the road just past what is now Yoder's Furniture, Russ had this guy on the ground with his hands behind his back." Jakob slid his gaze back to Claire's. "I . . . I don't think I can ever explain just how taken I was with that — how in *awe* I was of Russ and the entire police profession even though I wasn't supposed to be in awe of anyone other than God."

Extricating her fingers from his, she scooted across the swing until they were practically nose to nose. "You actually don't have to explain a thing, Jakob. It's written all over your face."

He laughed and pulled her close. "I can't wait for you to meet him," he said against her temple. "You're going to love him."

CHAPTER 2

"I don't think I could have imagined a better day than this, could you?" Claire leaned back against Jakob's chest and watched as the rock he'd been saving for last skipped across Miller's Pond four times before sinking below the surface. "Summer is still here, but fall is most definitely knocking at the door."

"Fall has always been one of my very favorite times of the year." Jakob wrapped his rock-skipping arm around Claire and pressed his cheek against hers, his words serving as a tour of a life she could never seem to learn enough about. "Sure, I loved coming here in the summer with Martha. Splashing around, skipping rocks, trying to swim to the other side . . . It was all good stuff. So, too, was winter and waiting for that moment when the ice was strong enough that we could play hockey with whatever stick we could find."

18

"What did you use as a puck?" she asked as her mind's eye tried to place the man she knew with the boy he was describing.

"Most of the time we used a flat rock, like the kind I was just skipping. A few times, we used one of my shoes. And once, we used a baseball hat we found on the side of the road."

"Your mother didn't mind you taking off out of the house with an extra shoe?"

"When we used a shoe, it was always one of the ones I was wearing."

She cocked her head up so she could see his face. "But if the ice was hard enough to stand on, wasn't it too cold to be taking your shoes off?"

"Amish boys at that age aren't much different than English boys. You see an opportunity to play, you play. No matter what."

Bringing her focus back to the water in front of them, she took in the sunlight dancing across the top, the squirrels chasing each other on the opposite shoreline, and the way the leaves on the nearby maple tree were beginning to hint at the autumn finery to come. Everywhere she looked, nature was at its best, but at that moment, thoughts of a young Amish Jakob, darting around the ice in one shoe, was all she could really see.

"So who did you play hockey with? Martha?"

His laugh rumbled against the back of her head. "Oh no . . . Martha would hang with the best of us when it came time for summer activities. But when winter came, she stuck close to home, preferring to read or work on a quilt during any free time we happened to have."

"Isaac?"

"No, not Isaac, either. By the time he was old enough to get out on the ice without worrying he'd do something silly, I was needed around the farm more."

"Ben?"

His chin nodded atop her head. "Man, we had such fun when we were kids."

She knew he was still talking, even managed to register the part about Ben donating his shoe on occasion, too, but mostly she was just thinking about the Amish man she called friend. Benjamin Miller was quiet, kind, hardworking, a phenomenal listener, and a respected member among his brethren. The fact that he'd actually proposed leaving his community to start a life with her the previous year had simply endeared him to her all the more. "Do you think he'll ever remarry?"

"I don't know. I hope so. Elizabeth has

been gone a long time." He released his hold on her long enough to push a strand of her auburn hair off his cheek. "I've seen him in the fields with the Stutzman boys and he's good with them. He *shows* them how to do things instead of just telling them, you know? Makes me think he'd make a good dad one day."

"I agree and . . ."

The rest of her sentence fell away as the *clip-clop* of an approaching horse claimed their collective attention and sent it toward the dirt pathway they'd navigated on foot not much more than two hours earlier. "Sounds like we're about to get some company."

"It does, indeed." Wiggling out from behind her, Jakob rose to his feet and then held out his hand to help her do the same. "C'mon, let's see who it is."

Together, they cleared the oak tree that had provided shade during their picnic, as well as back support for Jakob while they talked, and made their way toward the path. As they reached the edge, a familiar gray horse with a black mane and curly black tail stepped into their line of vision, pulling an equally familiar buggy.

Claire squealed. "Ooooh . . . It's Eli and Esther and the baby!"

Sure enough, Ben's younger brother, Eli, lifted his hand in a wave as his wife and Claire's former gift shop employee turned friend, Esther, broke out in a mile-wide smile. In her arms, nestled in a simple blanket, was their two-week-old daughter, Sarah.

Claire waited until Eli stopped the buggy under a grove of trees and then ran around to Esther's side. "Good afternoon, Esther! How is that precious little girl today?"

The smile Claire couldn't imagine being any bigger, grew exponentially. "She is good! She slept through her very first church service."

Esther exchanged a knowing smile with her husband, who, in turn, nodded like the proud new father he was. "It was a good thing, too. Mast had to be nervous enough without the fuss of a baby."

"Mast?" Jakob ran his hand down Carly's mane, darting his gaze between the animal and Eli as he did. "Is he a visiting bishop?"

"He is the new minister. As of today. It was between him, Bontrager, and Benjamin."

Jakob's answering whistle perked Carly's ears. "I can imagine Benjamin's relief when he heard it was not him."

For the first time since they came around

the corner, Claire peeled her attention off the blanketed bundle and looked from Eli to Jakob. "I didn't know Benjamin wanted to be a minister."

"No one *wants* to be minister," Jakob explained. "In fact, getting that tap on your shoulder, for lack of a better description, isn't necessarily a welcomed moment for the Amish."

"I don't understand. They're" — she motioned up to her friends on the buggy seat — "*you're* such God-fearing people."

Jakob gave Carly one more pat and then rejoined Claire. "Being minister or bishop is an added responsibility. They must still farm or do whatever it is they do to earn a living, but now they are also responsible for preaching and looking after the members of their district, as well." Rocking back onto his heels, he continued, his words stirring an occasional nod from Eli and Esther. "If the verse is in their hymnbook, they will do it, of course. It is something they vow to do when they are baptized. But *wanting* to do it and *doing* it are generally not one and the same in this case."

"But if Benjamin was being considered . . ." she prodded.

"His name was given to the bishop." Eli tucked the reins beside his feet and jumped

23

down from his seat. "Along with Mast and Bontrager."

"Given by whom?"

"People in the district. When there is a need for a new minister, everyone is asked to nominate someone and they do so, quietly. The top vote-getters become the candidates."

Eli took over for Jakob. "This morning, each opened their hymnbook to see if the slip of paper with the Bible verse was in theirs."

"Wait. So this is decided lottery-style?" Claire asked, glancing at Jakob. At his nod she turned back. "Wow. I had no idea."

Eli walked around the buggy and reached up for the baby. After a quick check of the blanket and a kiss on Sarah's head, Esther handed the newborn down to her husband as he continued. "It was Elmer Mast. He did not weep the way some do."

"Weep?" she echoed.

"You have to remember Claire, the Amish do not like to elevate themselves above others," Jakob said. "Being a minister is about leadership. It makes them uncomfortable. So if this Mast fella took it in stride, that's unusual but good."

She heard the name, even slightly registered a face to go with it, but at that moment all she could really focus on was the infant sleeping soundly in Eli's strong and capable arms. "Oh, Esther . . . Eli . . . I could look at that sweet face all day."

With little more than a grin, Eli transferred the baby to Claire's arms and then reached up to assist his wife down to the ground. Claire, in turn, blinked back the same tears she'd been unable to hold at bay during Esther's unexpected delivery at Sleep Heavenly earlier in the month. "Oh, Jakob, look . . . Isn't your great-niece absolutely precious?"

When he didn't respond, she looked up to see him watching her with a mixture of emotions she couldn't quite identify. "Jakob? Are you okay?"

"Yeah." He cleared his throat, stepped in beside her, and smiled down at Sarah. "I'm great. Just imagining, is all." Then, glancing back up at Eli, he got them back on track. "So this Mast fella? He really seemed okay with it?"

Eli nodded.

"Is he the one you told me about a few weeks ago?" Jakob slipped his arm around Claire, alternating his glances between the baby and Eli. "The one who came to look after the wife's kin and then opted to stay in Heavenly even after that kin passed?"

"Yah."

"And Bontrager?" Jakob asked. "Which one is he again?"

"John Bontrager . . . He farms the land across from mine. Has seven kids — all sons. Family keeps to themselves outside of Sunday service. Kind of surprised me to know his name came up to the bishop so many times."

"Especially when he has such trouble with Amos."

Claire glanced over at Esther. "Who is Amos?"

"John's oldest. He is on Rumspringa."

"Seven kids? Maybe it's best he didn't get the verse." Jakob pulled his hand from the baby's chin, stuck it inside the front pocket of his jeans, and pulled out his vibrating phone. "Oh, hey, it's the station. I better take this."

Claire watched him wander off toward the pond and then leaned forward to kiss Esther's cheek. "Can you three stay for a while? We haven't had our dessert yet and there's plenty for you and Eli."

"Eli?" Esther peeked at the baby and then smiled up at her husband. "Would that be okay?"

Eli motioned up at the sky. "Yah. It is the Lord's day, a day of rest and visiting."

Tightening her hold on the sleeping mound in her arms, Claire led the way toward the blanket and the picnic basket still housed in the shade of the largest oak tree. "I got up early and made a pan of brownies from a recipe of my aunt's. They have a drizzle of white chocolate on the top and the guests at the inn always seem to love —"

"Claire?"

Startled by the tone more than anything else, she looked over her shoulder, the sight of Jakob's ashen face sending a chill more befitting an early-December day down her spine. "Jakob, what's wrong? Has something happened?"

"I . . . it's . . ." He stumbled backward into a tree. "I . . . I have to take you home. Now."

"Is it Aunt Diane?" she murmured.

She heard Esther's gasp, even noted the flurry of movement that was Eli as he moved into place beside her, but at that moment all she really knew for sure was the blessed relief that came from the rapid shake of Jakob's head.

"Thank God! I thought that something . . ." The reality that was Jakob's widened eyes and wringing hands stole the rest of her sentence and had her passing

Sarah to Eli. "Jakob, please, tell me what's wrong."

Covering his mouth with his hand, Jakob squeezed his eyes closed for a second, maybe two. "I . . . I just can't believe it."

"Believe what?" Slowly, carefully, she captured his hand in hers and pulled it away from his face. "Jakob, please. Talk to me. Maybe I can help if you —"

"It's Russ."

"Your mentor?"

His answering nod was short, labored.

She glanced back at Eli and Esther, their confusion crossing into the same worry she felt clear down to her toes. "Jakob, I —"

He opened his mouth to speak only to close it in exchange for a hard, quick swallow. "He . . . he's *dead,* Claire."

CHAPTER 3

She was wide-awake and waiting when, at nearly two o'clock in the morning, she heard his footfalls on the exterior staircase that led from his parking spot behind Gussman's General Store to his second-floor apartment. Dropping her feet onto the living room floor, she made a mad dash toward the door in an effort to keep him from having to fiddle with the lock in the dark.

"I'm here," she said, swinging the door open.

Jakob jumped. "Claire!"

Something about the look in his eye and the way his hand moved to his hip sent an uneasy shiver through her body. "I'm sorry . . . I . . . I probably shouldn't have let myself in, but I was worried about you."

He righted himself with the help of the vestibule wall and then stumbled past her through the doorway. "No. It's fine. I gave you the key. I just didn't see Diane's car."

"It's out front. On the street."

"I didn't notice." Pulling her to him, he lingered a kiss against the top of her head. "I'm glad you're here, Claire. I really am. It's just really late and I hate that you've been waiting up for me this whole time instead of —"

She shushed the rest of his words away with a gentle kiss and then, stepping back, cupped his face in her hands. "Can I get you anything? A glass of water? A soda? Anything?"

"No." He slid her right hand around to his lips, kissed it, and then used it to lead her over to the couch. "Can we just sit? Together? I think I need that more than anything right now."

"Of course." She sank onto the cushion beside him, pulled the quilt off the back of the couch, and draped it across their laps. "How are you holding up?"

"I think I'm numb. I mean, I did everything I needed to do with the scene but I still just feel —"

"The *scene*?" she echoed, drawing back. "What *scene*?"

His Adam's apple jumped with his swallow. "Russ was murdered, Claire."

"Murdered?" she echoed. "But I thought his daughter found him . . . I assumed he

had a heart attack or something . . ."

"No," he said, only to wave his answer away. "I mean, *yes,* Callie found him, but it wasn't a heart attack."

"But h-how? W-when?" she stammered as her brain worked hard to catch up with her ears.

Cocking his head against the back of the couch, he stared up at the ceiling. "He was stabbed. Time of death appears to be sometime between two and four a.m. last night."

"Where did she find him?"

"Outside. Not far from the detached garage."

"At two a.m.?" She tugged the nearest throw pillow to her chest as she mulled his words. "Wait. That was the same night he was out at that bar he wanted you to come to, yes?"

Jakob nodded.

"Do you think someone may have followed him home from there?" she asked.

"I don't think so. The investigation is still early, of course, but the one thing I know for certain is that he'd been back in the apartment for a while before this happened."

"I thought he was staying with his daughter while he was in town."

"He was. Callie's place has an apartment

over the detached garage. She thought her father would get more sleep over there what with the kids being such early risers and all." He raked a hand through his hair and then released a sigh so long and so loud it echoed around the narrow room. "The only blessing in all of this is that her ex-husband took the kids to the park in the morning, arriving and departing with them via the main house. Kept the grandkids, if not his daughter, from seeing him like that."

She closed her eyes against her own memory involving a dead body and willed herself to breathe, to step outside her own head space and imagine what it would be like to find a loved one dead like that. Yet just as she did, her thoughts yanked her back to Jakob's words . . .

"Jakob?" She waited for him to look at her, but when he did, the pain she saw there was so raw, so intense, she had to look away for a moment just to maintain her composure. "How can you be so sure Russ had been back at his place for a while before this happened?"

He blinked hard and then stood, his feet taking him on a path toward the fireplace and the mantel adorned with a half dozen or so framed photographs that always made her smile.

The winter shot of Lighted Way . . .

The close-up picture of Eli and Esther's entwined hands on their wedding day . . .

The one of her making a snow angel in the snow . . .

The —

"He left me a voice mail after he got back from the pub. I didn't notice it until I was out at the scene." He smacked his hand down on the mantel so hard, the framed photograph Aunt Diane had taken of them on the swing earlier in the summer jumped. "He *called* me, Claire! At one o'clock in the morning. Because he wanted to talk! And me? I didn't *hear* the call come in because I'd left my phone out here." He swept his hand toward the end table next to the couch, his face contorted in disgust. "Then, on top of that, I managed to miss the message indicator when I looked at the phone in the morning before coming out to your place!"

"Jakob, it was *one a.m.* You were *sleeping.*"

"I'm a detective, Claire. Emergencies come in at all hours of the night. My phone should've been by the bed."

"It usually is, isn't it?"

"It *always* is." Again, he smacked the mantel, the sound of the frame falling over

33

muted only by his frustrated groan. "Except. Last. Night."

She'd never seen him quite like this. The anger. The regret. The self-loathing. More than anything, she wanted to go to him, to hold him until he let go of the parts that didn't matter in order to focus on the parts that did. But something inside her made her stay where she was, giving him the physical space he seemed to need.

Still, maybe a few questions would get him focused on what mattered most now. Her mind made up, she tossed the pillow back into its original place and leaned forward. "What did the message say?"

Something about the question or the sound of her voice seemed to snap him out of his funk long enough to see the knocked-over frame and right it. "I'm sorry, Claire. I'm not angry at you — *never* at you. It's just . . ." He stopped, took a deep breath, and then slowly turned. "He said that, come morning, he was going to be able to put in dibs on that fishing trip to Lake George I promised him a few years ago."

"Fishing trip?" she prodded.

"I don't know, Claire." He lowered himself to the hearth and dropped his head into his hands. "I mean, I remember talking about it at some point, but I can't, for the life of me, remember the context in which I said it or why on earth he'd call me at one in the morning to let me know he was ready to collect. It makes no sense and isn't ringing any of the bells I need it to ring right now."

She stood, crossed to the hearth, and squatted down in front of him. When he lifted his head, she grabbed his hands and held them tightly. "Jakob, you just lost someone very important to you. In the most horrible and unexpected way. You've been scouring a murder scene for hours. You're *exhausted.* No one can think clearly under those kinds of circumstances. *No one.* You need to try and get some sleep. None of what happened is going anywhere anytime soon. But maybe, with sleep, you'll be able to think — to remember the things you're trying to remember."

He hesitated as if he was going to argue, but, in the end, he nodded. "I know you're right. I really do. It's just that . . ." He inhaled slowly and quickly released the same breath with a whoosh. "I just don't know if I can sleep. I mean Russ is *gone,* Claire. I just can't wrap my head around it enough to believe it, you know?"

Pitching forward onto her knees, she rested her forehead against his. "I know. And I'm so sorry. But I'm here, and I know you're going to figure this out. I know it just as surely as I know I love you."

She tasted the saltiness of his single tear as he buried his head in her shoulder. For a while, she simply held him as he cried, and then, after several minutes, he mustered a deep breath and sat back, his eyes red. "Thank you, Claire. You have no idea what it means to have you here with me right now."

"There's nowhere I'd rather be than here with you." And it was true. Jakob was her future. She knew that. Believed it.

Hooking his finger beneath her chin, he managed a version of the smile that had gotten her through more than a few trials of her own. "I love you, too, Claire. And you're right. I *will* figure this out."

She was halfway between the inn and her shop when the vibration of her phone against her side led her to her purse. Reaching inside, she pulled out the phone, checked the screen, and held it to her ear.

"Hey, you . . ." At the sound of an approaching car, she held her free hand over her open ear. "How are you feeling? Did you get any sleep after I left?"

"I had no idea you'd left until I woke up shortly after nine."

"So that's a *yes* — good." She sidestepped a still-muddy rut from a hard rain the previous week and continued walking. "I stayed with you until you fell asleep and then I let myself out."

"You could have stayed. I'd have taken the couch."

"You needed some real sleep and I knew I needed to be at the shop by eleven this morning. This just made both those things easier."

She rounded the final corner between the inn and the Lighted Way shopping district and took a moment to breathe in the calming sight. The cobblestone roadway . . . The row of buildings, all painted white, lining both sides of the road . . . The English cars and Amish buggies parked behind one another in front of the shops . . . The hatted and unhatted passing each other on the sidewalks, each intent on whatever had brought them to the busy thoroughfare on that particular day.

Her gaze moved to the right side of the street and the shops that lined it — Glick's Tools 'n More, Shoo Fly Bake Shoppe, and, just beyond the mouth of the alleyway, her own Heavenly Treasures. A few steps past Glick's, Jakob's continued silence marched to the forefront of everything else.

"Jakob? Are you still there?"

"Yeah . . . yeah, I'm here. Sorry. Tom just dropped off the pictures from the garage apartment and . . ." His words gave way to what sounded like the shuffle of paper, followed by the telltale creak of his chair as he pushed back from his desk. "Claire, I've gotta go. I'll give you a call or stop by later."

And then he was gone, any residual background sounds muted by the rhythmic *clip-clop* of the horse pulling into the alley just ahead and the end button on the detective's phone. She quickened her steps past the bake shop and followed the charcoal-colored buggy toward the back of the buildings. When the buggy stopped, she was waiting.

"Hello, Martha." She slipped her phone into her tote bag and pulled out the envelope she'd carefully filled in the wee hours of the morning. "I have your money from last week's sales right here. And you did really well — not that that's anything out of the ordinary."

Martha dipped her kapped head in response and then rested the reins atop her lap. "I stopped by to see if Esther needed anything before I came to town."

"I planned to bring Esther's money to her after I close up this evening, but I can give it to you if that would be easier."

"I am sure she would enjoy a visit with you." Martha fiddled with the edges of her burgundy-colored dress for a few moments, her gaze moving from Ruth's bake shop, to Annie's horse, Katie, and finally onto Claire. "She spoke of seeing you and my brother by Miller's Pond after the church meal yesterday afternoon."

Unsure of what to say in light of the trouble Esther could get into for speaking to her banned uncle, Claire used her own glance back at the road to compose her thoughts. "Jakob and I were having a picnic by the pond when Eli and Esther drove up with the baby. I even got to hold her while she slept."

"That is good." Martha, too, looked back toward the road before dropping her voice to something just above a whisper. "Esther said news of a friend passing upset him? Is that so?"

Shielding the sun from her eyes, Claire looked directly at Martha. "It is. It was a man he knew as a child — during his Rumspringa and beyond. His name was —"

"Chief Russ?" Martha half whispered, half gasped.

"Yes."

Martha's hand flew to her mouth as her gaze flitted off Claire and onto the sky above. "Was he sick?"

"No. He was murdered."

This time, Martha's gasp was so loud a pair of birds inhabiting the trees behind Heavenly Treasures flew off. "But he was a good man! A good friend to Jakob! He . . ." Martha squeezed her eyes closed only to open them directly onto Claire. "He will need someone to listen. He will need *you,* Claire."

The emotion in the normally stoic woman took her by surprise and, for a moment, she wasn't sure what to say. On one hand, she wanted to encourage Martha to reach out to her brother herself. But on the other hand, she knew that wouldn't — *couldn't,* as Jakob was quick to remind — happen. Blood or not, the moment Jakob walked away from his baptismal vows to pursue a life among the English, his relationship with his sister was essentially null and void.

Still, life had a way of superseding the Ordnung on occasion, necessitating conversations in spite of the generations-old unwritten code that forbade them. Sometimes those conversations had been official — questions that needed to be asked and answers that needed to be given in relation to a crime that affected Jakob's former brethren. But sometimes, those same conversations led to something more genuine, like the shy smiles or seconds-long eye contact the detective treasured like others treasured warm hugs and affectionate pecks on the cheek.

It was the one part of Amish life Claire would never understand. The fact that someone as good and decent and honorable as Jakob was denied relationships with his loved ones because of a choice to protect and serve was simply too bitter a pill to swallow.

Yet every time she lamented that practice, it was Jakob who always defended it, reminding her that he'd known the repercussions of his decision when he opted to become a police officer after baptism. That the fault for the aftermath of that choice rested solely on himself.

"When Jakob first told me of his decision to leave, I was angry at Chief Russ. I believed it was *his* fault. That *he* was the reason I would no longer have Jakob as my brother."

"Jakob *is* your brother," Claire insisted. "His decision to become a police officer didn't change that. *Your reaction* to it did."

The second Martha stiffened, Claire knew she'd crossed a line. But for some reason, the apology she knew she owed the woman

41

wouldn't come. Instead, she let her rebuttal hang in the air as she handed the envelope up to Jakob's sister and then crossed in front of the buggy.

"He was baptized, Claire. He chose to leave."

At the base of her shop's steps, she turned back. "You're right. He did. Because a member of your community had been killed and he felt compelled to find answers. He didn't leave to sully God's name. He didn't leave to lead a sinful life or to speak ill of the Amish — quite the contrary, in fact. He is a man of honor and respect and loyalty to the people he holds most dear. Which, in case you're unaware, includes you, your parents, your brother, Isaac, your husband, your children, and now your grandchild."

She pulled open the screen door but stopped short of actually stepping through it as she looked back at Esther's mother one last time. "It was good to see you as it always is, Martha. The items you make to sell here at the shop are routinely my best sellers. I hope nothing I just said changes that, because I don't want it to. I treasure my friendship with you and with Esther. But I needed to say the things I just said. Not because I think anything will change, but because I just had to this one time. Your brother is very special to me. And I promise I will be there for him as he mourns the loss of his friend."

43

CHAPTER 4

There was something about watching Esther with her newborn that Claire found calming. Maybe it was the peaceful smile the new mother seemed to wear as effortlessly as the kapp on her head . . . Maybe it was the softly spoken Pennsylvania Dutch she cooed in the infant's ear as she moved about the kitchen preparing the evening meal . . . Or maybe it was simply being in the presence of such pure, unconditional love . . . Whatever it was, though, it was exactly what Claire needed in the wake of her conversation with Esther's mother in the alleyway.

Sure, she believed everything she'd said — believed it with her whole heart, actually. But knowing her words would have upset Jakob made shaking off the guilt she didn't want to feel even harder.

"Perhaps holding Sarah will help you to smile." Temporarily abandoning her one-armed dinner preparations, Esther strode over to the table. "Holding her always brightens *my* day."

Without so much as a hesitation, Claire accepted the baby from her friend and stared down at the perfect mixture of Eli and Esther. "Oh yes . . . This is exactly what I needed," she said, her tone hushed. "*Exactly* what I needed."

Esther fidgeted the side of her dress with her newly freed hand. "Is it true? What Mamm said when she came by again this afternoon? That my uncle's friend was murdered?"

"Yes."

Sinking onto the bench on the opposite side of the long wooden table, Esther closed her eyes for as long as it took to sigh. "I do not understand why people make choices that are for God alone to make. It is not right, it is not good."

"You're right, Esther. It's not right. And it's not good." She tucked the thin blanket under the baby's chin and tried her best to keep her posture at ease. "Jakob cherished that man and this is tearing him up inside."

Esther stood, made her away around to Claire's side of the table, and then squatted down beside her. "With you by his side, he will get through this. It is like it is for me

45

with Eli. When something goes wrong or I am worried about something, knowing I have Eli helps me to be stronger. It is that way for Jakob with you. I see it. Eli sees it, too."

"I hope you're right. I hate seeing him hurt like this." She lifted Sarah to her lips and then slowly, reluctantly, lowered her back down. "I think I may have upset your mother today and that wasn't my intent."

Esther's brow furrowed as she stood. "I am sure you did not upset Mamm. How could you?"

"By speaking of her relationship with Jakob when I know I shouldn't. It's just that . . ." She nibbled back the rest of her sentence and looked away.

"It is just what, Claire? Tell me."

Her eyes traveled back to Esther's. "I know it is the Amish way. I know this. But I hate watching him love all of you as fiercely as he does only to be held at arm's length — if he's even lucky enough to get that close — in return. It's heartbreaking to watch and almost as heartbreaking to have to stand by and accept it as" — she quoted her fingers around the baby — *"the way that it is."*

Esther's smile slipped from her face, taking the happy set to her shoulders and her overall demeanor with it. "I am sorry,

Claire. I do not mean to hurt my uncle. It is why I asked you to bring a guest to my wedding and hoped it would be Jakob. It is why I invite you to bring Jakob over for dessert sometimes — so we can sit on the porch and face out at the fields when we visit. I try to find ways even when I know I am not supposed to."

"And I'm a fool." Squeezing her eyes closed, Claire exhaled away her frustration. "I know you try. And I know the efforts you and Eli make mean the world to Jakob. I . . . I shouldn't have said any of that. It's just that, well, he's hurting right now and I don't know how to fix it. So I'm grasping at straws trying to fix something, *anything,* where he's concerned and now I've just made more problems."

"I'm sorry, Esther."

"Do not be. I would do the same for Eli." Esther pointed at a plate of cookies to the left of her mixing bowl. "When I worked at the shop with you, cookies always cheered you up. Perhaps they will still do the same?"

Claire smiled down at the baby, who was beginning to show signs of stirring. "Ohhh, Sarah, just wait until you are old enough to eat your mamm's cookies. They are the best."

"I think it is a good thing she can't

understand you." Esther plucked the plate from the counter and carried it over to the table and Claire. "Eli says I make too many cookies. Before Sarah, he thought I made so many because I was eating for two. But I am no longer eating for two and I still make many."

It felt good to laugh. It felt even better to see Esther's precious little girl open her eyes. "Ohhhh, I could sit here and hold this little one all day . . . She is so perfect."

"It is God who is perfect. Not man."

Startled, she looked up, her friend's kapp and aproned dress rooting her in a reality she'd almost forgotten. "I'm sorry, Esther. I . . . I didn't mean any harm. It's just" — she dropped her focus back to the now wide-eyed child in her arms — "that I'm kind of in love with your daughter."

"I am, too." Esther helped herself to an oatmeal cookie, broke off a morsel, and carried it down the short hallway to the front window. "I thought Eli would come inside when he saw that you are here. But — wait! I see him. He is speaking with Elmer and John."

Turning on her well-worn boots, Esther hurried back into the kitchen and over to a second, larger plate of cookies sitting on top of the refrigerator. She took it down, grabbed an empty plate from the cabinet, and carried both to the table. "I think there are enough here to put on two plates, don't you?"

Claire nodded even though Esther had moved on to dividing and redistributing, sans answer. "I didn't mean to make so many cookies while Sarah was napping this afternoon, but I just kept adding and stirring until I had more dough than I needed. I wanted to give some to Mamm when she stopped by again after her visit to town, but I forgot." The new mother stopped fussing with the cookies to peg Claire with a raised eyebrow. "Perhaps I should make three plates so you can take one?"

"No, no, it's okay. But who are *those* for?" she asked, pointing.

"The Bontragers have many mouths to feed."

"Bontrager," she repeated. "Why does that name sound familiar?"

"Because John is outside."

"No, I think — yes! I know! That's the one who owns the farm across the street, yes? The one you and Eli were talking about out at the pond yesterday?"

"Yah." Esther placed five cookies on the second plate, only to bring it back down to four just as quickly. "Elmer and Miriam do not have extra mouths. They will be fine with four."

Then, lifting both plates off the table, Esther motioned toward the door with her chin. "Come. We can say hello, and I can get rid of some of these before Eli wonders why I made so many."

Slowly, carefully, she stood with the baby and trailed Esther to the door. "Elmer is the one who *did* get the job of minister, right?"

"Yah."

"And you think he'll do a better job than your neighbor across the street?" She stepped out onto the porch and let her eyes travel the dirt lane to the trio of men at the end. Eli stood beside one man, while another sat on a buggy seat, sweeping his hand toward the fields on both sides of the road.

Esther led the way down the steps. "John would have done fine, I am sure. But there are many in our community who think he must focus on his son Amos."

"That's the son who is on Rumspringa, right?"

"Yah."

Rumspringa, she knew, was a window of time when Amish teens experimented with the ways of the English world. Most limited such experimentation to music and technology, but there were always a few who went too far. "I'm guessing the trouble John is having with the boy extends beyond the home?"

"Yah."

"And this Elmer? The one who *did* get the minister job?"

"Six months ago, the added work would have been difficult for Elmer, too, but it is different now. Good, even."

"What do you mean by different?"

"Elmer and Miriam do not need to look for Miriam's uncle in the fields or in the woods any longer. They do not need to sleep with one eye open or to put cans above the door to know when he got out. His passing was a blessing in that way."

Claire stopped making silly faces at the baby in the hope that would help her focus. But it didn't. "Cans above the door?" she echoed.

"Barley got to wandering the last year or so. In the beginning, when someone spotted him, he'd just say he was out walking. But by this time last year, before Miriam and Elmer came, he didn't say much when Eli would find him in places he shouldn't have been. He'd just stare and shake his head." Esther slowed long enough to peek at the baby before lowering her voice still more to keep from being overheard by the men now turning in their direction. "The cans were Elmer's idea. And it was a good one. Kept Barley safe right up until his passing over the summer."

"This Barley . . . Did he have Alzheimer's?" Claire asked.

"I think that's the word Miriam used. I just know he wasn't the Barley I remember growing up. *That* Barley knew everyone. The Barley *at the end* didn't know anyone. Not me, not Dat, not Mamm, not the bishop, not even Miriam and Elmer, themselves." Esther slowed her steps in a near-perfect match to the whisper she adopted. "Mamm said Barley started getting like that when he lost his wife. Said he couldn't think straight without her."

At about ten paces out, Esther cleared her throat, squared her shoulders, and smiled at Eli and his visitors across the remaining stretch of lane. "I saw you standing out here and thought I'd take a chance that you could both use some cookies in your home this evening. They're oatmeal."

"I won't turn 'em down." The hatted man on the buggy seat reached down, took the plate Esther handed up to him, and then patted his slightly rounded stomach. "I've always been partial to oatmeal. Though you won't catch me passing up chocolate chip, neither."

Esther returned his smile and then handed the other plate to the man standing beside Eli. "There's enough on here for your boys to have two each if they'd like, John."

The tall, lanky man took them but said nothing. If his lack of response bothered Esther as it did Claire, the Amish woman didn't let on. Instead, she spread her now-empty hands in Claire's direction. "This is my friend, Claire — Claire Weatherly. She owns Heavenly Treasures on Lighted Way. Claire, this is Elmer Mast" — Esther motioned first toward the buggy seat and then to the man standing beside Eli — "and this is John Bontrager. John and his wife, Liddy, farm the land across the street with their seven boys."

"*Seven* boys?" Claire repeated, grinning. "Wow, I imagine you must go through a lot of food."

"They eat what we put in front of them." John took a step toward the street and his farm but stopped as Eli waved him back.

"John, Claire might be someone you should get to know. She sells many things made by Amish in her shop. Esther's dolls and quilts and Martha's milk cans and wooden spoons, all sell well there. So, too, do Benjamin's birdhouses and my foot-stools. Might be a place for you to think about selling those doghouses you've taken to building."

Intrigue made her tighten her hold on the baby as she took a half step closer to Eli and Esther's neighbor. "You make dog-houses, John?"

"Yah."

"For big dogs or little dogs?"

"Both."

"A lot of the tourists seem to have little dogs," Claire mused. "Perhaps you'd like to leave one with me and we'll see how it goes. If it sells, we can talk about me taking more and —"

"I will sell them on my own."

His blunt reply had her recovering her step. "I'm sorry. I didn't mean to be pre-sumptuous."

"I'd think twice before being so hasty, John. Getting to put what you make on someone else's shelf sounds pretty worry-free to me." Elmer reached up, gathered the ends of his Eli-length, salt-and-pepper beard between his fingers, and narrowed his eyes in thought. "Heavenly Treasures, you say? Isn't that the shop across from the police station?"

Claire nodded. "It is. Though the best

54

landmark for directing people to my store is to tell them it's next to Shoo Fly Bake Shoppe. *Everyone* knows where Ruth Miller's bakery is."

Esther wiggled her finger at her daughter a few times and then turned back to Elmer. "Claire spends much time in the police station."

"Oh?" Elmer readjusted his hat atop his head. "You do not look like someone who would find herself at the police station . . ."

"She doesn't go because she has done something wrong," Esther explained. "She goes to see the detective."

Elmer lowered his hand back down to his lap. "Detective?"

"Yah. They are to marry one day."

"Esther!"

Esther leaned forward, cupping her hand around her mouth as she did. "Claire doesn't like it when I say that, but it is true. I have seen them together. There will be a wedding soon, I am sure."

Propelled by the sudden and face-saving series of vibrations in her front pocket, Claire handed the baby to Esther to check the display screen on her phone. Jakob's name had her requesting a moment and taking a step or two back from the curious glances of the group.

"Hey there . . . I've been thinking about you all day. How are you? Are you doing okay?"

"Any chance I could see you tonight? I think I need to talk about Russ . . . Maybe reminisce out loud for a little while, if that's okay? Might help me get through what I need to get through in order to get to the business of figuring out who did this."

"Of course!" Glancing back at the group, she tried to smile away Esther's worry, but it was no use. Esther's antenna was up. So, too, was Eli's if the way he kept rubbing his jawline was any indication. "Do you want me to stop by your place? I can be there in ten minutes — fifteen, tops. I just need to say good-bye to everyone here."

"That's fine. But let's make it the inn instead of my place, okay? Maybe Diane would like to reminisce, too."

CHAPTER 5

There was no mistaking the dark circles lining the underside of Jakob's eyes or the uncharacteristic slump to his shoulders as he turned to look out over a town and its people he'd loved for more than three and a half decades. He was hurting and it was painful to see. Still, Claire had spent enough time with him over the past year to know that when he wandered over to a window — whether it be in his office, his apartment, her shop, or here at the inn — he was working to compose his thoughts.

She'd asked him about it once and, for a few moments, he'd seemed at a loss to explain something that was clearly a subconscious act. But, after some careful thought, he referenced back to his Amish upbringing and the peace he always felt when exploring or working the land.

"There's an old Amish proverb that says, 'Many times we are climbing mountains when we ought to be quietly resting,' " he'd said at the time. "Looking out at what God has provided reminds me to breathe. When I do, I'm always able to see things more clearly."

So she let him breathe. And while she did, she soaked up the quiet strength that still managed to fill her aunt's parlor despite the sadness clearly weighing on his heart. She took in the khaki-colored trousers, the white, long-sleeved shirt, and the sandy blond hair that stopped well shy of his collar. What she couldn't see from her vantage point on the couch, her mind's eye filled in — the strong jawline, the amber-flecked hazel eyes, the clean-shaven skin, the dimples that melted her heart every time he smiled at her . . .

"When I was that little kid riding in that buggy that day, Russ was this larger-than-life unknown who ran after a bad person and made things right." Slowly, he turned until his focus was squarely on Claire. "And you know what? That never changed. He was always this larger-than-life character to me — running after bad people and making things right."

She patted the cushion to her left and, when he didn't take her up on the suggestion, she pulled her hand back onto her lap.

"Then he taught you well because that's how *I* see *you*."

"Trust me, Claire, I'm no Russ Granger."

"To me you are. You run after bad guys and make things right, too."

"In the moment, maybe. Like he did when I first saw him from the back of Dat's wagon, I guess. But that instinct, that drive was as much a part of Russ as that crazy webbed toe he had going on his left foot. He was always looking to make things right even when it wasn't his problem to worry about." Jakob wandered over to the mantel and then across the hooked rug to the computer desk, his fingers touching things it was clear his eyes weren't really seeing. "Like this one time, shortly after I got on with the force in New York, he called to check on me and see how things were going. I told him about this kid in Brooklyn who'd been kidnapped by his biological father. Next thing I knew, he was asking questions and I was hearing his infamous thinking grunts on the line."

"Thinking grunts?" Swiveling her body toward the armrest, she watched him make his way toward the shelves and the smattering of knickknacks and books that lined them from floor to ceiling. "What are those?"

59

"They were these sounds he made when he was working through a case. And Russ made them all the time. I remember trying them out on the way back to the farm after spending time at the station during Rumspringa. The cows weren't as impressed as I was, unfortunately."

Her laugh prompted him to turn just shy of the final shelf and head in her direction. "Anyway, the next day, I got called in off the road by one of the detectives in my precinct. He'd gotten a call that morning from Russ, who had a theory on where the father had taken his kid. The detective checked it out and — bingo! They found the kid."

"Wow."

"And that's just *one* example, Claire — one of probably hundreds. Russ never stopped being a cop. Not on vacation with his wife . . . Not when he was working on that hot rod he claimed was his way to unwind . . . Not when he was sleeping . . . And not on a trip to see his daughter, from what I saw this afternoon . . . Being a cop was in his blood in a way I'm not sure it's truly in mine."

"You're great at what you do, Jakob," she protested.

"But I don't think about it when I'm with

you. When we're taking a walk, I'm not thinking about my reports or what the next crime I might need to solve is going to be. I'm ready, if I get a call and the station needs me to come in, but I'm not waiting at home with my ear pressed to the scanner in the hope I might get a jump on something that hasn't happened yet."

"Russ was like that?"

"I don't mean that the way it probably sounds — like he cared about nothing else. Because that wasn't true. He just . . ." Jakob stopped, glanced off at something far beyond the walls of Diane's parlor, and then, after a quick shake of his head, shifted his attention back to Claire. "There were times he thwarted stuff from happening simply because he had a gut. Watched him do it myself at least a dozen times during my Rumspringa days. It was like he had a sixth sense when it came to crime solving — a sixth sense he was completely incapable of shutting off even if he'd wanted to.

"I mean, look at the kitchen table in his daughter's garage apartment. He got here, when? Late Saturday morning? And even though he'd had a full day with Callie and the grandkids and took a few hours to hit up a favorite haunt that night, his case files not only made the trip *with* him, they were *out* on the table. Like he'd been studying them, looking for the missing nugget, just like always."

He took the final step or two over to the couch, prompting her to drop her feet onto the floor. "I take it you mean files for crimes he wasn't able to close?" she asked.

"Oh no, Russ closed all crimes related to his department. Some faster than others, of course, but he closed them all. The guy wouldn't rest until he did. That's just the way he was."

She waited for him to get settled beside her and then turned her body so she could see his face. "Then I don't understand. What case files?"

"Anything and everything he could get his hands on. That's why, when he went south for retirement, he got himself a part-time gig working the desk at a station down there. He said it was to keep himself busy so he didn't drive his wife, Amelia, nuts. But if that's all he was looking for, he could have thrown himself into golfing or tennis or reading. Or found a part-time job at a million other places. But he chose a police station because it was in his blood. He couldn't walk away from it, any more than he could voluntarily walk away from breathing."

"Wow."

"I know."

"So these files he traveled with were from the station in Florida?"

"Some, yeah. But he made it a habit to be up on everything — even things that happened elsewhere but came through his department as a BOLO or whatever."

"Bolo?"

"It's an acronym for 'be on the lookout.' If a department has reason to believe a suspect might be headed for a particular area, they send a BOLO out to the stations in that area. It gives a picture of the suspect, a description of the suspect and the crime, and a number to call for the detective or department working it. The FBI sends them out, too. It's just a way to have more eyes open out on the streets at all times, you know?" Jakob let his head drift back against the couch. "Russ loved those things. He'd study them, memorize them, and then, if he wasn't actively working on something of his own, he'd start researching everything he could get his hands on about that particular crime. I used to give him garbage about being attached to his computer so much. But I'm telling you, it was *that* research, coupled with his sixth sense, that helped nab a few suspects for other departments."

"I don't know what to say other than I wish now, more than ever, that I'd gotten to meet him."

His eyes came to rest on hers. "So do I, Claire. So do I."

A flurry of movement at the parlor door had Claire glancing over the back of the couch in time to see Diane breeze in with a plate of cookies in one hand and a book in the other. Tucked into the front pocket of her apron was the dust cloth Claire knew wouldn't remain unused for long. "I'm sorry it took me so long to get these cookies to you. I got a little sidetracked looking at a cookbook the Andersons in Room Two gave me after dinner this evening."

The sixty-two-year-old innkeeper cleared the back of the couch and extended her plate-holding hand in their direction. "I made snickerdoodles."

Jakob's eyes crackled to life for the first time all evening. "I see that." He waited for Claire to take one and then helped himself to two. "I talked to Callie at length this afternoon. She's taking her dad's death extremely hard."

"I imagine she is. It wasn't all that long ago that she lost her mom. Amelia and Russ were her lifelines during the separation and divorce from Kyle Davidson." Diane set the plate on the table next to Claire and then retreated across the hooked rug to her favorite chair. "Her mom helped keep her calm during the roughest waters, and Russ, of course, put the fear of God in Kyle when it was needed."

"Fear of God?" Jakob repeated.

Diane sat down but kept her paperback mystery novel closed on top of her lap. "It was a contentious divorce, to say the least. There were times I wished, for Callie's sake, her parents were still living here. There were also times I was glad they weren't, because Russ might have gotten himself locked up otherwise."

Jakob stiffened next to Claire. "Why? What happened?"

"Let's just say Kyle is a bit of a hothead."

"How do you know this?"

"Callie told me. I saw her out and about a few times when it was all going on."

"Did he hurt her?" Jakob demanded.

"No, but he certainly threatened her a few times."

"Threatened her?" Jakob repeated, leaning forward. "Threatened her how? And why am I just now hearing about this? Why didn't Callie call me? Why didn't *Russ* call? And why on earth did he not mention this when I'd call him about one of my cases?"

"I can't answer that. But I can tell you this much: I know Kyle showed up at Callie's workplace a few times during the early stages of the separation. And I know, once it became apparent she wasn't going to change her mind about the divorce, he threatened to take the kids and leave the area." Diane pushed at the air as if it contained an invisible weight. "From what I understand, Russ got him on the phone and basically let him know if he tried something like that, Russ would make it his life's work to track Kyle down and see to it he never saw his children again."

Jakob let loose a long, low whistle. "Knowing Russ the way I did, I'm betting that's not all that was said to this guy . . ."

"Probably not." Diane ran her hand across the cover of her book but, still, it remained closed. "Regardless, the heat turned down enough that they were able to come to some agreements concerning the kids."

"I know this guy had the kids on Sunday when Callie found Russ. And she was beside herself with relief that he did as it spared the children from possibly being the ones to have found their grandfather like that." Jakob palmed his mouth and then used the same hand to push off the couch. "I didn't get any sense there was an issue there with the ex."

Diane waved off his growing angst. "I don't really think there is one anymore. The schedule they hammered out in court seems to be working."

Jakob made his way back over to the window but not for long. "Russ wasn't the type to forget threats, idle or otherwise. In fact, once a threat was made, the person having issued it was forever on Russ's radar from that day forward. So I'm guessing he wasn't a fan of this guy even if the custody stuff was moving along okay."

"I suspect you're right," Diane mused.

Claire watched Jakob as he wandered around the room for the second time that evening, noting the difference in his gait compared to the first go-round. Before, his trek had been about grief and trying to get a handle on his emotions. This time it was about something much more. "What are you thinking?" she asked.

He stopped near the parlor door and then doubled back to the couch, his feet moving with a purpose they hadn't shown earlier. "I'm thinking about the timing. Wondering if maybe Kyle saw Russ when he showed up to get the kids and — no. That doesn't work. The medical examiner said Russ was killed sometime between two and four Sunday morning. Kyle didn't pick up the kids until" — he checked the note section of his phone — "ten. So that's between six and eight hours later."

"Did Kyle know Russ was coming for a visit? Could he have seen him out at that pub on Saturday night? Maybe known Russ would be staying in the garage apartment rather than in the house with Callie and the kids?"

His eyes came to rest on Claire's. "All good questions. And all questions I will find answers to. Though this is exactly the kind of case I'd have called Russ about."

Diane peered at Claire across the rim of her glasses. "Are you suggesting Callie's ex could be behind what happened to Russ?"

"I don't know. Maybe." Claire pulled the closest throw pillow to her chest. "It's an avenue worth exploring, I imagine."

Jakob reclaimed his spot next to Claire, nodding emphatically as he did. "It's absolutely an avenue worth exploring. If someone had threatened my daughter in the past, I'm not sure *I'd* be able to let bygones be bygones, either."

"But things have been better," Diane protested. "Maybe even — dare I say — *peaceful* between those two. Callie told me that herself the last time I saw her at the market."

"And maybe it *has* been peaceful. But that doesn't mean Russ or, in this case, *Kyle,* put it behind them. Some guys take a real issue with being called out for things. Even things that are more than justified."

"But to suggest they might *kill* because of that?"

"Trust me, Diane, people have been murdered for far less. Far, *far* less."

The woman pushed the book from her lap and reached for her dust cloth, instead. "I'm going to hope you're wrong, Detective. I think facing a reality like that would be a bitter pill for Callie to swallow on top of the grief she's already —"

The peal of the kitchen phone startled the rest of the innkeeper's statement away and brought Claire to her feet. "I'll get it, Aunt Diane."

Grabbing the cookie plate for a possible reload, Claire headed out of the parlor, across the dining room, and into the large country-style kitchen. Halfway through the fourth ring, she picked up the receiver.

"Good evening, Sleep Heavenly, how many I assist you?"

"Claire?"

She breathed in the warmth of the surprisingly still familiar voice and flapped her free hand at her side. "Bill? Is that you?"

His answering smile was audible. "It is, indeed. I'm surprised you remember my voice."

I'm not, she wanted to say. Instead, she stepped over to the center island and flopped down on one of two stools, the image of the early-summer guest who so obviously fancied her aunt filling her mind's eye.

"So how are you?" she asked.

"I'm restless."

She pulled the phone closer to her ear in an attempt to block out any background noise. "Did you say 'restless'?"

"I did. Been that way since I met you folks back in June. At first, I thought it was just about reacclimating myself to the change in pace between Heavenly and just about anywhere else."

"Okay . . ."

"But I just kept feeling out of sorts until I admitted to myself what the real cause was."

Her visual inventory of the kitchen and any jobs that still needed to be done before Diane would concede to retiring for the night ceased. Crossing the fingers of her free hand, she leaned forward against the edge of the counter. "And what might that be?"

"I can't stop thinking about your aunt. I

think about her when I'm eating. I think about her when I'm working. I think about her when I settle down in front of the television in the evening. And I think about her every time I so much as see food of any kind because I know it won't be as good as hers."

Claire pumped her hand in the air in silent victory. "So come back."

"That's why I'm calling. To see if maybe she has an opening at the inn later this month or early next month." His inhale filled her ear, the apprehension and hope it held making it so she wasn't sure she'd ever be able to stop smiling. "But with you answering the phone, I can ask something I wouldn't be able to ask Diane."

"Yes, Annie can man the shop one day so I can cover things here."

He laughed. "How'd you know I was going to ask that?"

"I *hoped* . . ."

"Thank you, Claire. Your aunt is a mighty special woman."

"She is, indeed." Sensing the next question, she slipped off the stool and headed toward the kitchen door. "Would you like to speak with her?"

The hopeful inhale was back. Only this time, instead of being mixed with a pinch of apprehension, there was a healthy helping of excitement. "I would."

"I'll get her." She made her way through the dining room, across the wood floor in the hallway, and into the parlor, her eyes seeking and finding her aunt in short order. "Aunt Diane? You have a phone call."

Diane scooted forward and off her chair. "I do?"

"Yup." Then, to the man waiting expectantly on the other end, she added, "Here she is."

"Who is it?" Diane asked as she took the handheld phone from Claire.

She waved off the question and then hurried over to the couch and Jakob as the same hope and excitement she'd heard through the phone just moments earlier filled the hallway outside the parlor.

"Bill! What a lovely surprise . . ."

CHAPTER 6

She studied the placement of Martha's painted milk can in relation to the autumn frames and scented candles and gave Annie a thumbs-up. The Amish teenager returned the gesture in kind and headed back toward the display of place mats in the front-left corner of the showroom.

Lifting her face to the late-September sun, Claire breathed in the cool crispness of the air. "Well, that's another item off my to-do list," she murmured.

"You sure do have a way of putting the rest of us to shame."

Startled, she spun around, her surprise giving way to a grin at the sight of the familiar bald man studying her front window. "Harold! You must be awfully light on your feet as I didn't hear you come up behind me."

"I'll take that as a compliment these days." The hardware store owner and fellow

Lighted Way tenant patted his ever-growing stomach with an equally pudgy hand. "Seems I just changed my front window to summertime and here you are showcasing fall."

"According to the calendar and" — she splayed her hands upward — "the weather, autumn officially starts tomorrow. Which means people will be looking for rakes before long."

"Rakes . . . spreaders . . . limb cutters . . . you name it." Harold Glick rocked back on the heels of his sneakers, rubbing his chin between his thumb and his index finger as he did. "Think maybe I could gather up some of them early-changing leaves from the tree behind my shop and scatter them in the window alongside the fall tools? Think that'd be appealing the way your window here is?"

"I think it would be a perfect touch! And if you don't want to use real leaves, you can get some fake ones at one of the big-box craft stores."

"Nah. God didn't make leaves so we could go buy fake ones." Harold pointed at Claire's shop. "Annie working today?"

"She sure is. I wouldn't be able to spend so much time fussing with my front window if she wasn't here being the complete godsend that she is." Claire turned back to Harold. "How's your part-timer working? Still happy with him?"

"I get to be out here talking to you for a spell, don't I?"

She laughed. "True enough."

He stepped closer, all but eliminating the gap between them. "How's your young man doing, Claire? I know he was mighty close to Chief Granger."

And just like that, the joy she'd managed to find in the day via Annie's comradery, the opportunity to be creative with the window display, and memories of Diane's voice when she spoke to Bill, disappeared. In its place was the same helplessness she'd felt watching Jakob walk out to his car at the end of the evening, his sadness weighing on her very being. "He's struggling, Harold."

"I figured that'd be the case. Them two were like two peas in a pod back when Jakob was in his experementin' year. Jakob followed Russ around like a puppy, and Russ ate it right up." Harold patted the top of his stomach. "More than once I had people askin' if Jakob was Russ's son."

She squeezed her eyes closed around the image the man's words conjured and then opened them to find Harold studying her

75

closely. "A few of us old-timers around here — the ones who remember when Russ was chief here in Heavenly — are wanting to do something in his name. A fund-raiser for his grandkids, a scholarship for a local high school kid interested in law enforcement, or maybe a plaque in town hall honoring his service to our community . . . Don't know which we'll do yet, but those are the three things we were talking about after closing yesterday. Hard to narrow it down when we wish we could do all of 'em."

"Oh, Harold, those are all lovely ideas. And while I didn't know him, I'd very much like to be a part of whatever it is you choose to do. I'm sure Aunt Diane would, as well."

"We'll be sure to let you know what we decide." Harold hoisted his wrist into sight and then lowered it back down to his side. "Looks like it's time to start heading back to my shop. It's been good chatting with you, Claire, and I'll give that leaf thing a whirl and see how it looks. If I get stuck, mind if I give you a holler?"

"Of course." She leaned forward, kissed her friend on his round cheek, and hooked her thumb over her shoulder at her own shop. "I better head back inside, too. The more things I check off my to-do list, the better chance I have of getting out of here right after closing."

He took a few steps in the direction of Glick's Tools 'n More and then stopped. Glancing back at Claire, he nodded, his normally jovial demeanor subdued. "Best thing you can do for that young man of yours is be there for him. With you by his side, he can get through anything."

"Thanks, Harold, I'll do that. And let me know how you guys decide to honor Russ." She returned the man's parting smile, watched him walk past Shoo Fly Bake Shoppe, and then stepped back inside Heavenly Treasures, the door-mounted bell bringing Annie to her feet.

"Claire! I was hoping you'd come back in." Annie smoothed the wrinkles from her mint green dress and then swept Claire's focus toward the place mat display she'd just finished. "What do you think? Would it make you want to buy them for your table?"

Claire stepped around the table of Amish dolls to get a closer look at the young girl's display. The table Annie had selected for her display was now covered with a simple harvest-wheat-colored cloth — nothing too distracting, yet quietly pleasing. The place mats themselves were fanned out across the center of the table to showcase the plentiful array of autumn colors. Nearby and artfully arranged were a few of Claire's autumn-scented candles along with a cute shelf-sitting scarecrow.

"Oh, Annie . . ." She walked around the table, slowly taking in the rainbowlike assortment of fabric-covered napkin rings scattered about. "You did a fabulous job with this, kiddo. You not only managed to showcase the place mats in an appealing manner but you also put some of our other items on the radar in a way that makes the customer want *all* of them."

The teenager's wide-set brown eyes danced with the praise. "That is what I hoped! To be able to do what you do."

"I think you surpassed anything I could have done with this." She pointed at the almost kaleidoscope effect from the napkin rings. "Somehow you managed to place these in a way that makes me think of fallen leaves . . ."

"That is good, yah?"

Rounding the table, she stopped beside Annie and pulled her in for a quick hug. "It is most certainly good — *great,* even. You have a real eye for this kind of stuff."

A second swell of pride sent Annie's attention to the ground before returning it, sans sparkle, back to Claire. "I hoped this would make those lines between your eyes go away, but it did not."

"Lines between my eyes?" Claire turned and made her way over to the counter and the small handheld mirror she still kept beside the register even though Esther was no longer working at the shop.

Holding it close, she stared at her reflection — the slightly forced smile, the tired eyes, the lines between her eyebrows . . .

"It is like it always is when you are worried or sad."

She peeked around the mirror to find Annie studying her closely. "What is?"

"The lines."

Again, she took in her appearance, the lines Annie spoke of suddenly making her look far older than she was. She scrunched her nose, widened her eyes, even stuck out her tongue at herself, but try as she could, the only thing that made the lines go away was the smile she couldn't maintain with any conviction. Instead, she returned the mirror to its usual place and flopped down onto a stool. "I guess my limited sleep the past two nights is refusing to be denied."

"That is what *your eyes* are saying, Claire. The lines say more. They say that you are worried." Annie marched to the center of the store only to retrace her way back to Claire. "It is lunchtime. The shop is always quiet at lunchtime. Customers will come again when their stomachs are full. That is what they always do."

It took her a moment to follow the intent behind her employee's words, but when she did, she waved them away. "I'm not worried about the shop, Annie. We've had a really good month and I don't foresee October being much different."

"Then why *these*" — Annie pointed at her own smooth-as-silk forehead — "if it is not the shop that has put them there?"

"It's Jakob."

Annie drew back. "Are . . . are you not courting anymore?"

"No, it's not that. It's just . . ." Claire exhaled through pursed lips. "He's struggling with his friend's loss. It's hard to see him like that and know that there's nothing I can do to fix it or even lessen it. Only time can do the latter. Time and memories."

"Henry says the man was murdered. Like Henry's dat."

"He was."

"Will you dress up again to catch the person?" Annie asked as she, too, took a spot on a stool.

Propping her elbow on the counter, Claire allowed herself the small smile that came with the memory of lacing up the same style boots Annie wore . . . pinning her hair beneath a white kapp . . . tucking her cell phone out of sight . . . Sometimes her brief yet no less memorable foray into Amish living seemed so far away, yet at other times — like that moment — it seemed like just yesterday.

"No. I will help Jakob if I can, but he is the detective, not me."

Annie grew quiet for a moment, her fingers quietly fidgeting the edges of her dress. When the teenager finally spoke, her hushed words snapped Claire into the present. "What happened?"

So Claire told her. She told her about Russ's work as a police officer and how he worked his way up to chief in their town. She told her about the moment Russ captured Jakob's attention. She told her about the many ways in which Russ had served as both a mentor and a guiding hand for Jakob as the now-detective learned to navigate not only a new career but a new life, as well. And, finally, she told her about the last communication Russ and Jakob had and how, later that night, Russ was killed outside the garage apartment where he was staying while visiting his daughter and grandchildren. When she was done, she abandoned her perch and wandered over to the window that overlooked the alley between her shop and Ruth's bakery, the worry she'd clearly worn on her face now pressing on her heart.

"I don't know how to help him, Annie." She leaned into the window, the coolness of the glass a welcome yet momentary distraction from her sadness. "I don't know how to make him hurt less."

"When you lose someone you love — as I did with Mamm — it never hurts less. It is always there. But with time, you can get to a better place. A place where you can smile through the hurt with good memories."

"But how can I help him get there?" she asked. "Besides just giving it time, like it took for you?"

"Henry says you and your detective helped *him* get there."

She parted company with the glass pane to study the teenager. "How did we do that?"

"He says that before you dressed up as Amish, he would wonder who hurt his dat and why. He would think about finding the person and . . ." Annie stopped, swallowed, and averted her eyes from Claire's.

"Tell me, Annie. Please."

Slowly, Annie looked up, her cheeks red. "He would think of hitting the person."

"That's natural."

"We are not to think like that."

"I know and I won't tell anyone." She crossed back to the counter and Annie. "So please . . . Go on."

"Henry says that when you and Jakob found the bad person, he could think only of his dat again. And that was good."

"I wish I could do that for Jakob. But I didn't know Russ. I just know what Jakob and my aunt have told —"

"Claire?"

She shook the rest of her statement from her thoughts and forced herself to focus on the girl nibbling her lip on the other side of the counter. "What's wrong, Annie?"

"Some bad people do not get caught, yah?"

"Yes. Sadly."

"So they are still bad."

Unsure of where the teenager was going, Claire simply nodded. And waited.

"Police — like Jakob and this man — chased many bad people, yah?"

"Sure."

"When I go to Eva's house, I play with the children. Most times we play hide-and-seek because it is a game they all like. When we play chase, Joshua does not play. He does not like to be chased."

Reaching out, she nudged Annie's gaze back onto hers. "You've lost me, sweetie. I thought we were talking about Jakob and his friend."

"Maybe someone he chased didn't like it, either."

"Someone he chased didn't like . . ." The rest of the words faded away as the meaning behind Annie's words sent her scrambling for her phone. "Oh, Annie, this is perfect. You. Are. A. Genius."

CHAPTER 7

There was no denying the smile on Annie's young face as she guided her horse, Katie, down the alley and onto Lighted Way. It had been there since the moment Claire had called Jakob, widening exponentially as Claire had shared the teenager's theory on Russ's murder.

The idea, of course, had already crossed his mind, but that wasn't something Annie needed to know. Instead, as she'd hung up, Claire had relayed the detective's gratitude for Annie's assistance, thus earning herself and a few customers the auditory pleasure of an answering squeal in the process.

And that was okay. Because whether Jakob was already on it or not, it had been a good idea. A *clever* idea. But even more than that, Annie's desire to help had built a temporary bridge between the bishop's daughter and a man Claire could no longer imagine life without. Maybe, just maybe, if she could help facilitate more temporary bridges between the detective and his childhood roots, her Amish friends would see —

"I am trying to decide if you are happy or worried, but I cannot tell for sure."

Startled back into the moment and her surroundings, Claire lifted her hand as a shield against the day's waning rays and scanned the opposite stoop for the face that matched the voice. Sure enough, with a six-inch shift to the left and a quick dodge of her head to the right, her attention came to rest on the dark-haired Amish man with eyes as blue as a summer sky. "Ben, hi! I didn't see your buggy."

"It is on the road." Benjamin Miller stepped off Shoo Fly Bake Shoppe's side stoop and made his way across the cobblestoned alleyway separating his sister's store from Claire's. "Ruth needed some fresh milk and Emma was on her way to the market."

"Emma Stutzman?"

The startling blue eyes he shared with his sister, Ruth, disappeared behind the brim of his straw hat with a nod. When they returned to view, she searched them for anything that would back up Jakob's hunch regarding her friend and his feelings for the recent widow. But if there was any truth to the detective's musings, it was hidden behind the Amish man's bent toward stoicism.

"How is she doing?" Claire finally asked. "Emma, I mean. Is she finding any semblance of a routine in the aftermath of Wayne's death?"

"Emma still mourns but she is a strong woman. With Henry and the rest of the children's help, they are making do. Having Rebecca here has helped her, too."

Something in his voice caught her up short. "Rebecca? Who is that?"

"Emma's sister. She is visiting from upstate."

"Ahhh, I haven't met her yet."

"You will. Soon."

"I know your help has been invaluable to Emma, as well." At his questioning eyes, she rushed to continue. "Annie is friends with Henry. He speaks of your help."

Benjamin's shoulders rose and fell with a slight shrug. "To fulfill the law of Christ, brethren must bear one another's burdens."

"And it's appreciated, I'm sure." Motioning over her shoulder, she smiled up at her friend. "Would you like a water? I have some in my office."

"No. I am not thirsty."

"Would you like to sit, then?" she asked,

87

pointing at the stoop. "I don't think I've seen you since that evening up at the rock when you delivered the hope chest Jakob asked you to make for me."

"Yah."

She lowered herself onto the top step and gazed up at him when he opted to remain standing. "What have you been up to besides helping Emma and her kids and — wait! I . . . I haven't seen you since the baby was born!" Pulling her legs upward, she rested her chin on top of her knees and gave in to the grin that was a guarantee whenever she so much as thought about Esther and Eli's daughter. "I have to say, Benjamin Miller, your new niece is completely and utterly adorable."

"You have seen her often?"

"Every chance I get." She released her hold on her legs and, instead, leaned against the trim of the screen door at her back. "In fact, I was fawning over her on Sunday afternoon when your brother and Esther mentioned how close you were to becoming a minister."

"It is God's will that it is Elmer."

She considered asking him whether he was relieved, but decided against it. Esther and Eli, with Jakob's help, had probably shared more than they should have about the process. "I met Elmer yesterday after work. Out at Esther's. He was out near the road speaking with Eli and John."

"Bontrager?"

"I think so. He lives on the farm across the way from Eli and Esther."

"Then that is Bontrager."

"I don't think he was too fond of me, for some reason."

Benjamin drew back. "Why do you say that?"

"Because he wouldn't look at me when Eli introduced me, and then, later on, when Eli suggested he speak with me about selling one of his smaller doghouses on consignment at the shop, he dismissed it *and* me immediately." A speeding car on the busy roadway stole her focus just long enough for her to realize the subject at hand didn't matter. But when she looked back up at Ben, it was clear he didn't agree.

"It was not you, Claire. Bontrager is . . ." Clearly uncomfortable at the notion of speaking ill of someone, Benjamin let his gaze briefly travel to the stretch of woods behind Claire's shop. If his thoughts traveled back to the offer he'd once made to leave the Amish in favor of a life with her, it didn't show. Instead, he cleared his throat and tried again. "He has been that way since he moved to Heavenly from Smoketown. It is the way that he is."

She sat up, pushed herself off the stoop, and stood. "Thank you for saying that. I really wasn't sure if I'd unknowingly said something to offend or if it's because of my connection to Jakob."

"Bontrager is like that with everyone. It is why I was surprised his name was given to the bishop by so many."

"Don't forget *your* name was given by many, too."

"Yah. But I have lived here my whole life. It was not a surprise. Elmer is quiet and hardworking, but he has earned the respect of many since he came here. Soon, in another year or so, if there is a need for more names, maybe Eli's will be given."

A mixture of smells — most notably baking apples and cinnamon — wafted across the alley, prompting her to lift her nose for a long, drawn-out inhale. "Ohhh, I hope not. Eli and Esther need time together with the baby and the other little ones that will surely follow."

"Being ready to serve is part of baptism. Eli knows this." Benjamin wandered over to the section where Annie kept Katie during the workday and ran his hand over the hitching post. "It is why I was ready, why

Elmer and John were ready, too."

She watched him for a moment before abandoning her premium olfactory vantage point. "Eli said that whoever found the verse in their hymnbook had to get up right then and there and lead that morning's worship service. That had to have been a little nerve-racking."

"Maybe. A little. But" — he turned back to her — "it was God's will for it to be Elmer."

A flash of something behind his eyes caught her by surprise and she stepped forward, effectively reducing the gap between them to a mere foot, at best. "Ben? Are you okay? I feel like . . . I don't know . . . like maybe you're upset about something."

A chill skittered up her spine as his gaze dive-bombed down to the cobblestones. "Ben, please. Talk to me."

Finally, after what seemed like an eternity, he folded his arms across his suspendered chest and met her eye. "Is he okay?"

"He?"

"Jakob."

Something a lot like relief started in her chest and spread outward, enveloping her in a euphoria she wished with all her might Jakob was there to feel for himself. For nearly eighteen years Jakob had been cast aside by a people and a community he treasured. Not because he'd been mean-spirited or destructive or horrible in any way, but, rather, because he'd felt compelled to help solve a crime against the very people who subsequently turned their backs on him. Yet now, the one person he'd repeatedly referenced as his best friend during his early childhood years — before jealousy (his) and a culture's rules (Benjamin's) brought an end to it — was standing there, less than a foot away from her, clearly worried about the detective.

Aware of a sudden moisture gripping her palms, Claire willed herself to breathe, to answer Benjamin's question in a way that would be respectful of Jakob's privacy while also continuing to stoke the very real thawing that had begun between the pair back in the spring. "I take it you heard? About his friend?"

"I remember the first time Jakob spoke of the man. We met up at the pond with our frogs on the way home from school. Jakob did not argue when I told him my frog was to win the race. I said it a second time and he still did not argue. Before I could say it a third time, he spoke of seeing this man chase a thief down the street." Ben stepped around Claire and made his way back to the stoop, this time claiming the top step as a seat. "I tried to get him to stop talking. Dat was in the fields and I needed to help. But Jakob would not stop. He spoke of the man's uniform. He spoke of how fast the man ran. He spoke of the way the man sat on the thief's back. He spoke of the way the man took back the things the thief had stolen and handed them to the shopkeeper they belonged to. And he spoke of how he wished his dat had stopped the buggy when Jakob asked."

She trailed her way back to the steps and Ben, only this time she was the one who remained standing. "I can't believe you remember that so clearly."

"Jakob got excited when his frogs won our races, but I had never seen him like he was that day. After that, whenever he would see that man again, he would speak like that . . . In a way he never did about our races ever again."

"They became very close during Jakob's Rumspringa. And that relationship only deepened over the years." Claire glanced down the alleyway and across the street to the corner of the police department she could just make out from where she stood. More than anything, she wanted to reach into her pocket, pull out her phone, and ask

Jakob to join them, but, short of that, she needed to speak for him, from her heart. "I think, from what I've been able to piece together, that Russ helped fill at least a little of the void that came from losing his entire family and community in one fell swoop. So, with that in mind, I'm sure you can imagine just how hard he is taking Russ's murder, and how badly he wants to find the person who did this to him."

The brim of Ben's hat dipped forward only to return to start again as he sought her face. "Jakob helped me to find answers about Elizabeth. I would like to help him find answers about his friend."

She opened her mouth to speak but closed it as the emotion responsible for the sudden misting in her eyes saw fit to wedge a pretty decent-sized lump inside her throat, as well. Before she could get herself together enough to finally speak, though, he continued, his tone hushed yet firm.

"Please, Claire. Please tell Jakob I want to help. We are getting close to the harvest so I must be in the fields during the day, but at night, when I am done, perhaps he would like to sit and talk. I could go to the rock on the hill or to your aunt's inn when he is there and he could talk. Maybe when he talks, I will hear important things the way he heard important things when I spoke of Elizabeth in the spring."

CHAPTER 8

Claire held her hands under the water and watched as the flour she'd already gotten off her forearms slowly disappeared down the kitchen drain. "I think I know why I volunteer for biscuit-making duty anytime they're on the menu," she mused, reaching for the soap dispenser.

"I would imagine the fact that the guests always rave about them has something to do with it, no?"

"It's a side benefit, sure. But it's more than that." With the soap rinsed away, she shut off the water, grabbed a hand towel, and made her way over to the counter and her aunt. "Do you remember how I'd disappear into my own little universe every time you'd bring out the Play-Doh during a visit?"

Diane's laugh filled the spacious kitchen as she placed the lid on the butter dish and carried it to the refrigerator. "I used to joke to your father that a herd of elephants could walk right past you when you were playing with that stuff and you wouldn't notice."

"Probably." She transferred the salt and pepper shakers from the serving tray to their home in the glass-fronted cabinet to her left and then returned to her spot at the counter. "Although I didn't really have any stress in my life back then, I still liked getting away from everything right there in the middle of your living room. I'd roll the dough into a ball between my hands, flatten it out with that little plastic rolling pin you got me, and then cut it or mold it with all those cookie cutters and cookie stamps you kept in that dark brown basket just for me. Something about the steps I needed to take to get to the final shape soothed me in the same way making biscuits for your guests does now."

"I'm glad. Though" — Diane pulled her cleaning cloth from the waistband of her apron and shook it at Claire — "I don't like hearing you *need* to be soothed. I'd prefer to think your life here is peaceful and happy all the time."

Claire looked around the room for anything that still needed to be done before they could officially call the evening tasks complete and was pleased to see there was nothing. Every plate and glass had been loaded into the dishwasher she'd finally gotten Diane to use, the counters were clean, the perishables put back in the fridge, and the guests themselves had scattered in different directions, leaving Claire and Diane with some quiet time. "My life *is* peaceful here, Aunt Diane, you know that. I couldn't love it here any more than I do. Still, I'd be lying if I didn't say it's fun — therapeutic, even — to lose myself in something so completely that I can disappear into my own thoughts. Sometimes it's just about vegging out or shutting down after a particularly busy day. Sometimes it gives me the opportunity to step back and look at something differently. Sometimes it lets me plan out my evening or the things I need to do at the shop the next day."

"And what was tonight?"

"I guess I was just thinking about Jakob this time."

Diane scrubbed at an invisible spot on the countertop and then tucked the cloth back in place. "Anything new on Russ's murder?"

Claire pulled out a stool with the intention of sitting but sidestepped it instead for a look outside the kitchen window. Here, unlike in the parlor, the Amish countryside didn't claim every square inch of her sight line. Instead, while she could see some of it by pressing her nose to the glass and looking to the left, the majority of what she could see was the small parking area under the shade of a massive oak tree and the cars that traveled the English end of Lighted Way in the distance.

"Claire?"

"It won't be long before the leaves start changing colors, huh? You can actually see a little browning happening along the edges of some of the oak leaves."

"Yes. But I was asking about Russ's murder, dear . . ."

"Right. Sorry." She took one last look at the tree and allowed herself a deep inhale before turning her back to the window. "Annie said something today that I thought was really smart. She wondered if, perhaps, someone Russ had crossed paths with in the past decided to exact revenge."

Diane perched on the edge of the stool Claire had bypassed, her brow furrowed. "By 'crossed paths' do you mean someone he'd put in jail in the past?"

"Exactly. I mean, surely he made some enemies along the way. People who were angry they got caught, or were made to serve time, or had to pay money to someone because of something they stole or defaced . . ."

"Hmmm." Diane nodded. "And *Annie* came up with this?"

Leaning back against the sink, Claire folded her arms across her chest. "She did. She's a smart kid, Aunt Diane. A *really* smart kid."

"Even supposing Annie is right, John Zook's murder is the only one that happened here during Russ's time with the local police force."

"I don't think it would necessarily have to be a murder, do you? I mean, just last year, those kids from the high school got caught for all that graffiti on the underside of the covered bridge out on Route 50, remember? Two or three of them even got kicked off the football team by the coach because of it, right?"

Diane was nodding again before Claire had completely finished. "They did, indeed. In fact, one of them was a senior hoping to get recruited. Made it so a lesser school came knocking. But that was last year. Russ Granger hasn't been with the Heavenly PD for ten years."

"I know. I really just used that as an example of someone who could turn their anger over getting caught onto the person who did the catching." She released her arms back down to her sides and ventured over to the center island. "Surely, in his time on the force here in Heavenly, Russ was instrumental in making more than a few people face up to the consequences of their illegal actions. Especially with the way Jakob described him as being all cop, all the time."

"Oh, he was. Very much so."

"Needless to say, the notion of someone with an ax to grind being behind Russ's murder had me on the phone with Jakob the second Annie was done talking."

"And?" Diane prodded. "What did he say?"

She pointed to the cookie jar next to the stove and, at Diane's nod, peeked inside to find a fresh supply of oatmeal scotchies. "Oooh . . . When did you make these?"

"Today. While you were at work. I went through every single cookbook I own in the hopes of finding a different recipe for them, but nothing spoke to me."

Closing her eyes, she took a bite, her taste buds reveling in the butterscotch flavor now bursting inside her mouth like little fireworks. "That's because it's absolutely impossible to improve upon perfection, Aunt Diane. I mean, come on, everyone knows this."

"Perfection?" Diane echoed. "I think you're biased, dear."

101

"Nope." Diane's laughter accompanied her back to the cookie jar for seconds. "I just know my treats, that's all."

After a beat or two of silence, Diane got them back on track. "What did Jakob say about Annie's idea?"

"Oh. Right." She gave some thought to a third cookie but wandered back to the island instead. "He said he'd already thought of that and was looking into it."

"Did he find anything?"

She shrugged. "I don't know. I didn't want to interrupt whatever he was doing with a bunch of questions he probably didn't need me asking at that exact moment."

"And now?"

"What do you mean?"

Diane directed Claire's attention to the clock above the doorway leading to the dining room. "It's seven o'clock. Surely the detective is done working for the day . . ."

"I wouldn't be so sure. Especially when his singular focus right now is finding the person who killed his friend."

"That may be true, dear, but that doesn't mean he wouldn't like a visit from you as a little break." Diane stepped down off the stool, opened the refrigerator, and removed a covered plate from the top shelf. "Besides, he loves my apple pie and it would be a shame if he had to wait until tomorrow to have a piece. It's never as good the second day."

This time it was her own laughter that echoed around the room as Claire met her aunt en route to the back door. "Don't *you* want to give it to him, Aunt Diane? I know you like the way he gets all excited about your edible surprises . . . And, let's face it, his hugs *are* pretty darn spectacular, if I do say so myself."

"I think, after the day that man has likely had, any excitement will come from seeing you — not this pie. The pie is just my way of nudging you to stop in and see him. I suspect it will be the highlight of his day. And as for the hug part, something tells me he could probably use one of those from you right about now." Holding the plate with her right hand, Diane extracted her key ring from the catchall table beside the back door and handed it, along with the pie plate, to Claire. "Take my car. There's no rush to get it back, so take your time. The only plan I have for my evening is to read or to do a little crocheting during that dance show with all the celebrities. Other than that, I'll be at the computer, searching all the lesser-known baking sites to see if I can come up with a better scotchie recipe."

Claire peeked at her reflection in the mirror but abandoned it in favor of the woman looking at her with such love it nearly stole her breath from her lungs. So much of her happiness could be traced right back to here — to this home and this woman. Sometimes, at night, when she was staring up at her ceiling waiting for sleep to descend, her thoughts would wander back to her time in New York City and the utter loneliness she'd felt night after night as she waited for her then husband, Peter, to return from whatever business meeting had won out on the priority list that particular evening. His lack of interest in coming home had left her feeling inadequate, uninteresting, and unimportant. But here, with Aunt Diane quietly cheering her on every step of the way, she felt free. Free to be who she was always meant to be, and free to have the confidence that came from knowing that was enough.

Holding her aunt's gaze until the last possible moment, Claire turned from the mirror and gathered the woman's hands inside her own. "While I truly believe Bill likes oatmeal scotchies, I'd be willing to bet everything I own on the fact that what he loved most about them when he was here over the summer was the fact that *you* made them. So leave the recipe be and know that the reason he wants to come back isn't about cookies, getting the lay of the land for an upcoming tour group, or snapping pictures for whatever flyers he does or doesn't have to mail out to the appropriate customer base. He wants to come back to see *you,* Aunt Diane."

CHAPTER 9

Claire pulled into the narrow lot behind
Gussman's General Store and glanced up
at the second-floor window. Even from her
limited vantage point she could see through
the open blinds to the darkened living room
beyond. Still, she pulled into the parking
spot normally taken up by Jakob's car and
cut the engine.

Her brain told her he wasn't there. If he
was, she'd be parked one spot over and the
reading lamp beside his couch would be
casting his shadow onto the scrap of wall
she could see as she exited Diane's car and
headed toward the back staircase. But her
heart and the hope she was wrong had her
carrying the pie plate up the stairs anyway.

There was a chance he'd simply left his
car at the station and walked the block and
a half back to his apartment. He did that
sometimes. Particularly if he needed fresh
air. And as for the lack of light in his living

room, that could simply mean he was reading in his room . . .

At the top of the wooden steps, she shifted the plate into the crook of her arm and knocked. When she got no response, she knocked a little louder.

Reaching into her front pocket, she pulled out her phone and dialed the station's non-emergency number.

"Heavenly Police Department."

"Hi, Curt, it's Claire Weatherly. How are you this evening?"

She leaned back against the railing as her favorite of the dispatchers gave his usual what's-going-on rundown for each of his three teenage sons, putting her on hold only twice to check the status of other incoming calls. After returning to the line the second time, he chuckled. "Seems something has been feasting on the mums outside Glorious Books. My guess is one of our new Amish drivers parked his dat's wagon a little too close to some planters this afternoon."

"It sure sounds like it." Gussman's back door squeaked open beneath her and, seconds later, an Amish woman emerged with an open-top cardboard box stuffed with groceries. Wedging the phone between her cheek and her shoulder, Claire watched the woman limp her way toward the road as

Curt returned to the line after yet another brief hold. "I can see that you're pretty busy this evening, so I won't keep you. I was just calling to see if Jakob is still there by any chance? I'm outside his place with some pie from my aunt and I don't know if he's not here or if he's sleep—"

"He's here, Claire. In his office. And every time I've passed by it since my shift started at three, he's either been pacing, ripping through department files, or having a pow-wow with the chief about the Granger case."

She wasn't surprised, really. In fact, she'd have been more surprised, albeit pleasantly, if he'd actually been inside sleeping.

"I'm betting a piece of pie and a visit from you would be mighty welcomed right about now." Curt's chair squeaked in the background. "And if it helps your decision to stop by any, the chief is gone for the day."

"Roger that," she said, grinning. "I'm on my way."

Tucking the phone into her pocket, she headed back down the stairs and over to Diane's car. For a brief moment she considered just walking to the station, but the reality that was Jakob's current situation had her dismissing that idea and sliding into place behind the steering wheel. With the pie plate secure on the passenger seat, she started the engine and headed out of the lot. A glance to her left as she reached the exit netted no oncoming traffic and a second sighting of the limping, box-carrying Amish woman who was now mere steps away from disappearing into the growing darkness.

Momentarily torn between the need to see Jakob and doing the neighborly thing, she made herself turn onto what remained of the cobblestoned road, open her window, and slow to a crawl alongside the kapped woman Claire guessed to be in her early to midforties. "Looks like you have some pretty full arms there. Can I give you a ride to your farm?"

"No. I am fine. It is good to walk."

She felt the cobblestones give way to thin gravel as she creeped forward. "I love to walk, too. Especially if I'm heading out for a visit with Eli and Esther, but it's only going to get darker, and pretty soon you'll be really hard to see walking on the side of the road by yourself."

This time, when the woman turned toward the car, it was with her whole body rather than just her head. The residual light from the gas-powered lampposts that ended with the cobblestoned road cast just enough of a glow to make out the snippet of dark hair, the standard lace-up boots, the hunter green dress beneath the apron overlay, and the single kapp string that dangled across her shoulder in much the same way Esther's once did.

"You know Esther and Eli Miller?" the woman asked.

"Esther is my best friend. She used to work with me at my store before she and Eli were married."

"You have a store?"

She nodded. "Heavenly Treasures. It's the gift shop next to Shoo Fly Bake Shoppe."

Slowly, the woman inched her way over to the car with the box still balanced atop her arms. "What is your name?"

"Claire — Claire Weatherly." The woman hesitated, her dark brown eyes moving past Claire's and into the car. Claire, in turn, followed them to the wrapped plate nestled in a corner of the passenger seat. "My boyfriend is a huge fan of my aunt's apple pie and I figured I'd bring him a piece before calling it a night. Only he wasn't home so now I need to bring it to him at work."

"He works at night?" the woman asked, swinging her attention back onto Claire.

"He does. He's a police detective." Claire hooked her thumb in the direction they'd both just come and sighed. "He's working a

110

case that will likely have him burning the midnight oil, so I'm hoping a little pie will give him the boost he's surely needing right about now."

The woman's gaze strayed back toward the tourist-friendly thoroughfare for a few beats before finding Claire's once again. "I would be grateful for the ride home, if you are sure. I cut the bottom of my foot on a piece of glass out by Miller's Pond the other day and it has yet to heal."

"*Ouch.* Come on, I'll make room." She hit the unlock feature on the passenger-side door, moved the pie plate to the floor of the backseat, and smiled as the woman and her box got into the car. "I'm sorry, I don't know your name so I'm not sure which farm to take you to."

"I am Miriam Mast."

"Mast . . . I feel like I know that — wait! I do. You're Elmer's wife, right?"

"You know Elmer?" Miriam busied herself with the contents of her box, shifting the bag of flour to the side only to shift it back when she realized the balance was off. "He has not mentioned you."

"I don't know him well. In fact, I just met him yesterday after work. Out in front of Eli's house. I understand your husband is a new minister in your church community . . ."

"He is a good Amish man. Very devoted to God, very respected for his work." When Miriam had the contents the way she wanted them, she scooted the box forward on her lap just long enough to fasten her seat belt across her chest. "You must wish your police friend wasn't so busy so you could get out of this place for a little while — maybe see a movie or go dancing or hang out with other people."

Claire laughed. "I actually like the quiet that is Heavenly. Suits me just fine. Jakob, too. So . . . Where is your farm? I'm drawing a bit of a blank."

Miriam pulled the box flush against her stomach and rested back against the seat. "You take the road that is just past Eli's parents' farm and we are at the end there. In the valley."

Claire returned her foot to the gas and continued into the Amish side of town, bits of conversations with Esther dropping into place. "You live on your uncle Barley's farm, right?"

"You knew my uncle?" Miriam asked.

"I'm afraid I didn't. I just remember Esther telling me about him and what a nice man he was." She scanned the road in front of them for any sign of the reflective orange triangles mandated by the state to keep Amish buggy drivers safe in the dark and, when she spotted nothing, peeked over at Miriam. "I'm sorry to hear of his passing. I understand he was ill for a while."

"He remembered nothing and no one and he kept us on our toes, but that's what family is for, isn't it?"

"It is, but that doesn't take away from what you did coming here and caring for him until his passing." She slowed as the turnoff to Benjamin's place approached. Sure enough, just beyond it on the right, was the narrow lane she and Jakob took on occasion when out for a Sunday drive. Unlike the main road, it took a while to come to the first farm, and still longer to reach the second. Since Miriam said nothing, she kept driving. "So where did you and Elmer come from again?"

"Indiana."

"The Shipshewana area? I've heard it's really beautiful out there. I'd like to see it sometime."

"This is it." Miriam pulled her hand from the side of the box and pointed to a dirt lane up ahead on the right. "It ain't much to look at, but it'll do, as Elmer says."

Claire turned at the rusted mailbox and slowed still further to accommodate a series of deep ruts capable of rocking the car from side to side in almost violent fashion. The lack of any exterior or interior lights in either the house or barn made it difficult to make out much beyond basic structural lines. "So what do you grow out here again? Barley?"

"Yes . . . Oh, look, there's Elmer now! Come out to see who's driving up in a car, I'm sure." Powering down her window, Miriam stuck her face into the night air. "It's just me, Elmer. Me and the policeman's nice girlfriend who didn't like seeing me walk home in the dark."

Claire stopped next to the man's horseless buggy and leaned across the center console, the man's height making it difficult to make eye contact through the open window. "Good evening, Elmer, it's nice to see you again."

The apprehensive lines around his eyes and mouth softened as recognition took over. "It's Claire, isn't it?"

"I see you have a very good memory." She pointed to the box on Miriam's lap. "I saw your wife as she was leaving the market in town and offered her a ride."

"That was very kind of you, Claire, thank you." Reaching out, he opened the car door and stepped back to allow Miriam room to exit with her box. When she was clear, he closed the door and leaned in through the open window. "I hope everything was okay after your phone call from your fella last night? You seemed in a rush to leave. Wasn't sure if it was because of the call or because of John and his . . . *ways.*"

"I'm sorry about that, Elmer. I didn't mean to rush out on our conversation the way I did. It's just that I thought Jakob had gotten a lead on the case he's working on."

"What kind of a lead?"

Shaking her head, Claire retreated back to her spot behind the steering wheel. "Nothing, actually. He just needed to talk."

"He's at the station working," Miriam said around Elmer's shoulder. "Claire says he's burning the midnight oil on this one. That's why she was out just now. Because she was bringing him a piece of pie."

Elmer's left eyebrow rose as he scanned the area around where his wife had been sitting just moments earlier. "Pie? I don't see any pie." Then, turning around, he looked at Miriam. "You didn't go with her to drop —"

"No, no . . . It's right here." Reaching into the back, Claire plucked the wrapped plate from the floor and placed it back on the now-empty seat. "I'll bring it by the station when I leave here."

"That's assuming he's still there," Elmer offered.

She returned her hands to the steering wheel and readied her hand atop the gearshift. "Knowing Jakob the way I do, he's still there. And he *will* be until he's figured out what he needs to figure out."

"Hardworking. That's what I like to hear." Stepping back from the car, Elmer reached down, took the box from Miriam's hands, and nodded at Claire. "Don't be a stranger, young lady. Bontrager is the only off-putting one we've met around here. The rest of 'em are nicer than you'd think."

She returned his nod and added a smile. "Trust me, I know. It's why I stayed."

CHAPTER 10

She was rooting around in her purse for a piece of paper and a pen for note-leaving purposes when Jakob strode into his office. Tossing his keys onto his desk, he met her in front of the chair she'd been inhabiting for nearly a half hour and pulled her up and into his arms.

"Curt told me I missed you by less than ten minutes, so I'm really sorry that took so long. It shouldn't have, and it wouldn't have if . . . Well, it doesn't matter." He turned his head so his lips grazed her temple and then he stepped back, the smile he wore stopping just short of his hazel eyes. "Wow. Having you here like this? It's exactly what I needed right now."

He pointed her back to her seat while he perched himself against the lip of his desk. "I'm sorry I didn't call earlier. I was going to. In fact, I was using that as my personal carrot once the chief headed home, but then

117

that's when the call came over and I decided to take it as a way to clear my head first. Big mistake, I'll tell you, but whatever. You're here now and, well, things are looking up, in spite of Bontrager."

"Bontrager?" she repeated. "As in John Bontrager — the farmer who lives across from Esther and Eli?"

Running his palm through his hair, he nodded. "One and the same. You met him out at Eli's yesterday, didn't you?"

"I did. Briefly."

"And?" He dropped his hand back down to the edge of his desk. "What was your first impression? Out of curiosity, of course . . ."

She shrugged. "He's a little standoffish, I guess. But then again, maybe it was just a case of him not knowing me."

He rose to his feet and made his way around the desk to his own chair. "I wish I could see the vibe you got from him as some sort of validation that it had nothing to do with me out there tonight, but considering you're my girlfriend and he's likely well aware of my Amish roots, I doubt it."

"What happened?"

The chair creaked beneath him as he leaned back, tenting his fingers. "A call came over shortly after dusk about some English kids and a baseball bat heading

118

toward the countryside in a rusted-out SUV."

"Uh-oh," she said between groans.

"School is back in session and football season has started. So it's par for the course this time of year, unfortunately." Resting his chin atop his fingers, he rasped out an exhale. "But they're usually smart enough to wait until after midnight, when the likelihood of seeing any other cars on the road is pretty nil. People might hear the sound of the bat hitting the mailbox while they're sleeping, but even if they figure out what it is and get out of bed to look, the perpetrators are long gone."

"Okay . . ."

"Not this time. This time they weren't so smart. A local electrician spotted them and figured they were up to no good. So he called it in. I heard the call and decided to ride along with one of the cops. Sure enough, as we made our way out into the country, there was a line of mailboxes either on the ground or sporting big dents. One had even been knocked into the middle of Hershberger's field."

Her answering laugh lacked all shred of humor. "I will never understand how destroying other people's property can be construed as fun. I just don't get it."

"I know. But it's been going on for years." He drummed his fingers together for a few seconds and then dropped them down to his lap. "Anyway, as we were rounding the corner just before Esther's place, we see Bontrager's mailbox flying through the air and the SUV that was called in by the electrician slowing to celebrate the hit. So Damien swerves up alongside them and lights them up with the roof rack and the floodlights."

"You got them?"

"Two of them. The other one took off across this Bontrager guy's field. I started to go after the kid, but that's when Bontrager comes out and tells me to get off his property." Jakob hiked his left foot onto his right knee and again released a frustrated breath. "I try to tell him what happened, but he takes one look at me and all he can see is an Amish defector. He doesn't care that his mailbox is halfway into his field. Or that they damaged his fence post in the process. No, sirree, he just wants me off his property. And he wants me off it that instant."

She stared at him for a moment, waiting for any evidence he was kidding, but there was nothing. Only disgust, anger, and a hint of the sadness she suspected would never truly disappear regarding his exit from Heavenly's Amish community postbaptism. "You're serious . . ."

His nod was slow, labored.

"But you were trying to catch the kids who took down his mailbox," she protested.

"True. But he'd have just as soon they take down his entire fence and maybe run over a few cows before letting someone like me step foot on his property." The chair creaked again as he dropped his foot back down to the ground and leaned forward against the desk. "Now, don't get me wrong, it's never fun to run into that when I'm simply doing my job, but when that dismissal extends to the other cops because of me, it gets under my skin in an entirely different way."

"So this rudeness extended to Damien, too?"

"It did."

She considered his description of the encounter and matched his lean from her side of the desk. "Any chance his behavior is more about the police in general than it is about you being former Amish?"

He paused, thinking, his gaze lifting just above hers. "Is it possible? I suppose. I mean, the Amish don't care for the police — that's a fact. But to be so openly hateful to them? I've not seen that before."

"Except toward you?"

"No. Not even then. They'll turn their back on me. They do it all the time. And when I need to speak to them for a case — it's never easy. But this reaction from Bontrager was *hatred.*"

"So then maybe it wasn't about you as Jakob Fisher, former Amish. Maybe it was something else." She reached underneath her chair for the covered pie plate she'd yet to give him and rested it on her lap, just out of the detective's view. "I found him to be quite cold when I met him yesterday before your call."

"I might consider that a possibility if you weren't seen as being tied up with me, the Amish defector."

"The new minister — Elmer — doesn't seem to be a fan of John Bontrager, either. Calls him off-putting."

Jakob seemed to drink that in as he, once again, rested back against his chair. "Interesting . . ."

"Anyway, I think I have just the thing to help you shake off this man's rude behavior."

The left corner of his mouth lifted a half second before being joined by the right. "Oh? What's that?"

"Close your eyes."

His eyes registered a quick yet unmistakable glint. "Close my eyes?" he echoed.

"That's what I said."

He did as he was told. "They're closed."

"Keep them that way." She stood and walked around the desk. "Now hold out your hands."

"Eyes still closed?"

"Eyes still closed."

Lifting his hands from their respective armrests, he held one of them out, palm-side up. "Both of them," she instructed.

He added the second.

"Better," she said, placing the covered plate on top of his hands. "Now open your eyes."

A long, low whistle filled the room as he looked from the plate to Claire and back again. "Is this what I think it is?" he asked, leaning in for a smell check. "Ohhhh . . . Wow. I've forgotten what I've been yammering about for the past ten minutes already."

Laughing, she reached over, pulled back the covering, and froze. "Uggh! I completely forgot to bring a fork."

"No worries. I keep one right here" — he set the plate on his desk and pulled open the drawer on the bottom-right side — "for just such occasions."

"Women bring you pie often?" she teased.

He extracted a fork along with a pile of napkins and shut the drawer. "My coworkers all seem to be married to women who are on diets at the moment. Which, translated, means pantries are being emptied out all across Heavenly . . . With the contents ending up here, at the station. Though now that I say it, I've only needed an actual fork for that kind of stuff once and it most definitely wasn't one of your aunt Diane's apple pies."

She crossed her arms at her chest. "What makes you so sure I didn't make that pie?"

He paused, his first forkful of pie less than a centimeter from his mouth. "Did you?"

"Nope. Why would I? They don't come any better than hers." Perching on the edge of the desk, she watched as the stress he'd worn since he walked in his office slowly ebbed away. And, as it did, she made a mental note to thank Diane for suggesting the gesture.

He grinned at her across the tines of his fork. "You're smiling . . ."

"You're right, I am."

"Why?"

"Because you are. And I've been worried about you." She opened her mouth to the forkful of pie he offered and, when he went back for another bite of his own, she gestured toward the whiteboard and the absence of anything resembling possible suspects or motives in the Russ Granger case. "Still nothing, huh?"

Just like that, any joy the pie had managed to bring was gone as he pushed back the plate, stood, and wandered over to the window overlooking the same fields he'd once farmed alongside his father. "I need suspects in order to be able to write stuff down."

"Isn't Callie's ex-husband a possibility? With revenge being the motive?"

"Maybe . . ."

"And what about the notion that someone Russ may have had a hand in putting behind bars decided to exact revenge?" she asked as she, too, abandoned the desk. Only this time, instead of leaving him to digest in front of the window alone, she closed the gap and rested her hand on his back. "Maybe what you're looking for is as close as the department files from Russ's time here in Heavenly."

"Which I've been poring over all day." Turning, he captured her hand in his and directed her toward the door with his chin. "Come on, let me show you."

In the hallway, he released her hand in favor of the small of her back and guided her to the left, passing first the chief's office and then the break room. At a door just beyond the records department, he reached into the darkened room and flipped on a fluorescent overhead light.

Sure enough, spread out across a large fifteen-person conference table, were open files, mug shots, arrest records, and what appeared to be handwritten notes on standard five-by-seven-inch notebook paper.

"Welcome to my day," he said, sweeping his free hand toward the table. "And this only represents two years of the twenty Russ was with this department. I've got eighteen more to go."

"Wow," she whispered, stepping forward. "And have you come across anything at all in these two years?"

"I still have about six months to go but these are from his first two years — which makes them almost twenty-five years old. Add in the fact that he was early in his career and thus not the arresting officer in most cases, I'm not thinking I'll find anything here."

She ran her hand along the top of a folder marked with the month and year and then glanced back at Jakob. "Yet you're still looking."

"I don't want to miss anything, Claire. I *can't* miss anything."

"Is that why you're starting with the older files first?"

"I'll get to all of them sooner rather than later, but the last ten years of his career here were as chief, which means he was inside more than outside."

"So you're thinking any true involvement worthy of revenge would have happened earlier in his career?"

"Seems most likely, yeah. But I'll look at them all even if that has me in this room straight through to tomorrow night."

"It won't take that long because I'm going to help." She pulled out the chair closest to the untouched pile. "Just tell me where I need to look to see if he was involved with a particular case and I'll set those aside for you to review. That should make the process go faster and free you up to put your concentration where it needs to be."

"Awww, Claire, I can't ask you to do that. It's" — he looked at his watch and the darkness outside the conference room window — "already coming up on nine o'clock at this point. You have to get up early to help Diane prep for the guests' breakfast before heading off to the shop . . . This is my job, not yours."

Plucking the top file off the stack, she set it directly in front of her and flipped it open. "I may not have met Russ in person, but I've heard you talk about him so many times I feel as if I did. He was special . . . like you. And if anything like that had happened to you, I'd want every able-bodied person in a five-state radius doing what it took to find the person responsible. So I'm your five-state radius. Right here. In this chair. For however long it takes."

"I'm not going to change your mind, am I?" At her emphatic *no,* he moved in behind her chair and pointed across her shoulder at the top sheet in the file. "Okay, so this is an incident report. It tells us what the incident was, *here* . . . . The time that it occurred, *here* . . . Which officers were involved, *here,* and so on."

She followed his index finger to the bottom half of the page as he explained the section devoted to the officer's verbal description of the event. A second page noted the name of the arresting officer if there was one, as well as the names of any other officers on the scene and the action that was taken — warning, ticket, or arrest.

"If you see mention of Russ's name anywhere, set that file in between us. If you don't, stick it in a pile to your right. Sound good?"

"Absolutely."

He headed toward the chair he'd obviously been sitting in for much of the day, but refrained from sitting as he made eye contact again. "And you're sure you really want to do this? Because I don't expect —"

"I'm really sure." She dropped her attention to the first file, scanned the report for any sign of Russ, and set it off to her right. "One out of the way . . ."

The next file yielded Russ's name in the witnessing officer field and so she set it between them and moved on. File by file she made her way through what was left of the original pile and then got a new set of folders from Curt. As she worked, she began breaking down the Russ pile into smaller, priority-based stacks. One for minor issues like traffic stops, one for standard issues such as peace disturbance calls, and one for bigger things like domestic calls, destruction of property, and anything else that resulted in an actual arrest — with Russ as the arresting officer.

Twice they stopped for a break, one called by Jakob and one called by Claire. Jakob's break involved a hug, a little pacing, and a stop at the station's vending machines for a soda and a bag of chips. Claire's break also included a hug, but then branched off into a few quick stretching exercises and a vending machine stop for a chocolate bar and a bottle of water. But even with the breaks and the additional priority sorting she'd taken on, she made her way through twenty-five years of files by the time dawn started peeking through the window. And in doing so, Jakob's pile grew exponentially.

"I'd hoped my being here would help lessen your load." She set the last file in its correct pile and took a long, hard look at the center of the table and the three distinct stacks making it so all she could really see of Jakob was from the nose up. "Yet, looking at this, I have to think I made it worse."

He looked up from the report in front of him, his brow furrowed, his expression one of distraction. "Huh?"

"This." She splayed her hands to indicate the Russ-related files and the now-empty stretch of table directly in front of her seat. "My part is done, yet yours is *mountainous* now."

"No, it's . . ." His gaze dropped back down to the paperwork in front of him. "Listen to this: 'I stopped at Dottie's Diner on Route 35 for a sandwich around noon on March fourth. While I was returning to my car I witnessed Mr. Tom Shaunessy driving past the parking lot, drinking from a flask and swerving. I got in my car and pursued the suspect. The suspect ignored the sirens and kept driving, stopping only when his car struck the children's school bus shelter. The bus shelter was empty. When I approached the vehicle, the suspect was actively drinking from a flask. When instructed to put it down, he threw it at me, dousing my uniform in whiskey. I placed him under arrest and brought him back to the station where the suspect proceeded to fail the alc test.' "

Jakob flipped the page over, sifted through the remaining paperwork, and smacked his hand down on the final page. "Yes, I thought it was him . . ."

"Him? Him, who?" She pushed back her chair and came around behind Jakob, her eyes narrowing in on the familiar face. "Wait. Isn't that the guy who ran for mayor of Cedarville this past spring? The one who was absolutely slaughtered in the press for . . ." Sucking in her breath, she palmed her mouth and slowly lowered herself onto the vacant chair directly next to Jakob. "Oh. Wow."

"You can say that again. He was publicly

humiliated in the press both before and after the election. Do you remember the signs his opponent's team held up outside the polls on election day? The ones calling him a danger to the town's children? And calling him out as the very definition of poor judgment?"

She nodded. "And when was this? The arrest, I mean?"

"Ten years ago. Just before Russ retired and moved to Florida. Shaunessy lost his license for a year, had to attend counseling, had to submit to random urine tests for two years, and was sentenced to two hundred hours of community service."

Ricocheting her focus between the file and Jakob, she worked to steady the sudden acceleration of her heart. "Do . . . do you think this could be it?"

He stared at the former mayoral candidate's picture for a few more moments and then made his way back through each and every document in the man's file, his eyes scanning every line of every page. Eventually, he set it down to face Claire. "I don't know. It's too early to say. But he'd certainly have one heckuva motive."

CHAPTER 11

"Claire?"

Lifting her head off the cool metal, she forced her eyelashes apart enough to make out the Amish teenager standing just outside her office door, a curious look on her young, makeup-free face. "I'm here . . . I'm here."

"I'm sorry to wake you but your detective is here to see you."

She wiped the odd dampness from the right side of her chin and slowly pushed back her chair. "I wasn't sleeping, Annie. I was just resting. That's all."

The corner of Annie's mouth twitched with a smile she fought valiantly to hold back. "Perhaps you would like to look in the mirror before you come out."

"I don't need to . . ." The rest of her protest disappeared as, at Annie's suggestion, she located her compact in the top drawer of her desk and took a peek. Sure enough, in addition to the hooded eyes and flattened hair, there was also a sizable red patch on her right cheek that served as proof of time spent on her metal pillow. "Oh. Oh my."

"I came in to see if I could get you something at Shoo Fly during my lunch break and you did not move. So I ate at the counter."

She glanced at the clock above the door and sagged back against her chair. "Oh, Annie, I'm so *so* sorry. I didn't mean to fall asleep like that. It's just that I was awake all night, helping Jakob with something at the station, and I guess it caught up with me. One minute I was looking at the books" — she pointed at the open notebook next to where her head had been — "and, well, I guess I must have nodded off. Hard."

"It is okay," Annie said, smiling. "It is not good to be awake all night."

Nodding, Claire rose to her feet, balanced herself against the desk, and when she was sure she could stay upright, crossed to the door and Annie. "Thank you, kiddo. For covering for me like you did. I'm just sorry you had to."

Annie's narrow shoulders rose with a shrug. "I am glad you could get a little sleep. Perhaps you should go home after you speak with Jakob and get some more — in a real bed. I can close the shop on my own. I have done it many times."

"I know you have and I know you can. But it's *my* day to close and *your* day to leave at three. I don't want to change that and mess up any plans you may have."

"Dat will not be home until supper. He has a meeting with the new minister."

"I met Elmer the other night outside Eli's house, and then again last night, when I drove his wife, Miriam, home from the store. He is a very nice man."

"Yah. Dat says he has good ideas for many things. Henry, too, says he is nice."

She grinned at Annie's chosen barometers for a person's character and then motioned toward the shop's main room. "I am afraid I have kept Jakob waiting too long as it is. Let's go back inside now and see if everything is okay."

Annie led the way through the narrow hallway and into the showroom with Claire following at a slightly slower pace. Still, the moment Claire rounded the corner into the shop and spied Jakob standing by the window overlooking the alleyway, she managed to rustle up every ounce of energy she had to have a smile in place when he turned. "Hi there. I'm sorry it took me so long to get out —"

"What happened to your face?" He crossed the distance between them with just a few long strides. When he reached her, he cupped her cheek in his hand. "Did you fall?"

"Oh, I fell, alright . . . I fell *asleep*. On the desk in my office. And by *asleep* I mean, 'out cold.' " She captured his hand with hers, moved it around to her mouth for a kiss, and then lowered it down to the space between them. "But yet, I'm looking at you — who was awake all night, as well — and I'm not seeing any sign of tiredness at all. Did you go home or something?"

He laughed. "Uh . . . no. In fact, until I left to come here, I haven't been outside the conference room since I walked you out this morning."

"Jakob! That's not smart! You need your sleep."

"And so do you. Yet" — he released her hand in favor of spreading his to indicate the displays around them — "here you are. At work."

"Sleeping in my office, you mean." She grinned in the direction of the counter and the almost-seventeen-year-old who was trying not to appear as if she was listening. "Fortunately for me, I have Annie Hershberger picking up my slack, isn't that right,

Annie?"

Annie returned the smile, her cheeks taking on a crimson hue.

"Annie, that reminds me . . ." Jakob made his way over to the counter, clearly gauging how close he could get before the bishop's daughter grew uncomfortable. When she began shifting her weight from leg to leg, he opted to cover the remaining distance with a smile. "I want to thank you for that great idea you had yesterday in regards to my friend's — well, in regards to the case I'm working on. It was quite clever. In fact, it's the thought that someone may have been out for revenge that had Claire and me up all night."

The girl's eyes dropped to the ground and then shifted to Claire before fixing, finally, tentatively, on Jakob. "Is that what happened? Is it someone who did not like to be chased?"

"Last night, I saw it as a possibility. Now I'm starting to see it as a probability. But I have a lot more work to do before I can even think about making an arrest and setting the wheels of justice in motion for my friend and his family." He took another half step forward and, when Annie didn't stiffen, he made it a whole step. "Claire has said many times in the last six months that you are smart in your work here at the store. Now I can add that you are smart in many ways. Like having good hunches."

Clearly uncomfortable with Jakob's praise, Annie smoothed the sides of her pale blue dress with her hands and then grabbed the clipboard with the day's to-do list. Still, as she ran her finger past the checks she, herself, had likely made while Claire was sleeping, the tiniest hint of a smile played at the corners of her lips. A glance at Jakob proved that he, like Claire, saw it, too.

She joined him near the counter as Annie headed across the room to the candle display. What the girl was going to do, Claire had no idea, but there was no denying Annie's eye when it came to arranging things in a way that called to shoppers. She watched for a few moments as Annie fussed with the candles on a neighboring shelf and then turned back to Jakob. "I hated leaving you with such big piles to go through this morning. If it was something I could've helped with, I would —"

He stopped the rest of her apology with a gentle finger against her lips and then followed it up with a quick peck designed to minimize any discomfort for Annie. "Trust me, Claire, your help last night was invaluable. It filtered out things I don't need to waste my time on so I can concentrate on the items that might actually lead me to the doorstep of Russ's killer."

"You'll find him. I have no doubt." She reveled in the energizing boost that was his embrace and then stepped back. "So did you come across anyone else who might be a possibility?"

"Not really. Not yet."

"Keep looking. You just may end up finding a few that'll rival the kind of motive that mayoral candidate certainly has."

He rubbed at his stubbled jawline and then pulled her close once again. "Which brings us to why I stopped by. I'm sorry but I'm going to have to bail on our movie night this evening. I hate to do it as I've been looking forward to it since last week, but I really don't have a choice."

"That's okay. I understand. You really need to get some sleep."

"I'm not bailing out on our date so I can get some sleep. I just feel like I need to stop in and check on Callie and the kids. See how they're doing. The visitation is tomorrow and the funeral the day after, and I know it's going to be hard. Losing one parent is heartbreaking. Losing both, in a relatively short time period, is unthinkable."

She took a half step back and then reached

up, cupping the side of his scruffy cheek in her hand. "You're amazing, you know that?"

"Thanks, Claire." Leaning forward, he lingered a kiss on her forehead. "I still can't believe he's gone . . ."

"I know. And I'm so sorry. Just know you can still visit him in your memories and I'm always here to listen when you want to talk."

He pulled back, reached for her hand, and squeezed. "I know, and I'm grateful."

"I don't know if I mentioned this or not yet, but Harold and some of the other shopkeepers here on Lighted Way are working on a way to honor Russ and his service to Heavenly. Some of the ideas they're batting around are very special and I told them I'd like to help, too."

For a moment she wasn't sure he'd heard. But when she looked up at him to see if he'd been distracted by something, she saw him valiantly fighting back tears. "Oh, Jakob, I wish I could take this from you," she whispered.

He breathed in deeply through his nose and then released it slowly through his mouth. A second round of the same, followed by a third, soon had his eyes clear. "I'd like you to go with me to the visitation or funeral if you can spare the time."

"I wouldn't think of being anywhere else."

"Thank you. And if it's okay, I'd like to swing out to that bar out on Route 65 after the visitation if you're game? If not, I can just drop you back at your aunt's and then head out there myself."

She tried to keep her surprise in check, but even with the effort, she was pretty sure a slight wince got through. "No, of course I'll go with you if that's what you want to do . . . But if you're thinking you'll be upset and needing to talk, maybe something quieter like Heavenly Brews might make it easier for me to hear you."

"If it was about wanting to talk, I'd take you back to the inn or to my place. But it's not about that." He glanced at the candle display and then lowered his voice so as to be heard only by Claire. "I want to see if the bartender tomorrow night is the same one that was there on Saturday night."

"Saturday night?" she echoed. "I don't understand. What difference does it make what bartender was working . . ." The rest of the question faded away as the answer filtered through her thoughts and out her mouth. "Scratch that. That's the night Russ asked you to meet him there."

Jakob's jaw tightened with the memory a split second before his amber-flecked eyes disappeared in a longer-than-normal blink.

"Jakob?"

Slowly, his eyes returned to hers, only now, instead of just sadness, there was . . . *anger*?

"Jakob, what's wrong?"

"I should have gone, Claire . . . Russ was my mentor. *My friend.* And because I didn't want to be up too late, I pushed him off until Sunday afternoon." His voice grew hoarse. "If I'd gone . . . If I'd spent that time with him . . . I'd have been able to tell him more about you . . . I'd have been able to tell him how much he meant to me . . . And maybe I'd have noticed Shaunessy eyeing him up from whatever dark hole he may have been slithering around in that night . . ."

She pulled in a breath. "You think this guy was at the bar that night?"

"It would certainly nail the timing if he was."

Jakob was right. It would. Still, everything else he'd said was wrong.

"You have to know you had nothing to do with what happened to Russ," she pleaded. "Please. Please tell me you know that."

She followed his focus down to their intertwined hands and felt the answering squeeze. "I would, if I could, Claire."

CHAPTER 12

Somehow she managed to get through the rest of the day — the customer questions, the purchases, the shelving, the cleaning, and, finally, closing on her own. Regardless of how busy she was, though, her thoughts were never far from Jakob and the heartbreaking admission he'd made just moments before returning to work.

She'd tried to make him see he was wrong, that Russ's death happened outside his daughter's guest house, miles away from the bar the retired chief had suggested for a meet-up with Jakob. But when he'd headed out the door for the station, she knew she hadn't made even so much as a dent in his conviction.

"Claire?"

Startled back to her surroundings, Claire glanced up at Shoo Fly Bake Shoppe's front porch and the twenty-four-year-old Amish woman watching her intently. "Ruth, hi.

I . . . I didn't see you standing there."

"That is because you were looking down instead of up." Eli's twin sister, Ruth, crossed to the top of the three-step staircase and ran her ocean blue eyes from Claire's auburn-colored hair to the tips of her brown ankle-length boots and back. "You are missing your usual happy smile."

She opened her mouth to protest her Amish friend's assessment but closed it in favor of a shrug. "I'm just tired, is all. I didn't get any sleep last night and it's caught up with me, I guess."

"Then come. I have something that you will like." Beckoning Claire onto the porch, Ruth turned and led the way inside her shop, a potpourri of cinnamon, vanilla, and all things delicious greeting them just as surely as any bell or person ever could. "I have made some black-and-white cookies — the kind you said you liked when you lived in the city."

"You made . . ." The words faded away as her gaze traveled from her friend, to the glass display case, and finally, to the simple plate stacked with the yin-and-yang-like cookies now calling to her from the top shelf. "Oh, Ruth. I haven't had one of those since the day I left New York City. It was my parting gift to myself."

"I am glad you left New York. It means you could come here."

Then, without another word, Ruth slid open the glass case from the back and reached inside. Claire, in turn, worked to mute the anticipatory rumble of her stomach with her hand while studying her shy friend. Clothed in traditional Amish dress for a young, unmarried woman, Ruth was, in a word, stunning. Her blonde hair, parted severely down the middle and covered with a kapp, set off the breathtaking blue eyes she shared with her older brother, Benjamin. Her high cheekbones and perfectly arched brows completed a face more befitting a high-fashion runway than an Amish bakery. Yet as beautiful as the exterior was, it didn't hold a candle to who Ruth was on the inside.

"You are to take two. One to eat now and one to eat on your walk home." Ruth set the two cookies on a plain white napkin and handed them to Claire across the top of the case. "Perhaps that will help you stay awake as you go."

"This probably sounds crazy, but these right here" — she held up the cookie-topped napkin — "are one of my only good memories from that time in my life. In fact, there were days when the promise of one of

145

these kept me from sobbing."

Ruth slid the case closed, her delicate mouth sagging downward at the corners. "I am sorry your marriage did not work. But you are happy now, yah?"

Claire shook off the unwelcome trip down memory lane and wandered over to the single table in the corner. When Ruth accepted her invitation to sit, Claire did, as well. "I'm *very* happy now, Ruth. I fit here. In . . . in a way I never did in the city. I fit with you, and Annie, and Esther, and your brothers in a way I never did with anyone there."

"And Jakob? You fit with Jakob?"

"Oh yes." She turned her still-uneaten cookie over in her hand, the very thought of Jakob bringing the aforementioned missing smile to her lips. "With Jakob, I can be me. I can talk about and enjoy the things that make me happy and know that he enjoys them, too. He puts people over things, and he's kindhearted. *To everyone.*"

Ruth dipped her head in a quick nod and then let her own gaze travel out the front window and down the street past Heavenly Treasures. "I feel those same things about Samuel. He is a good man. A hardworking man like Dat. Even though he does not need to, he looks out for me as Eli does.

And when I speak or have an idea, he listens to me as Benjamin does."

Claire looked down at the black-and-white cookie and took a bite off the chocolate side. "Benjamin really is an amazing listener. We had some truly wonderful talks up on the hill by the covered bridge."

"Yah."

Moving on to the white side of the cookie, she took another bite, her eyes practically rolling back in her head. "Oh, Ruth. The chocolate side is good, but . . . wow. The vanilla is amazing."

"I am glad you like it. I hoped you would."

"Samuel better be careful once you're married. He may need to consider something other than furniture making to keep himself fit."

Ruth's cheeks flushed red. "Samuel says the same thing."

It felt good to laugh. Even if the simple act ushered in a reminder of how tired she was at that moment. "Are you excited about your wedding?" she asked, stifling a yawn. "Because nine and a half weeks isn't all that far away, you know."

"Last night, Dat and Benjamin spoke about the room they will build for the wedding."

She took another, smaller bite and compared her friend's anecdote to what she'd learned about Amish weddings since moving to Heavenly. "I still can't believe that the Amish erect a room, considered a permanent addition in an Englisher's home, in a matter of *days.* Only to take it down when the wedding is over."

"There will be many people at the house that day," Ruth ran her finger along the edge of the table and then dropped her hand into her lap. "Many mouths to feed. But Mamm and I will make much food, and Samuel's mamm and sisters will help, too."

Claire nodded. "I helped make bread for Esther's wedding. Aunt Diane and I both did. I have never made so many loaves of bread at one time. Then again, I've never been to a gathering with almost three hundred people at it before, either." She nibbled a little more off the vanilla side of her cookie and then set it back down on her napkin. "Will you have that many people at your wedding, too?"

"Yah. Perhaps more."

"Wow."

Ruth fiddled with the edge of her apron overlay and then lifted her eyes back to Claire's. "You will come, yah?"

"I wouldn't miss it for the world, Ruth." And it was true. Ruth was special. She was

148

kind and thoughtful and the first shopkeeper on Lighted Way to . . . Propping her elbows on the table, Claire settled her chin on her palm. "I'll never forget my first day at the store. I was a nervous wreck. But you came in with that comforting smile of yours, welcomed me to Lighted Way, and handed me a chocolate chip cookie fresh from the oven. And more than anything else that first day, *you* doing *that* made me absolutely certain I'd made the right decision."

Ruth's cheeks flushed red again. "It was just a cookie."

"Trust me, Ruth, it was way more than just a cookie."

Again Ruth's attention dropped to her lap, only to return, rather hesitantly, to Claire. "Will you bring Jakob?"

"Bring Jakob?"

"To my wedding."

She felt herself stiffen at the question and, rather than beat the drum about the Amish and their treatment of Jakob, she used the time it took to finish her cookie to get her emotions in check. When she was sure she could speak without sounding accusatory, she did. "If I am allowed to bring a guest, I would like to bring Jakob, of course. He is important to me and I know he cares very much about you and Samuel. But if that isn't okay with your family or your community, I will simply come alone. Or, perhaps, bring my aunt."

"Jakob can come. Backs will be turned to him, but he can come. Dat, Benjamin, and Eli said it is so."

She made a mental note to thank Ruth's brothers the next time she saw them and pushed back her chair. "Thank you, Ruth. That means a lot." Then, rising to her feet, she scooped up the napkin with the second cookie. "Will you still make dinner sometimes for Ben? I know you worry about him being lonely and all."

Ruth, too, stood. "I do not worry so much about my brother anymore."

"Oh?"

"He eats at Emma's farm many nights now."

Surprise propelled Claire to grab hold of the chair for support. "I . . . I knew Ben was helping Henry and the other boys with the farm in the wake of their father's death, but I didn't realize he was staying for supper now, too."

"Yah."

"But . . ." She stopped, swallowed, and tried again, quietly praying her question reflected the concern she felt, rather than the nosiness one might assume. "Isn't

Emma's period of mourning supposed to be longer? I mean, Henry was killed, what? Three, maybe four months ago, tops?"

Ruth smoothed her hands down the sides of her dress and then quietly surveyed the counter and her surroundings for what Claire assumed were any last-minute tasks before heading home. When she saw nothing that needed to be done, she turned back to Claire, her eyes shiny with excitement. "It is not *Emma* that invites Benjamin to stay."

"Oh. I get it. The kids like having him there." She slid her now-empty chair back into place against the table and stepped toward the door. "I guess that makes sense. Probably helps fill the emptiness a little."

"It is not the *children* who invite Benjamin to stay, either."

Claire paused, midstep, to stare at Ruth. "Then I don't understand."

"It is Rebecca."

"Rebecca?"

"Emma's sister who has come to stay and help with the children." Ruth rose up on the toes of her simple lace-up boots and quietly clasped her hands beneath her chin. "I think she might be the one, Claire — the one to make Benjamin think of getting married again."

Something that felt a lot like joy, but also a little like sadness, rushed her from all sides, rendering her momentarily speechless in the process. But it didn't matter. For Ruth, who was more apt to speak when spoken to, was in full-blown gush mode as she painstakingly described Emma's sister, Rebecca . . .

Eyes: Green. Like a barn cat's.

Smile: Big and warm.

Hair: Blonde, but a little darker than Ruth's and Eli's.

Personality: Sweet and shy, but funny sometimes, too.

Ruth unclasped her hands and reached, instead, for Claire's. "When Benjamin is in the fields with Henry and the other boys, Rebecca brings him a glass of cold lemonade and a wet cloth to help him cool down."

"So this Rebecca is thoughtful, too . . ."

"Yah. And Benjamin says she is a good cook. Like me, he says."

At a loss for what to say, Claire looked out at the road and tried to process the words still pouring from Ruth's mouth. "Sometimes, when I know he is to be returning from dinner at Emma's farm, I make sure to be outside on the porch with my knitting or my quilting. And that is when I see, when I know . . ."

"See and know what?" Claire echoed, turning back to her fellow shop owner and friend.

"That he is not lonely anymore. That he is *happy* in the way I want him to be. In the way I know *you* want him to be, too."

CHAPTER 13

On any other day, she'd have set out for the Amish side of town to be alone with her thoughts. Something about walking along the quiet roads alone, regardless of the season, soothed her soul. But the stop at Ruth's had made it so her window between closing the shop and helping Diane with dinner at the inn was diminishing. Rapidly. So instead of turning west, she headed east, the day's waning rays doing little to offset the hint of a nip in the air.

Twenty minutes earlier, her mind had been filled with just two thoughts — Jakob and sleep. Now, thanks to the Amish bake shop owner, a third had been added to the mix.

If Emma's sister, Rebecca, made Benjamin happy, then yes, Claire was happy, too. She'd been hoping and praying the kind-hearted widower would find someone special ever since she'd turned down his offer of a life together. At the time, she'd known in her heart it wouldn't work. Jakob had paid dearly for his decision to leave. The last thing she wanted to do was see Ben go through the same thing.

But it had been more than that, too. She loved Ben as a friend. Period.

So why, then, was news of a possible love interest for her friend rattling her so much?

"I want him to be happy," she whispered as her feet parted company with the cobble-stoned portion of Lighted Way. "He deserves that."

"Can I give you a lift the rest of the way?"

She turned toward the familiar voice, squinted through the open passenger-side window of the now-stopped white sedan, and let loose a not-so-tired squeal at the sight of the grinning man seated behind the steering wheel. "Oh my gosh, Bill! You're . . . *here.* You're really, really here!"

The travel agent's laugh floated from the car as she ran around the hood and over to the driver's side. "I . . . I thought you were coming next week."

"I was. But then, when Diane mentioned something about having a few empty rooms going into the weekend, I decided to take a chance." His smile slipped momentarily as she followed his gaze to the lone bend in the road that stood between them and Sleep Heavenly. "You don't think she'll be upset with me just showing up, do you?"

"Upset? Are you kidding me? She'll be thrilled."

His eyes moved straight back to hers. "A friend of mine told me he hasn't seen me act like this about anyone in decades, if ever."

"Like this?"

Pulling his hand from the steering wheel, he pushed it, instead, through his salt-and-pepper hair. "I don't think I've attended a party, gone for a run, put together a travel itinerary, or had a single phone conversation with anyone where I haven't brought Heavenly, Pennsylvania, into the mix."

"It's a nice place," she teased. "I talk about it a lot, too."

"Yeah, but if you polled all those people I've mentioned Heavenly to over the past few months, they'd think it's a town inhabited by one."

She settled her hand at the base of her neck and batted her lashes. "I'm honored to know I left such an impression."

His complexion reddened. "I've mentioned you a time or two, of course . . . You know, your shop, your detective boyfriend —"

"Hey . . . it's okay. I'm just playing with you a little." Leaning through the window, she planted a kiss on the top of the sixty-something man's head. "I know who you're talking about. And truth be told, I couldn't be more pleased."

He cleared his throat of any shred of discomfort as his gaze traveled through the windshield once again. "Your aunt is a very special person, Claire."

"I couldn't agree more. Which is why I'm going to take you up on that lift." She headed back around the front of the car to the passenger side and opened the door. "That way I get home in better time than I seem to be making, and I get to see her face when you come through the door."

When she was settled in her seat with her seat belt fastened, he slid the car into gear yet kept his foot on the brake. "Just now, when I was coming up behind you, it seemed like you were a million miles away. Is everything okay?"

"I'm just tired. I was helping Jakob with something at the station and I pretty much went from there to work with a quick stop back at the inn to shower."

"I would imagine, if you two pulled an all-nighter, it must be something pretty important?"

Giving in to the sigh the subject all but demanded, she flopped her head back against the headrest. "Jakob's mentor was killed over the weekend. Here. In Heavenly."

"Oh, Claire, I'm sorry. Was it a car accident?"

"No. He was murdered."

Bill's answering gasp was quickly followed by the feel of his hand on hers. "Is — is there anything I can do?"

"You can say a prayer that I can find a way to convince him it wasn't his fault."

"His fault? Why? What happened?"

She fingered a piece of lint on her slacks for a few seconds and then brushed it onto the floor. "Russ apparently came to town to see his daughter. He and Jakob planned to get together and catch up Sunday evening. But on Saturday, Russ called and asked Jakob to meet him out at a pub on Route 65. Jakob said he opted against it because we had plans to spend time together the next morning and he didn't want to chance oversleeping or being too tired for that."

"Jakob doesn't really strike me as a bar kind of guy, anyway."

"That may have been a factor, as well, but either way, he told Russ he'd just see him Sunday evening as originally planned." Pausing to collect her thoughts, she let her attention wander to the water bottle in the center-console cup holder, the GPS system plugged into the cigarette lighter, and the various coins separated by value in their applicable spot. When she was ready, she continued with the part of the story she wished she didn't have to tell. "Only it never happened. Because while we were at the pond, having our picnic after church, the station called. Russ's body had been found outside the garage apartment where he'd been staying while visiting his daughter and grandchildren."

Bill took a moment to process Claire's words. When he had, he shook his head. "So why is Jakob blaming himself?"

"Because he thinks that if it was someone who maybe followed Russ home from the bar, he could have stopped it, I guess. But here's the thing. From what Jakob has told me about the case so far, Russ had been back at the apartment for a while before he ended up outside again. So the way I see it, even if Jakob *had* met Russ at the bar, the likelihood he would have still been with Russ at the garage apartment was next to nothing. Yet he's still beating himself up."

"Give him a little time, Claire. He's probably still in shock over the loss of his friend. The fact that it happened at the hands of a murderer in his own town, surely makes it even worse." Reaching across the center console, Bill quietly tucked a strand of hair behind Claire's ear. "And while I know I only met him a few times when I was here back in early June, Jakob struck me as a smart man. Sooner or later, he'll be able to see through the pain he's in right now to the reality of the situation. When he does, he'll know the only one at fault is the person who took his friend's life."

"I hope you're right, I really do." She managed a smile and then gestured toward the road. "Anyway, I'm pretty sure you didn't drive all this way from Kentucky just so you can sit here, on the side of the road, talking to me."

"I didn't, but that doesn't mean I'm not enjoying it." Bill rested his own head against the seat. "All this time, I've been trying to explain to my friends what it is about this place that I can't forget — beyond your aunt, of course. But sitting here, talking to you, it's suddenly so clear I can't believe I couldn't put it into words before now."

Releasing her seat belt, she squared her back against the door and took a moment to really study the person seated not more than a foot or two away. Bill Brockman was a handsome man. The salt-and-pepper shade of his hair lent itself well to the distinguished flare he wore as easily as the playful glint in his blue-green eyes. His affinity for running had him in good physical shape, yet, from what she remembered, he was always willing and able to enjoy a good meal, too.

"I like the whole package of being here," he said. "I married young and, since it didn't work out and there were no kids in the mix, I never really found myself looking in the rearview mirror all that much. I traveled. I ran. I worked. And I found people along the way that enjoyed those things, too — travel buddies, running buddies, colleagues, that sort of thing. And it worked for me, because I didn't have anything to compare it to until now. Or, rather, until I was here back in June. This" — he moved his index finger back and forth between their seats — "is just shoring it up in broader terms."

She leaned forward. "Tell me."

He was silent for so long, she actually wondered if he'd heard her. But just as she was getting ready to repeat herself, he took a deep breath, lowered his gaze from the ceiling to her, and splayed his hands. "Every time I sat in the parlor, or the dining room, or out on the porch with you and Diane, I felt like I was part of something bigger. I liked hearing what you were up to, and meeting your young man. I liked watching Diane's face light up when she talked about the horses out at that Amish barn she took us all to. I liked learning fun facts about the different breeds because it mattered to her. I liked sitting on the porch swing sometimes at night, looking out over the fields and not having to talk because the silence was comfortable. I liked talking about my travels in a different way with her than I ever have with anyone before. And I wanted — no, *needed* — to know that the person behind that Amish farmer's murder had been apprehended."

She felt the emotion rising in her throat and did her best to swallow it back down, but it was hard. Especially when those same emotions were magnified tenfold across Bill's face as he continued. "Even now, when I pulled up alongside you and saw your face, I knew something wasn't right and I wanted to fix it. Still do."

"I'm okay," she whispered, closing her hand around his. "I just have to have faith that Jakob will see he's not responsible for Russ's death, like you said."

He flipped his hand inside hers and squeezed. "He will. With your help."

"Thank you."

"So . . . How has everything else been with you? Shop going okay? Finding a little time to enjoy your friends?"

"The shop is good. Annie is a godsend." She pulled her hand from his in favor of fidgeting with the strap of her purse. "And my friends are . . . good."

"Uh-oh."

She laughed in spite of the heaviness she couldn't quite shake off. "I can be a little transparent, huh?"

"I wouldn't say transparent. Rather, I'd like to think that even though I only stayed at the inn for a grand total of two weeks back in June, I was present during our conversations. And when a person is present, they start to pick up cues. At least they do if they care. Which I do, by the way."

"I know. That's part of the reason you didn't feel like a guest. You felt like . . ." She cast about for the right description only to have Bill sum it up in one word.

"Family." Then, turning his attention forward and onto the road, he nodded. "That's it. I felt like I was with family when I was here, and I've felt like something has been off ever since I left."

She followed his gaze through the windshield, past the trees and their changing colors that dotted the edges of the road, and then closed her eyes, the need to talk through what was troubling her heart winning out over her discomfort at sharing something so personal with a man who felt like family yet wasn't.

"My friend Benjamin has found someone special — someone his sister thinks could be the one."

"Benjamin . . . Benjamin . . ." Pitching forward, he snapped his fingers. "I remember Ben. He's Amish. Used to be childhood friends with Jakob . . . Lost his wife shortly after they got married . . ."

"That's him." She fidgeted the edge of her slacks between her fingers only to release the fabric along with a sigh. "And I'm . . . I don't know . . . Torn, I guess?"

"Why? Do you have feelings for this man, Claire?"

She let the question hang in the air long enough to truly consider it. Did she? Did she feel more for Benjamin than she'd allowed herself to believe? Did —

"No. Not in the way I think you mean, anyway." Oh, it felt good to talk, good to get it all out, even if the words that came pouring out seemed to be doing so of their own volition. "When I first came here, after my divorce, I was pretty lost. I'd failed in marriage and I was angry at myself. I spent the first six months of my being here, holed up in the inn. I read, I went for walks, and I cried on Aunt Diane's shoulder so much, I'm still shocked she didn't float away. But, eventually, with her help, I decided to open Heavenly Treasures — something that was *all me* with no ties to Peter or New York. Benjamin was one of the first people I met that day, after his sister, Ruth. He was kind. And, for whatever reason, he seemed to be interested in what I had to say in a way Peter never had been. He listened to my ideas for the shop and encouraged my efforts. And, along the way, I began to wonder if I was having feelings for him. I mean, I thought about him all the time. I'd get excited when I heard his buggy in the alley, and I'd get excited when I looked up from whatever display I was working on and he'd be standing there, smiling back at me. Soon, the brief moments during the day turned into hanging out on the hill overlooking his farm. I'd talk about the shop and my past, and he'd talk about the farm and his siblings, and, after a while, we started to share dreams — or, I guess, I did, anyway. But he always listened. He made me feel like I was interesting, like I was something special."

"That's because you are, Claire. Don't

ever doubt that."

"But I did. All the time. Until Ben."

"What about Diane?" Bill reminded her.

She took in a breath. "Ben's patience and kindness helped me heal in a different way than Aunt Diane did."

"How so?"

"Aunt Diane was like . . ." She paused and collected her thoughts. "Aunt Diane was my lighthouse in the storm, so to speak. Her smile, her hugs, her motivating words . . . Those are the things that helped me get me back on my feet and believing that I could start over and be okay. And without that — without *her* — I'm quite certain I wouldn't have Heavenly Treasures and all the wonderful friends I've made because of it."

A sweet smile claimed the left side of Bill's mouth. "She'd have made a great mom."

"You're right. And I know this, because she's made one heck of an amazing aunt."

His gaze wandered through the windshield once again, only this time, instead of continuing down the road in front of them, it seemed to seek a shortcut through the trees to the same destination. But just as she was getting ready to suggest they move along again, he turned back to her. "And Ben?

What part in the healing process did he play?"

"He was like the surgeon who helped sew my heart back together." Resting her cheek against the seat, she shrugged. "Which is why I was able to give it to Jakob."

"Ahhhh . . ."

"Ben wanted to leave his community behind for me. He wanted to marry me, Bill."

Surprise lifted his brow, but he said nothing.

"But I turned him down. Because as important as he was to me, I knew he wasn't the one for me. Not in that way, anyway."

She could see her aunt's friend trying to take everything in. She could also see the confusion her words caused. "Trust me, Bill, I've been trying to figure out why the notion of Ben falling for someone else is weighing on me like it is. I don't get it, either. I don't have those kinds of feelings for him, I really don't. In fact, I pray every single night that he'll meet someone as special as he is."

Sitting up tall, she splayed her hands. "Yet now that it appears as if that might actually be the case, I'm like" — she waved inward — *"this."*

"Do you not like this woman?" Bill asked.

"No! I haven't even met her!"

Bill traced his finger around the steering wheel, stopping as he reached the top. "Maybe that's the issue. Maybe you need to know in that heart of yours he helped patch, that he's going to be okay."

She looked a question at him.

"That's the way it is when you love people, isn't it? Their happiness and safety matters as much to you as your own, yes?"

Claire nodded.

"Then it seems to me it's only natural that you're worried about him. He lost his first wife, didn't he?"

Again, she nodded.

"And he was a crucial part in your own healing process after your divorce . . ."

"Yes."

"You want him to be happy, Claire. That's all. And until you meet this woman and can see for yourself that she's worthy, you're going to be like" — he matched her earlier wave — "*this,* as you say."

She stared at him as his words filtered their way from her ears, to her brain, and, finally, to her heart.

"Seek her out, Claire. Maybe, once you do, you'll be able to see that your prayers have been answered in the best possible way."

It all made so much sense. It really did.

Reaching out, she plucked his hand from its resting spot against the steering wheel and squeezed. "I'm so very, *very* glad you've come back, Bill."

Chapter 14

She was rearranging the shelf of Amish dolls when the jingle of the door-mounted bells sent her focus to the front of the shop, and the face that had a way of brightening even the drabbest of days.

"Esther!" Tossing the last two dolls onto the rest, Claire took off across the store, her pace quickening as her gaze fell on the infant in the crook of her friend's arm. "And you brought Sarah to see me, too!"

"Yah."

She stopped, kissed Esther on the cheek, and then, after the nod of approval she sought, scooped the baby into her own arms. "Well, hello there, sweet girl. Are you having a nice day out with your mamm?"

"I took her next door for one of Ruth's brownies. She liked it very much."

Freezing, midcoo, she glanced up at her friend, her heart beginning to pound in her ears. "Esther, sweetie . . . You can't give a three-week-old baby brownies. Or" — she looked back down at Sarah — "solid food of any kind."

Esther's answering silence pulled Claire's attention back to her friend and the mischievous smile her former employee currently sported. "Wait! That was a joke?"

"Yah."

"Ha, ha." She turned her own smile back on Sarah. "Your mamm can be a very silly mamm sometimes, little one."

"Eli tells her the same thing."

Lifting the baby so her tiny ear was mere inches from Claire's lips, Claire added, "The two of you are going to have so much fun together, you just wait and see." Then, eyeing the child's mother once again, she nudged her chin in the direction of the folded newspaper wedged beneath Esther's arm. "What's that?"

"It is Eli's copy of the *Budget.* It came in the mail this morning." Esther crossed to the counter, transferred the clipboard with the day's tasks to its proper hook, and then unfolded the newspaper across the now-clear surface. "You have seen the *Budget,* yah?"

She followed her friend over to the counter and took in the simple headlines comprising the front page. "Samuel Yoder tends to

171

read the latest issue while waiting for our monthly business meeting to start, but I've never really looked too hard at an issue myself. Why?"

"The *Budget* is a national newspaper for Amish and Mennonites. Districts can send in news of crops and weather and special events. See?" Esther pointed to sections of the front page with town names as headings. "In Bordon, Ohio, they have had several days of sunshine and last week's church service was held at the home of Jonas Schlabach. Next time it will be at the home of David Miller. And on Tuesday, the Scenic View School took a field trip to the zoo and the children had a lovely time."

Leaning around Esther, she peeked at a section labeled *Bakerstown, Arkansas,* and read the item aloud. " 'Dennis Miller is okay after falling from a tree while picking apples. The gash on his head was able to be taken care of at home.' " Her gaze skimmed down several paragraphs. " 'Fannie Miller traveled to Holmes County, Ohio, on Tuesday to help with preparations for her sister, Mary's wedding. After learning of her aunt and uncle's health issues in the *Budget* last month, Mattie Troyer traveled to Labarge, Indiana, to help care for them in their final days.'

"Wow," she murmured. "They tell everything in here, don't they?"

"Sometimes it's the only way people know what's going on with their kin in another state. Weddings, illnesses, new babies, deaths . . . It's all in there."

Claire shifted her focus to the right side of the front page and the handful of names included under death notices. "We have obituaries in our papers, too, but not on the front page — unless the death came by way of a crime or something scandalous."

"There are other things inside the paper, too, like recipes and auction notices, and even a few advertisements. But it is these items" — Esther pointed to the sections they'd just read — "that I enjoy most. Mamm, too. When I was little, Mamm would read the section from Heavenly and Spencewood, Wisconsin, to Hannah and me over lunch sometimes."

Pulling her attention off the paper, Claire fixed it, instead, on Esther. "Spencewood, Wisconsin? Why?"

"That is where Mamm's sister went to live. Mamm said reading those bits made her feel close to Lena. Hannah and I liked the Heavenly bits more, especially when Mamm read a name we knew."

"Who writes these things?" Claire asked.

"Just someone in the community. Their name is at the end of the bit."

Sure enough, when Claire looked back at the section she'd been reading about Bakerstown, Arkansas, she saw the name *Melvin E. Hershberger.* "Ahhh. And who sends in the stuff for Heavenly?"

"When I was growing up, it was Annie's mamm. Now it is Annie."

She drew back. "Wait, Annie? As in *my* Annie?"

"Yah. Eli has always said she does a good job, and he is right."

Even without looking at her, Claire would have known Esther was smiling. She could hear it in her voice just as surely as she could see it on her pretty face. Only this time, there was no sign of mischievousness. Just . . . *pride?*

"Estherrr?" she prodded, slanting a look at her friend. "What's going on?"

Esther clasped her hands beneath her chin. "Turn to page nine. The numbers are at the top of the page."

She looked for any tells as to what was so exciting, but when Esther pointed her back to the paper, she obliged and turned to page nine. "Am I looking for anything in particular or —"

Halfway down the page, in the middle column, she saw it.

Heavenly, PA
Lancaster County

September 18 — Warm, sunny days are now followed by chilly evenings. Soon harvesttime will be here and coats will be worn by everyone.

Atlee Hershberger church was held at the home of Emma Stutzmann with Mose Fisher, Grace Fisher, Isaac Fisher, Abram King, Martha King, Hannah King, Eli Miller, Esther Miller, Benjamin Miller, Ruth Miller, Evin Yoder, Evelyn Yoder, Samuel Yoder, Daniel Lapp, Sarah Lapp, John Bontrager, Liddy Bontrager, Elmer Mast, Miriam Mast, Annie Hershberger, and many young children attending. Elmer Mast is the new minister.

Emma Stutzmann's sister, Rebecca, is continuing to stay with Emma to help with the children.

Lester Hochstetler, 6-year-old son of Luke Hochstetler, jumped off a haystack and broke both bones in his left arm. The other boys said he can still fork hay with his right arm so he'll be okay soon.

Published to be married is Samuel Yoder,

son of Evin A. Yoder and Evelyn Yoder, to Ruth Miller, daughter of Zebediah Miller and Mary Miller. The wedding is planned for Thursday, November 29th.

A baby daughter, Sarah Ann, is born to Eli and Esther Miller. Grandparents are Zebediah Miller and Mary Miller and Abram King and Martha King.

Claire glanced back up at Esther and then at the baby intently watching her every move. "Well, look at that . . . you're a little baby celebrity," she half whispered, half cooed. "Your name is in the paper with your mamm and dat."

"Eli says it is not important to see such things, but I caught him reading it *three* times — once before dinner, once after dinner, and once this morning before he went out to the fields."

"It's exciting stuff."

"Yah."

"Annie did a good job on her Heavenly report."

"Yah."

Clearing her throat of its sudden thickness, she looked again at Annie's report, her gaze moving up three paragraphs from mention of the baby. "Um, so I'm guessing, that since church was at Emma's house this past weekend, that you've met her sister, Rebecca?"

"Yah. Many times."

"Oh?"

"Benjamin brought her to dinner on Tuesday night. She is very nice. And funny, too."

"Funny?" she echoed. "But she is Amish, yes?"

Esther pulled a face. "*I* am Amish and I make *you* laugh."

"Yes, but I know you and . . ." She gazed down at Sarah and forced herself to breathe. When she thought she saw the faintest hint of a smile in reaction to her own, she squared her shoulders and turned back to Esther. "So . . . you really think she's nice?"

For a moment Esther said nothing, her hazel eyes, so like Jakob's, inventorying Claire's face in much the same way she might have done with a shelf of dolls or candles before marriage brought an end to her employment at the shop. But just as Claire was starting to become uncomfortable, Esther pulled her and the baby in for a gentle hug. "It is okay, Claire," Esther whispered. "She makes him smile. Even Eli sees it."

She tried to blink away the mist borne on her friend's words, but those three simple sentences said so much — not just about Ben, but also about Esther. Never, in her life, had she ever had a friend quite like Esther. Someone who got her better than she even got herself, sometimes. It didn't matter that they came from such fundamentally different worlds and upbringings; she of the modern world with all its trappings, and Esther of the Amish world with none of that. It didn't matter that Esther was ten years her junior, either. All that mattered — all that had mattered since practically the first time they met — was the overpowering sense that they had the capacity and desire to fill a special place in each other's heart.

For Claire, Esther was like the younger sister she always wished she'd had. For Esther, Claire was the big sister her own birth order had denied.

"You know me so well, Esther, it's almost scary." She kissed her friend's cheek and then stepped back, darting her focus between mother and daughter. "You are one very lucky little girl, Sarah."

When Esther said nothing, Claire pulled the baby to her chest and studied her friend across the top of the infant's soft hair. "Esther? Is everything okay?"

"Perhaps you would like to meet her?"

"Meet who?" she asked.

"Rebecca." Esther wandered over to the front window and its view of Lighted Way. "That way you can see for yourself that she is nice. And if they marry, as I think they will, you will be friends."

Claire drew back. "*Marry?* You think it's that serious?"

"Yah. He speaks of her often, Eli says. Sometimes, when we sit on the porch with the baby after dinner, we see them walking together on the road. And Sunday, after church, they spoke often. When they *were not* speaking, I would see Benjamin looking at her."

"What's she like?" Claire asked. "I mean, besides nice and . . . funny."

"I do not understand."

"Like, how old is she? And why isn't she already married?"

Esther gravitated toward Annie's candle display. "Rebecca is my age, I think. Maybe a little older. She didn't court because she was caring for their mamm, who passed three months before Emma lost Wayne. Benjamin said Rebecca and Emma's mamm was very sick for a long time."

"Oh. Wow. I . . . I'm sorry to hear that."

"I think it has been good for Rebecca to be here, helping Emma with the children. It has given her something new to do. And I know it has been good for Emma to see her sister smiling with the children . . . and Benjamin."

She lowered the baby from her chest back down to her arm and willed the sight of Sarah's sweet face to help keep her voice steady. "Does she show any interest in wanting to go back to upstate New York when Emma and the children are more settled?"

"I do not know." Esther studied the display from various angles and then nodded her approval of Annie's arrangement. "Eli has not said."

"Do *you* think Benjamin would move if he was to marry her?"

"If there is land, and it is important to her, yah. It is Benjamin's way."

Esther was right. Benjamin Miller was a good man. A kind and thoughtful man. If he'd been willing to leave everything he knew for a life with Claire twelve months earlier, surely a simple geographical move at the request of a potential yet grieving bride-to-be would be a given.

So, too, would be the hole in Claire's heart at the loss of her treasured friend . . .

"Is Annie working at all tomorrow?" Esther asked.

Claire shook off her woolgathering and forced herself to focus on the woman watching her from the other side of the room. "Annie? Um, yes. She'll be here by herself for much of the day so I can go to Russ Granger's funeral with Jakob in the morning."

At the mention of her uncle, Esther's smile traded places with worry. "Is Jakob okay?"

"He's struggling, Esther."

"Will you stay with him after the funeral?"

"I'd like to. Very much. But I suspect he'll go back to the office. He's putting in crazy hours right now trying to figure out who killed his friend."

Esther crossed back to the counter and reclaimed the baby from Claire's arms. "If he does, you must come to the farm. We can sit and visit and you can get to know Rebecca."

"Rebecca will be at your house tomorrow?"

"I think it is time we give her a proper welcome to Heavenly, don't you?"

CHAPTER 15

"After everything your aunt shared with me about the two of them, I'm glad to see your detective up there with the man's family."

Claire abandoned her view of Jakob and the line of mourners still waiting to pay their respects to Russ Granger's loved ones and managed a smile for her aunt's newest guest. "I am, too, although watching him deal with this kind of pain and not being able to do anything about it is really hard."

"I suspect just knowing you're here is helping him. I know it would help me if I were him." Bill unbuttoned the top button of his suit jacket and, at Claire's nod, sat on the simple folding chair to her left. "Anything new on your friend?"

She glanced back at Jakob. "It looks like I'm going to get to meet this Rebecca tomorrow afternoon. Over cake and tea at Esther's house." Then, realizing she was using names the travel agent probably didn't

know, she rushed to clarify. "Esther is my
—"

"Friend. She's Amish. She worked with you at the shop until she got married. And she's Jakob's niece," he said.

"How did you know that?"

"You talked about her often when I was last here. Plus Diane filled in a few gaps last night." His smile reached all the way to his eyes as they met Claire's. "We stayed up almost till morning talking in the parlor. I learned a lot, as did she, but there's a lot more still to cover. Hopefully tonight. And tomorrow. And the day after that, too."

"Ahhh, so that's why she wouldn't stop humming this morning while we were getting breakfast together."

"You didn't ask?"

"Oh, I *asked,*" she said, looking down their otherwise empty row. "She just couldn't seem to stop humming long enough to answer."

Bill's soft laugh eased the tension in her shoulders. "I did some humming myself this morning. Trust me."

"I do."

And she did. There was something about Bill that just rang true all the way across the board. The fact that his very appearance in the kitchen doorway the previous evening had garnered such a sweet and hope-filled smile from her aunt was simply the icing on the cake. Now all that remained to be seen was whether Bill might truly be —

"So this visit . . . With Esther having you and Rebecca over at the same time . . . Maybe by meeting her and getting to know her a little bit, you'll be able to quiet some of those worries you have. And who knows, maybe you'll even discover they're a perfect match — she and your friend, Ben."

"That's all I've ever wanted for him." She surveyed the rows in front and behind their own, then took in the mourners gathered around the easel-mounted picture boards. "Where is Aunt Diane? I haven't seen her since I sat down."

"She shooed me over to check on you when she spotted someone named Harold heading in our direction."

"Ahhh, okay. I can just make out the side of Harold's face back there by the hallway but I couldn't tell who he was talking to." She patted Bill's hand. "This'll be a while."

Bill's brow lifted in amusement. "He's a talker, I take it?"

"If it was an Olympic event, he'd get the gold. Every. Single. Time." She savored the lighthearted moment and the chance it gave her to catch her breath on what had been a nonstop kind of day. "Harold Glick owns the hardware store two doors down from my shop. He is a sweet, sweet man who loves to eat, loves to talk tools and gadgetry, and takes his self-appointed role as town gossip very, *very* seriously."

"Yeah, but she already knows about" — Bill nudged his chin and Claire's focus toward the receiving line — "*this,* so what else could he possibly share about Heavenly that's taking this long?"

"I'm guessing he started with this gossip or that gossip, but I'm willing to bet that by now, it's not about what *he's* saying so much as it is about what he can get *her* to say."

Bill pulled a face. "About?"

"You."

"Me?" Bill echoed.

"Harold is sharp. He knows all, sees all. He probably recognized you from your last visit to Heavenly the second you walked in the door tonight."

"Okay . . ."

"Now he's just trying to get the scoop on why you're back, and what it means." Claire tapped her watch and then her chin. "Which means, conservatively speaking, of course, that every single one of my fellow shopkeepers along Lighted Way will know who you are, where you're from, how long you stayed last time you were in town, what you do for a living, and what your favorite dinner is by nine thirty tomorrow morning."

Running his hand along his clean-shaven jawline, Bill glanced back at Harold. "So what you're telling me is I need to go tool shopping tomorrow morning."

"Tool shopping? No, I'm not saying that. Harold is a good guy. A gossip, yes, but no one you have to worry about or give a hard time."

Bill drew back. "I'm not suggesting I'd stop by his store to give him a hard time. I'm just thinking he might have something good to tell *me,* too."

"About yourself?" she asked, laughing.

"No. About your aunt."

Folding her arms, she eyed her companion. "If you want to know something about my aunt, ask her . . . or me. You don't have to ask *Harold.*"

"But Olympic gold medalists are good at what they do. Which means he should be able to tell me if I've got a chance."

"A chance?" When she saw a few heads turn in their direction from the vicinity of the picture boards, she lowered her voice to a near-whisper. "A chance with what?"

"Your aunt."

She dug her teeth into her lower lip in an effort to stop her answering grin, but it was no use. "You don't need a gold medalist to tell you that."

Hope pushed his left eyebrow practically to his hairline. "I don't?"

"Nope. In fact, any old gift shop owner can tell you that."

"Any old gift shop owner, eh?" At her slow, drawn-out nod, he leaned closer. "Well? Do I have a chance?"

"Yes, Bill, you most certainly have a chance — a *good* chance, in . . ." Her words trailed off as the movement of several heads around them led her eyes back to the receiving line and the young Amish couple approaching a clearly surprised, yet equally touched Jakob. "Oh. Wow. I . . . I guess I didn't think they'd come."

Bill, too, looked forward. "That's your friend Esther, isn't it?"

"Yes. With her husband, Eli. But I don't see the baby . . . They must have left her with Esther's mother, Martha." She inched forward on her chair and then stood. "I'm sorry, but I probably should say hello once they're done paying their respects to Jakob. I'll be right back."

"I understand. Go." Bill waved her toward her friends and then glanced back at Harold.

"Maybe I should rescue your aunt . . ."

"I think that's a great idea." Without really thinking, she kissed him on the forehead and then turned and made her way down the aisle toward the picture boards. She traded subdued smiles with a few familiar faces and then positioned herself in a spot where Eli and Esther would be sure to see her after viewing Russ's body.

While she waited, she, too, found herself looking toward the open casket and the man who had been both a mentor and a father figure of sorts for Jakob. So much of Jakob's adult life had been spent mourning familial relationships he could no longer have because of his decision to leave his Amish roots. To see him lose yet another important person from his life was downright painful.

"Claire? Are you okay? I waved to you as soon as I saw you but you did not wave back."

Shaking her thoughts back into the present, she greeted Esther with a kiss and Eli with a nod-smile combination. "I'm sorry. I was standing here specifically so you'd see me when you finished with the receiving line and the viewing, and then I disappeared into my head. Sorry about that."

Esther smoothed her hands down the sides of her navy blue dress and peeked

188

back at Jakob, her expression stricken. "My uncle . . . He looks so sad."

"Because he is." She, too, watched Jakob as he spoke quietly with yet another mourner before she turned back to her friends. "But having the two of you here, showing him your support, surely means a lot to him, as it does me. So thank you for that. I know you probably could get in trouble for being here . . ."

Eli inhaled himself to his full height. "Once, when I was young, Jakob's friend there" — he nudged his chin in the direction of the open casket — "found one of Dat's goats wandering around behind the police station and brought her back to the farm. He stayed and helped Benjamin and me fix the hole in the fence she'd used to get out."

"Yah. That is why we are here." Esther's hands moved quickly to her kapp and the lone strand of hair trying its best to escape. "It is why Elmer and Miriam were to come, too."

"You mean the new minister and his wife?"

"Yah. Eli told them of Mr. Granger's help when we were leaving to come here and Elmer said they would come, too. But just before we got here, we saw John's oldest."

"Bontrager?" Claire asked.

Nodding, Eli stroked the front of the nearly year-old beard that served as his wedding ring. "John sent Amos to town for something and he was coming back when we passed."

"He was carrying a box that was very big," Esther added. "He almost fell into a ditch because he could not see where he was going."

"If he did not look at us the way he did when both buggies passed, he would not have been so close to the ditch," Eli countered.

Shrugging, Esther lowered herself onto a nearby chair and brought her eyes, if not her words, back to her uncle. "That is when Miriam and Elmer turned back. He said it was getting dark and he could not sleep if he did not know the boy had gotten home."

"He'll be okay, Esther."

Esther turned back to Claire, confusion tugging at her features. "I know. It was not a long drive."

"I'm not talking about the Bontrager boy." Taking the chair next to her friend's, Claire slid her arm around the young mother's shoulders. "I'm talking about your uncle. I know you're worried about him and so am I. But I can tell you with absolute certainty that you and Eli being here tonight helped more than you can ever know."

Esther leaned her cheek against Claire's. "We did not come because of a goat."

"I know, sweetie. I know."

CHAPTER 16

They were out on the country road, heading away from Heavenly, when she finally broke the silence, the uncertainty she felt manifesting itself in a raspy whisper she tried to cough away. "I know how hard that must have been for you tonight."

"It was beyond hard, Claire. Like I'm playing a role in some show instead of actually being at my friend's visitation." He pulled his hand down the center of his face, rasping a breath as he did. "I mean, we're talking about *Russ* here. Russ *Granger.* He was practically bulletproof, you know?"

Nodding, she reached for his hand. "I'm so sorry, Jakob. I wish there was something I could do."

"There is and you're already doing it." He threaded his fingers through hers just long enough to lift them to his lips. "Being able to look up from time to time during the visitation and see you there helped more than you can possibly know."

He lowered her hand back to the top of his thigh and then returned his own to the steering wheel. "He would have loved you, Claire."

"I wish I'd had the chance to meet him."

"So do I." He let up on the gas as they rounded the corner and came upon a familiar orange triangle blinking in the darkness. Claire waved to the Amish buggy driver as they passed and then turned back to Jakob as he accelerated once again. "I feel so bad for Callie. Aside from her kids, she really doesn't have any family left. And as if the grief of losing her dad isn't enough, she's got some anger mixed up in there, too."

"Maybe when you catch the person who did this, she'll get to unleash some of that anger in a courtroom. They let loved ones address the killer sometimes now, don't they?"

"That's assuming I catch him."

She squeezed his thigh. "You already have two people on your watch list."

"Two?"

"Tom Shaunessy and Callie's ex, Kyle."

"I'm not so sure on the ex after seeing him tonight."

"He was there? At the visitation?"

Jakob nodded. "He sat in a chair off to

the side for most of the night. I was surprised to see him show up, but Callie said it was okay for him to stay, that he's been checking in on her and the kids since it happened. And I have to admit, every time I looked at him tonight, I saw nothing but concern for Callie."

"Okay, so maybe it's just Tom for now. Maybe you'll come across someone else, too. But either way, you'll find the person who did this, Jakob, and Callie will get to speak her mind. Have faith."

He opened his mouth as if to protest and then looked back at the road. "Even if I catch the person who did this and Callie gets her day in court, there's still a different anger. At Russ . . . At herself . . . At all the moments she can't go back and redo, and all the moments they won't have to try and do better."

"Did they have a strained relationship?" she asked as he passed yet another buggy on the dark, otherwise deserted road.

"Not in the way it probably sounds. Russ adored Callie and her mother. *Adored* them. But he was distracted a lot. With work. Both his and, sometimes — no, *many* times — others'."

Her answering laugh was void of any real humor. "When I was younger and a teacher assigned a group project for a class, I had a tendency to do everyone's part in addition to my own just so I could know everything would be done. I guess I just didn't want to be penalized for someone else's poor time management or preference for fooling around instead of working.

"I think I even did it at the store in the beginning, with Esther, and again when Annie first started. Fortunately, I stopped with both of them once I saw what kind of work ethic they had and that they cared about the shop as much as I did. Still, I guess some might see me as a bit of a control freak."

"It's *your* store, it makes sense you'd care about all the details."

"But maybe that's all it was with Russ, too," she mused. "Caring about the details. I would imagine you'd have to be pretty dedicated to your job to work your way up from patrolman to department chief, yes?"

"Absolutely. And he did that. But it's like I told you the other day. It didn't stop when he retired." He took a left where the road teed with another and, soon, lights began to appear out the window, a clear sign they were leaving the quiet, predominantly Amish-inhabited areas.

She pointed at a house already decorated

for Halloween despite the nearly five-week gap, and then brought her full attention back on the handsome man in the driver's seat. "I know that the whole workaholic thing can be destructive, it's what eroded my marriage to Peter. But you heard Diane the other night. She said Russ and Callie's mom were Callie's lifeline during her divorce. Surely that means he didn't completely block her out . . ."

"Callie respects everything her father did, and she respects the sacrifices he made and was prepared to make for the public's safety, if necessary. But it was the stuff he didn't have to do, the time she didn't have to lose with him that rankles most, I think."

"Meaning?" she asked.

"Meaning, like Saturday evening after he got back from Murphy's . . . Callie was awake. She called to him to come in. But he said he was tired."

"Okay . . ."

"The files on the table . . . the opened can of soda . . . the bowl of chips in that garage apartment say otherwise."

"Maybe he thought he could sleep but then couldn't. That happens to me all the time. Maybe he figured rather than toss and turn, he'd get some work done."

Jakob slid a knowing look in her direction.

"Oh, there's no doubt about that. The files alone say that. But here's the rub for Callie. The reason for some of her anger. Those files had nothing to do with Russ or his department. He was just going over old reports from various parts of the country, just like he always did."

"How do you know?"

"Because I saw them with my own two eyes when I was going through the apartment Sunday night. I, of course, almost laughed when I saw them because it was so him, you know? But for Callie? Those files stirred a very different emotion."

"Meaning?" she prodded.

"She's angry. Because, in her mind, he left her feeling as if he loved playing cop more than he loved being a dad."

"Oh." She sagged her shoulders into the back of the seat and let her head loll back a little, too. "Wow."

"Yeah."

At a loss for what to say, she simply looked at Jakob and waited for the part of the story he'd yet to share, a part clearly weighing on him if the lines etched across his forehead were any indication.

"She said she wanted him to come in because the kids were asleep and she felt like reminiscing about her childhood —

memories of her with her mom and dad."

"And he turned her down."

Jakob squared his jaw in conjunction with a sigh. "And he turned her down."

"I can't believe he meant any harm. Especially knowing, from you, what kind of man he was."

"He didn't. And deep down, I have to believe Callie knows that." He decreased his speed and moved onto the shoulder as the neon green sign for Murphy's came up on their right. With a turn of the wheel, he pulled into the lot and quickly located a parking spot not too far from the door. "She says she wishes he'd chosen a Dad Moment over a Cop Moment for once. So, if nothing else, she could have that memory to hold on to right now."

"Is there anything you think I can do for her? I know Aunt Diane knows her, but I'm not sure we've ever met. If we have, it was in passing."

He pulled the key from the ignition and looked out at Murphy's, a distinct cloud passing across his face. "Right now, I want to go inside and see what we can find out about Russ's time here on Saturday night. Tomorrow, on the way to the funeral, maybe we can come up with something we can do to help Callie out a little. Maybe we can invite her out for coffee with us one night, or offer to watch the kids so she can take a little time to herself. Sound good?"

"Sounds good."

"Then, let's go inside." He pushed open his door and stepped onto the pavement, his gaze moving between the people coming and going from Murphy's front door and the cars parked to their left and right. When she joined him on his side of the car, he guided her toward the door. "We're just going to go inside, sit at the bar, and see if tonight's bartender happens to be the same one who was working when Russ was here."

She walked through the door he held open, the quiet of the early-autumn evening wiped away by the sounds of billiards being played, glasses being clanked against one another, raucous laughter, and people jockeying for attention by being louder than everyone else. By instinct, she started to back up, to reverse course back to the parking lot, but Jakob's calming touch on the small of her back helped her to stand tall. Sure, if she had her druthers, they'd be settling in at their favorite two-person table in Heavenly Brews, ready to talk the rest of the evening away. But this stop wasn't about talking — not to each other, anyway. This was about listening and observing.

"This way," he said against her ear as he guided her toward the three-sided bar on the opposite end of the room from the pair of pool tables and the crowd of people gathered around its competitors.

A few steps from their destination, he pointed to a trio of empty seats on the left side. "Perfect. We can chat up the bartender while still being able to see everyone else."

She nodded. Or, at least she was pretty sure she did. Either way, she followed him to the open barstools and took the one he indicated. Once she was settled and her purse situated on a hook beneath the overhang, he took the stool to her right. "Do you want anything?" he asked.

"I guess I'll take a soda with ice."

He lifted his finger into the air briefly and then smiled as the fortysomething male bartender abandoned the section of bar he was wiping with a cloth and headed in their direction. "Welcome to Murphy's, I'm Todd. What's your poison this evening?"

"She'll take a soda and I'll" — she followed Jakob's eyes to the collection of bottles along the back wall — "just take a beer."

"Comin' right up." Plucking two cocktail napkins from a holder not far from Claire's seat, Todd set them down in front of their respective spots and then went about filling their order. When he returned, he placed the drinks on the napkins and nudged his chin in Jakob's direction. "You just get off work?"

Jakob took a sip of his beer and helped himself to a handful of peanuts from a bowl Todd slid closer to their spot. "You mean because of the suit?" At the bartender's nod, he popped a few peanuts into his mouth and shook his head. "Nah. A funeral — or, at least, the visitation part, anyway. Funeral service is tomorrow."

"Oh, hey, I'm sorry, man. Was it family?"

"Close enough." Jakob took another sip of his beer and then lowered it back down to the bar. "In fact, he was *here* . . . at this bar . . . not more than five or six hours before his death."

Surprise pushed Todd's head back. "You serious?"

"Unfortunately, yeah. ME says he died sometime between two and four Sunday morning."

"Wow. Heart attack kill 'im?"

Claire pulled her glass closer to her body but kept her focus on Todd as she waited for Jakob's answer.

Jakob, in turn, leaned back a hairbreadth on his stool. "Nope. He was stabbed. Outside his daughter's home in Heavenly. She found him shortly after noon on Sunday when she went looking to see if he'd like some lunch."

"And you say he was *here*?" Todd asked.

"That's right."

"And this was *Saturday* night?" At Jakob's slow, measured nod, Todd raked a hand through his thinning hair. "That was my shift . . ."

She felt Jakob stir in his seat as he leaned forward again. Only this time he dispensed with the whole beer-sipping, peanut-eating pretense. "Maybe you remember him?"

"If he sat at the bar, I imagine I would. If he was at one of the tables, then Lauri would have been taking care of him."

Jakob scanned the room and then pointed at a woman carrying a tray through the billiards crowd. "Is that Lauri over there?"

"It is." Todd grabbed up a cloth and used it to wipe the area around the tap. "So what was this guy's name?"

"Russ. Russ Granger."

"That's not ringing any bells so I'm guessing he wasn't a regular?"

"That depends." Jakob propped his elbows on the bar. "How long have you been working here?"

"Two years."

"Yeah, then he wouldn't be a regular to you." Jakob pushed the peanut bowl closer to Claire, pulled out his phone, and clicked on the photo icon near the bottom of the screen. When he found what he was looking for, he turned the screen so it was visible to the bartender. "He was back in town to visit the daughter I just mentioned."

"If this guy wasn't a regular, he probably wouldn't have found a space at the bar on a Saturday night. That evening's crew tends to arrive in the late afternoon and stay deep into the night." Todd stepped out from behind the tap and leaned in for a closer look. "Nope, if he was here, he didn't sit here at the bar. He musta been at one of the tables or playing pool or something."

"Which means Lauri, right?" Claire asked.

"Yep. I handle the folks here, she handles the folks out there." Todd held up a one-minute signal to a patron at the other end of the bar and dropped his cloth into a bucket beneath the tap. "The regulars tend to sit up here with me. Which is why I've gotta take care of old Doug down there before he gets cranky. And he *will* get cranky if I don't get him his beer."

Claire followed the bartender's attention to the fifty-year-old hunched over the bar with an empty shot glass on his left and an empty beer bottle on his right. On a hunch, she set her hand on the bar top and her sights on the bartender. "So not only do you know your regulars, you also know which days they tend to come in?"

She felt Jakob's eyes on the side of her face as Todd shrugged. "Sure. Helps me know what I need behind the bar on any given day."

"I heard Tom has been trying to catch up with me for a while now but we keep missing each other. Maybe the key is to pop in on him here."

"Tom Buggley? Yeah, sure, he's a Tuesday happy hour guy."

"No, not Buggley . . . *Shaunessy.*" She resisted the urge to look at Jakob and, instead, kept her focus on the bartender. "We — I mean, *our folks* were friends way back when and, well, my mom keeps asking me how he is when she calls. If I had something to tell her the next time she calls, maybe I could divert her from the whole when-are-you-getting-married? conversation."

Todd laughed. "I get the same question from my mother all the time, too. Wish she'd give it a rest but I don't see that happening anytime soon."

"There's one way to make her stop," she teased.

"Uh . . . no."

Shrugging, she took a quick sip of her soda and followed it up with a peanut. "So? When's the best time to catch Tom?"

"Saturday night. Comes in sometime between six and seven pretty much every Saturday, and usually stumbles back out around midnight." He pointed at her soda and eyed up Jakob. "Any friend of Shaunessy is a friend of mine. Her soda is on the house."

"Thanks, man."

"No problem." Reaching under the counter to the left of where they sat, Todd pulled out a bottle of beer, opened it with a bottle opener attached to his belt, and took off for the fiftysomething tapping his fingers on top of the bar.

The second the bartender was out of earshot, Jakob swiveled to face Claire. "Nice work there, Sherlock. That was smooth. Very, very smooth."

"Why, thank you. I try." She took a fortifying sip of her soda and then swiveled her knees to his. "So? What do you think?"

"I think you just put my only suspect in Russ's path that last night." Reaching into his inside suit pocket, he pulled out his wallet and plunked a ten down on the bar. "Which is exactly why we came tonight."

"Do you really think it's him?" she asked.

"I don't know. Too early to say. But it's certainly looking a bit more likely now, thanks to you." Leaning across the space between their stools, he kissed her on the lips and then gestured his chin toward her glass. "Let's take that with us and go sit at a table. If you're hungry, maybe we can grab a dessert or something."

She helped herself to a few more peanuts and then slid off the stool. "Sounds good. Maybe Lauri has a favorite she can recommend."

CHAPTER 17

It took about ten minutes to get a table and another ten to get menus, but eventually, the leggy brunette in the formfitting T-shirt slowed at their table long enough to size them up and pull a small notepad and pencil from the back pocket of her jeans. Extending her pencil toward Jakob's beer, she flashed a bored smile. "Want a refill?"

He took in his barely touched drink and then pointed at the menu. "Actually, we were thinking about ordering a dessert. What do you recommend?"

"Hey, I like your shirt, by the way — it's a real pretty color on you," Claire said.

Lauri's dark brown eyes shifted to Claire. "Thanks."

Smiling, she directed the woman's eyes back to the menu and the boxed section containing a list so paltry it would likely give Ruth heart palpitations. "We're torn between the cheesecake and the brownie à la mode. Which is better?"

Lauri considered Claire's question and then tapped her pencil down on the one choice they'd already dismissed. "My favorite of this sorry lineup is actually the fruit plate with the melted chocolate for dipping. Mainly because even Drake, our cook, can't mess up fruit. But if you're really set on one of these other two, I'd say the brownie."

"Shall we give it a go?" Jakob asked.

"It wasn't on my radar, but based on what she just said, I'm thinking yes." She lifted her eyebrow at Jakob's obvious amusement and looked back up at Lauri. "We'll take the fruit plate. With the melted chocolate."

Lauri scribbled their choice on her notepad. "Anything else?"

"No. That'll be perfect," Claire said.

The waitress turned to leave but stopped before she was more than a step or two away. "You two look mighty dressed up for this place. Coming from a nice dinner in Cedarville or something?"

"A wake, actually." Claire pulled her soda over to the edge of the table but stopped short of actually taking a sip. "Jakob's friend was killed over the weekend."

Lauri's demeanor morphed from bored to intrigued in rapid fashion. "Killed? Like in an accident or something?"

"He was murdered."

Sucking in a breath, Lauri took in the rest of her tables with one sweeping glance, and then scurried back to theirs, her eyes no longer showing anything even close to boredom. "*Murdered?* Really?"

"Really." Jakob's shoulders rose with the inhale Claire knew was more about steadying his emotions than anything else. "Seems someone lured him out of the apartment he was staying in at his daughter's house."

"He was visiting from Florida," Claire added.

Surprise traded places with intrigue. "Wait. This guy was visiting his daughter from Florida?"

Claire slanted a look at Jakob and, together, they turned back to Lauri. "That's right," said Jakob.

"Was he a cop or something out in Heavenly before he moved to Florida?"

Again, Jakob and Claire traded glances with Jakob breaking free first. "Yeah, he started as a cop and worked his way up to chief of the Heavenly PD . . . I take it you knew Russ?"

"Russ . . ." The name disappeared behind Lauri's palm as she lowered herself onto the bench seat next to Claire. "I met him here. Saturday night. He . . . he sat at that table over there."

They followed her finger to a table across the aisle as Lauri continued, the intrigue she'd shown at the notion of a real-life murder clearly muted by the reality that she'd talked to the victim just hours before his death. "He was so nice and so — so *interesting.*"

"So you talked to him, then?" Jakob asked.

"I did. He" — Lauri squeezed her eyes closed briefly — "was really excited to spend time with his grandchildren. Two of them had a soccer game coming up mid-week, and the other had some sort of special award thing going on at preschool. He was hoping it wouldn't be too tense for the kids."

Jakob stiffened on the other side of the table. "Too tense?"

Lauri shrugged. "Seems his daughter had been married to a bit of a jerk and this guy, being the kids' dad, was going to be at both things, too."

"And Russ was worried about that?" Jakob prodded.

"A little, I guess. I mean, he brought it up. But probably because I said something about my ex and having to deal with him all the time. He asked me if my dad got in his face at all. Told me it could help." A sad smile trembled its way across the woman's face only to be shoved to the side with a labored sigh.

"Did he say anything else about his daughter's ex?" Jakob asked.

"I'm not sure. I don't really remember him saying much else about — no!" Lauri sat up tall. "That's when Carla came in and waved me over to see her new tattoo. I hated having to end my conversation with your friend but I knew if I didn't look, Carla would get all miffed like she does. Though, when I saw that it was an exact duplicate of the one on her other ankle, *I* was a little miffed. Especially when I didn't get to say thank you for . . ."

Lauri's gasp pulled more than a few glances in their direction. "Oh no . . . You don't think . . ." The woman squeezed her eyes closed. "You don't think his daughter's ex had something to do with this, do you?"

"I don't know," Jakob said honestly.

"Should I . . ." The girl stopped, took a breath, and looked from Claire to Jakob and back again. "Should I call the cops? Tell them about the ex? You know, just in case this creep had something to do with what happened to your friend? I mean, he was such a nice guy . . ."

Jakob reached across the table and covered Lauri's fidgety hand. "You don't need to

211

worry, Lauri. I'm a cop, and Russ was my friend."

"You're a cop?" Lauri whispered.

"A detective now, but yes, I'm a cop. In fact, the whole reason I can even say I'm a cop is because of Russ. I saw him tackle a shoplifter from the back of my father's buggy when I was a kid and I was pretty much hooked on the notion of being a cop from that moment on, even if it took me entirely too long to recognize it." Jakob took a moment to rein in the emotion making its way into his tone and then cleared his throat. "It's just like you said a minute ago. He is — I mean, *was* an interesting guy."

Lauri clapped her hand to her mouth only to let it fall back to the table as she leaned forward. "Wait. *You're* the one? The Amish kid who became the cop?"

"He — he mentioned that?" Jakob stammered.

"Oh my gosh, yes! He said you were like the son he never —"

"Miss? Any chance I could get another beer? Preferably sometime this decade?"

"Yeah . . . sure." Bracing her hand on the edge of the table, Lauri stood. "I better get back to work before someone complains to my boss."

Still clearly affected by Lauri's words,

Jakob managed a swallow and a nod. Claire, in turn, extended her hand and smiled when the gesture was reciprocated. "We understand. Thanks for talking to us, Lauri."

The waitress started toward the balding man and his empty beer bottle and then stopped. "Maybe you could send my condolences to his daughter? He was a really nice man."

"Sure, we —"

"My name is Biegler. Lauri Biegler."

And then she was gone, her clipped persona winning out once again as she made a pit stop at the man's booth for his empty bottle and then headed toward the bar for a refill. When she was more or less out of sight, Claire reached across the table for Jakob's hand. "Hey . . . You may not have seen him that last day, but what Lauri just shared? About his feelings for you? It's quite clear he felt as strongly about you as you did about him. That has to feel good, yes?"

"Of course." He stared down at their entwined hands and then pulled his free to fist it against the table. "I just want to know who did this to him, Claire. I want him to pay."

"And he will. When you have everything you need to make a case stick." She held her hand out, palm up, until he took it again. "You now have confirmation that Tom Shaunessy — a guy with what could be a pretty decent motive for seeking revenge on Russ — was, in fact, here at the bar on Saturday night."

"Do we?" he asked, meeting her eyes.

Claire drew back, taking her hand with her. "You heard what the bartender just said . . ."

"I heard him say *most* Saturdays. He didn't necessarily say our guy was here this past Saturday . . ."

"Okay, then I'll ask him." She scooted down the bench toward the opening but stopped on Jakob's say-so. "What? It's a simple question. Besides" — she flashed a grin — "he comped my soda. That means he likes me."

Jakob returned the grin, although it failed to engage anything beyond the left side of his mouth. "How could he not? Have you looked at yourself in the mirror?"

"Your fruit and your melted chocolate is here." Lauri plopped a nondescript-looking bowl filled with strawberries and apple slices in the center of the table and a smaller, equally nondescript-looking bowl of melted chocolate at its side. "It's not gonna be the *best* dessert you've ever had in your life, but it's the best you're gonna get at Murphy's, that's for sure. I gave you a little more chocolate than I'm supposed to, but I figured I'd push it just this once on account of everything you're going through."

"Thanks, Lauri." Claire looked toward the bar and the dozen or so patrons bellied up to it on all three sides. "Do you know if Tom Shaunessy was in here Saturday night?"

"Yeah, sure, he was here. Carla called him over to see her tattoo, too."

Jakob dropped his carefully selected strawberry back among the rest. "Do you know if he saw Russ?"

"Who? Tom?" Pulling a few extra napkins from the dividing wall between their booth and the next one, Lauri dropped them next to the dipping cup. "I don't know. But he was still standing there, drooling over Carla, when I showed them the tip your friend left me."

"Tip?" Claire echoed.

Lauri scanned the booths around them and when she didn't see anyone needing her for anything, she turned her attention back to Claire. "Yeah. It was way bigger than he should have given me on a beer and a plate of wings. But considering how kind and decent he was, it fit. I mean, you read stuff in the papers about nice people giving waiters and waitresses big tips during the holidays and stuff. But it's September, and it's me . . . Stuff like that doesn't happen to me."

"Hold on," Jakob said. "Are you back to talking about Russ? Or Tom Shaunessy?"

Lauri snorted a laugh. "Uh . . . no. Tom isn't a big tipper. In fact, my bartender will tell you he's the quintessential non-tipper. Shows up with exactly what he needs for the eight to ten drinks he'll put away while he's here and leaves nothing for Todd. It's pathetic. But he's a customer and Todd's a professional and so he treats him just the same as everyone else. Week after week."

"So this tip?" Jakob wrapped his hand around the beer bottle but didn't pick it up off the table. "It was from Russ, then . . ."

"It was. Only I didn't know he was ready to leave. If I had, I'd have gotten him a proper check and offered to box up the rest of the wings he didn't eat. But when I finished seeing Carla's darn tattoo and listening to her yammer on to Tom and me about the colors and the design and whatever else she felt the need to share, I looked over at Russ's table and it was empty. I figured he'd just gone to the bathroom or something so I finished up with Carla and Tom and then grabbed the pitcher of water, thinking he might want a top-off when he got back to his table. I swear, Drake dumps so much hot sauce on our wings you need a fire hose to cool off after a single bite. But when I walked over to refill his water glass, I saw the hundred-dollar bill folded up underneath the salt and pepper holder." Lauri pointed toward the same holder on their own table. "A *hundred-dollar bill . . .* on a *fifteen-dollar check.*"

Claire and Jakob exchanged looks as, once again, the balding man two booths over yelled for another drink. Rolling her eyes, Lauri hooked her thumb in the man's direction and then tapped their table with her knuckles. "I better take care of this. I just wish . . ."

"What?" Claire prodded.

"At the time, I wished I'd had the chance to thank your friend for the tip. Now, I wish I'd had the chance to say good-bye."

CHAPTER 18

Claire followed Jakob's taillights until the
bend of the road and the line of English
homes dotting the eastern end of Lighted
Way stole them from her view. The ride
home from Murphy's had been relatively
quiet, with Jakob giving mostly monosyl-
lable answers to just about everything she'd
said. Eventually, she'd given up and simply
watched the moonlit fields zoom past as
he'd navigated the back roads with ease.

If he'd noticed her retreat, he hadn't let
on. And when he'd dropped her off in front
of the inn at the end of their drive, the
internal strain he was under had manifested
itself in very un-Jakob-like behavior.

"Claire? Is that you?"

Bracing her hands on either side of her
hips, she pushed off her temporary seat on
the top step and turned. "Yeah, Aunt Diane, it's me."

"Where is Jakob?" Diane pushed open the

screen door and stepped onto the porch, her wide-set eyes leading Claire's back to the driveway and the quiet road beyond. "I didn't hear you two out here talking . . ."

"That's because we weren't. He dropped me off and headed home."

Diane's gaze darted back to Claire's. "That doesn't sound like Jakob."

She made her way over to the swing and sat down, its answering sway releasing her long-held sigh. "Neither does a twenty-minute car ride that was virtually silent from start to finish. Save, of course, for the occasional *uh-huh* I got."

"Oh dear, did you two have a fight?" Diane claimed the edge of her favorite Adirondack chair and studied Claire closely.

"Nope. He's just . . ." She stopped, draped her arm across the back of the swing, and pillowed her cheek against her silky sleeve. "I thought that maybe what Lauri said would have helped him a little bit. You know, given him a little added reassurance that Russ thought the world of him. But he just seems so lost, so down on himself right now."

"This is all still new, Claire. Russ hasn't even been gone a week. You have to give him time."

"I know. But this is more than just mourning, Aunt Diane. It's . . . I don't know. I don't know how to describe it, exactly. It's like he's retreated so far into his own head that I can't reach him, and it's scaring me."

"Would you like me to talk to him, dear?"

Claire lifted her head and gave it a quick shake. "Not yet. Let me see how he is after he's had a little sleep. Maybe he'll be more willing to open up tomorrow on the way to the — wait. No. We won't be riding together because he's going to Callie's beforehand so he can ride to the church with her and her kids."

"Why don't you let him get through tomorrow and *then* talk. Maybe, once this part is done, he'll be more willing to share his thoughts and feelings on all of this. Men are funny that way, you know. Far too often their preferred way of dealing with things they can't control is to be quiet. But I don't think it will last too long with Jakob." Diane brushed at a speck of dirt on her armrest. "He treasures the time you two spend talking."

"So do I. That's why this not-really-talking stuff is leaving me so unsettled. I mean, even when I brought up what Lauri had said again, it was like he didn't hear me. And we learned some pretty helpful things, if you ask me."

"Who is this Lauri you keep mentioning? That's a name I'm not familiar with."

Claire stopped the swing's gentle sway with her foot and stood. With quick yet aimless steps, she eventually made her way over to the front railing and its uninhibited view of the moon-drenched fields that comprised the western side of Heavenly. "Lauri Biegler. She's the barmaid out at Murphy's. Jakob and I went out there after the visitation this evening so he could see if anyone would remember Russ from Saturday night."

"And? Did this Lauri Biegler woman remember him?"

"Oh yes. They spoke. At great length, actually. Russ told her about Jakob's Amish childhood and how Jakob left to become a police officer. He even told her Jakob was like a son to him."

Diane's sigh filled the night air. "I would imagine hearing that was both validating and painful for Jakob."

Aware of the instant deflation of her shoulders, Claire turned away from the fields and leaned back against the railing. "Oh my gosh, I'm such an idiot . . . I heard what Lauri said and all I could see was the validating part. I . . . I never stopped to think about how those same words could stir up Jakob's pain all over again."

"That doesn't make you an idiot, dear." Diane, too, stood and closed the gap between them with purpose. When she was just inches away, she reached out, tucked a strand of hair behind Claire's ear, and then rested their foreheads together. "Someone said something nice about a person you love. That's the part you wanted to get through to him because you're worried about him. I think that makes you *special*. Jakob does, too."

She closed her eyes and waited for her aunt's words to make a dent in her guilt. "Maybe you're right, Aunt Diane. Maybe I should give him a little time to process all of this without me talking in his ear the whole time. But I have to give him a quick call before he falls asleep. I have to let him know I understand his hurt. I owe him that."

Stepping back, Diane bookended Claire's face with her soft palms and lingered a kiss in the center of Claire's forehead. "You're the best medicine for that young man right now, dear."

"Thank you, Aunt Diane." She breathed in the courage that was her father's older sister and then motioned to the door. "You coming in, too? It's gotta be past your normal bedtime by now."

A flash of crimson brightened the woman's cheeks. "No, dear. You go ahead. It's a beautiful night and I think I'd like to sit out here for a little while and soak it in."

"Are you sure? Because it's starting to cool off and . . ." The words drifted into the night as a series of footsteps from the front hallway pulled her attention off her aunt and sent it toward the handsome sixtysomething now standing at the screen door, smiling back at —

Ahhhh . . .

"You're right," Claire said, grinning. "It *is* a beautiful night. Enjoy every moment."

Sinking against her headboard-propped pillow, Claire silently counted each ring. One . . . Two . . . Three . . .

Halfway through the fourth ring, he picked up, his tone void of its usual pep. "Hey, Claire."

"Hi." She took a moment to formulate her thoughts and then rolled onto her side, pinning the phone between the edge of the pillow and her cheek. "I thought I'd be okay with our good-bye when you dropped me off, but I guess I've grown more accustomed to our nightly phone calls than I realized."

When his only reply was silence, she reached down, grabbed hold of the afghan folded neatly at the bottom of her bed, and tugged it up to her shoulders. "I didn't wake you, did I?" she asked.

"I'm at the office."

She rolled onto her back. "The *office*? But, Jakob, you need to get some sleep. You've been going nonstop for days!"

"I can't sleep, Claire."

"Have you tried?" she asked.

"No."

She opened her mouth to argue but closed it as the reason she was on the phone in the first place reared its head. "Jakob, I want to apologize for earlier."

"Apologize?"

"Yeah. I was so intent on wanting you to truly hear what Lauri had said about Russ and you that I didn't stop to think that you *did* hear it, and that it probably just added to your pain."

The creak of his chair in the background told her he'd either leaned back or stood. The silence that followed had her pulling the phone from her ear and checking to make sure they were still connected.

"Jakob?" Sitting up, she shivered as the blanket slipped off her shoulders. "Look, I'm sorry I bothered you. I should have listened to my aunt and given you space to get through tomorrow. But please know I'm not trying to be thoughtless or dense. I'm just worried about you and I want to help. And I —"

She exhaled away the rest of the sentence as she swung her feet off the bed and into her waiting slippers. "Just please — please know that I love you with all my heart and I'm here for you. Day or night."

This time, when his chair creaked, she was virtually certain he'd abandoned it. Especially when the next sound she heard was the whoosh of his office window as he opened it to the autumn night. "I know how this is going to sound," he finally said, his words coming in starts and stops. "And it's why I didn't want to say anything on the way home from Murphy's just now. But I wish I could bypass the whole funeral tomorrow — or, better yet, put it all on hold until the timing is better."

"The *timing*?" she echoed.

"Trust me, Claire. I know how callous that sounds. But I want my thoughts to be focused solely on Russ when I say my final good-bye, you know? And, right now, they're not. Not in the way I want them to be, anyway."

"Tell me."

"At that gravesite, when I put my hand on Russ's casket for the last time? I want to be able to tell him I got our guy. I *owe* him that, Claire."

She wandered over to the window and its cushioned seat and nestled in against the cheerful throw pillows she'd made with Esther's help over the summer. More than anything, she wanted to walk up behind Jakob in his office, wrap her arms around him, and hold him close, but short of that, she needed to make sure her words conveyed the same.

"Okay, so maybe you can't say that to his casket. But you can say that you're working on it — that you're turning over every stone you can think of. You can tell him you love him and that you'll never forget him. And when you find your guy, as you say, you can stop out at the cemetery and tell him.

"My guess, though, is that he already knows you're going to figure it out. Because from what I've been able to piece together from Aunt Diane, and you, and Harold, and Lauri, Russ always had faith in you and your ability as a cop. If he didn't, he wouldn't have thought so highly of you. He knows you're going to find the guy who did this to him, Jakob. He *knows* it."

The utter silence in her ear was back. Only this time, after what seemed like an eternity, she heard a deep breath. "I don't know what

I did so right in this world to be blessed with someone like you, Claire Weatherly."

"I ask myself the same thing in regard to you all the time," she said.

"Thank you. For sticking with me. For reaching out. For listening. For knowing. For . . . being you."

She blinked against the emotion kicked off by his words and, instead, squared her shoulders. "Okay, so what do you think about everything we learned tonight at Murphy's? I mean, Tom Shaunessy was *there,* Jakob. As close as a few table-lengths away at one point. So maybe seeing Russ on his turf after all those years set this guy off . . . Maybe he really did track Russ down at Callie's house, lure him outside, and exact his revenge for Russ's perceived hand in his failed mayoral run."

"It could certainly fit, I'll give you that. But something isn't adding up between Lauri's account of Saturday night and this otherwise pretty strong theory . . ."

"Meaning?" she prodded.

"You remember what I told you about the way he went after that shoplifter when I was a kid, right? I mean, Russ was fearless with a capital *F.* He ran *toward* the bad guys, not away from them."

"Okay . . ."

"*Russ* is the one who pulled up stakes and ran Saturday night, Claire. Not Tom."

"Maybe his leaving had nothing to do with Tom being there," she mused. "Maybe his sudden departure and Tom being within eyesight was purely coincidental — at least on Russ's end."

"On Russ's end." Jakob exhaled into the phone. "You're right. There wouldn't be any reason for Russ to have left because of Tom. Tom's issue, at least as far as Russ was concerned, was years ago. What truly matters here is the one thing Lauri couldn't tell us."

"Which is . . ."

"Whether Tom noticed Russ sitting at that booth, and if he did, what kind of reaction he may have had in the moment."

Hiking her slipper-clad feet onto the window seat, she rested her chin on her knees and looked out into the blackness. "Definitely a wish-I-could've-been-a-fly-on-the-wall moment, for sure."

"You're telling me . . . Wait! That's it!"

She sat up tall, the phone pressed to her ear. "What? What's *it*?"

"What you said just now — about the fly on the wall. Murphy's is a bar! That means there's a better-than-average shot the owner has a few cameras set up around the place to make sure his staff isn't ripping him off! Maybe, just maybe, one of them is angled in such a way I'll be able to see whether Tom noticed Russ when he was checking out that patron's tattoo with Lauri . . ."

"This could be it, Jakob!" She dropped her feet back to the floor and stood. "This could be exactly the break you've been looking for."

"I'll send one of our guys out there tomorrow while we're at the funeral service. If he gets anything, I'll have to come back here to the office as soon as it's over. I hope you understand."

She headed toward her dresser and the top drawer reserved for pajamas. "Even without this tape thing, I figured you'd be back on the case the second everything wrapped up, anyway. So yes, I understand. Besides, Esther asked me to stop out at her place afterward and I'm thinking I'd like to do that."

"Can't stay away from my new little great-niece, can you?" Before she could answer, he moved on, his detecting wheels practically clicking in her ear. "I probably better get off the phone. There's a lot I still need to do before I can head out of here."

"Yes. Please. Get some sleep. Tomorrow is going to be a long day for you," she said.

"I know. And I will. But I'll see you at the service tomorrow? Eleven o'clock?"

"I'll be there."

CHAPTER 19

It didn't matter that there had to be close to a hundred people gathered along the sidewalk watching the pallbearers place Russ's casket in the hearse. And she suspected, at that moment, it didn't even matter that she was one of those people. Because one look at Jakob's face as he stood beside Callie and her children proved he was somewhere else in his thoughts — a place likely inhabited solely by memories of his mentor and dear friend.

"He looks positively broken, doesn't he?" Claire managed to whisper around the ever-growing lump lodged halfway up her throat.

Diane reached for Claire's hand and held it tight. "He's grieving, of course. But he's not broken, dear. Russ mentored him better than that."

She tried to nod, to show some semblance of a response, but her attention was riveted on the scene playing out not more than ten steps ahead in the church's driveway. The first of the three vigilant funeral attendants tapping the back of the hearse indicating the body was loaded inside . . . The second speaking in hushed tones to Callie, Jakob, and the children . . . The third attendant sliding into place behind the steering wheel of the car directly behind the hearse . . .

"Do you realize that aside from the family who prefers to pretend he doesn't exist, Russ Granger is probably the only other person who knew Jakob when he was a young boy?" Claire gently tugged her hand free and waved at Jakob as the car in which he was riding lurched forward for its journey to the private burial on the other side of Heavenly. "Think about that, Aunt Diane. With Russ's death, he's lost yet another link to his past."

"I remember him as a boy," Diane corrected. "Or, at least a young man in his mid to late teens . . ."

She tried to take some comfort in her aunt's words, to see it as something positive to offset the dread she felt for Jakob, but it was hard. Russ had been a piece of Jakob's past — a piece Jakob could see and talk to without worry of fallout.

"A past is special, Claire, there's no doubt about that. But life is about now. And aside from *this*" — Diane motioned toward the two-car funeral procession now several blocks away — "I think Jakob is happy. He likes his job, *your* job helped him establish at least a semblance of a relationship with his niece and sister, and, most importantly, he has you."

"But I don't have any connection to his past at all. I can't share stories of his youth because I didn't know him."

Diane wrapped her arm around Claire's shoulder and drew her close. "No, you can't speak of what he looked like when he was little or chime in with the part of a childhood story he may have forgotten. But you can listen when he takes you down his own personal memory lane, and you can ask questions."

"I just wish he had photo albums I could see."

"As do I. But I'm quite sure he has plenty of vivid memories stored right here." Diane tapped her temple knowingly. "Memories I would imagine he'd love to share with you."

Claire waited until the hearse and car were no longer in view and then kissed her aunt's cheek. "You're right. Thank you. And thanks for being here with me."

"Are you heading back to the shop now?" Diane asked. "Because I could drop you off there if you'd like."

She took in her watch and then the sky, the peeks of sun in the otherwise overcast day a nice counterpoint to the funk she was desperate to shake off. "Actually, could I drop *you* off, instead? I'd like to take the car out to Esther's for a little while, if that's okay."

"Of course! I think that's a wonderful idea." Diane's quick clap claimed the attention of a few lingering mourners. "Time with Esther and that sweet new baby will surely get that chin of yours up and off the ground."

Claire fell into step beside her aunt as they made their way around the back of the church to the parking lot and the no-frills white sedan parked two spots over from the used-clothes donation bin. "She wants me to meet someone."

Diane fished her keys from her purse and handed them to Claire. "Oh? Is it anyone *I* might know?"

"Her name is Rebecca. She's Emma Stutzman's sister." Claire slid in behind the steering wheel and waited for her aunt to take the passenger seat. "She's visiting from somewhere in upstate New York."

"How lovely. I imagine her being here has been a blessing for that poor young woman and her children."

Claire steered the car toward the lot's exit but refrained from actually pulling onto the street. "It's looking as if it might be a blessing for Ben, as well."

"Benjamin Miller?" Diane echoed. "Why? Because now he doesn't have to spend so much time at Emma's?"

"Actually, Rebecca being there might be a factor in *why* he's there so much."

"I don't understand what you're . . ." Diane's sentence drifted off as the reality Claire was trying to share seemed to click into place. "Oh . . . *Oh!*"

She didn't need to turn her head to the right to know her aunt's attention was now fully trained on her. She could feel it just as surely as she could the sudden acceleration of her heart at her decision to bring Ben into the conversation at all. *Uh-oh.* She licked her drying lips with the tip of her tongue and made a show of finally pulling onto the road and heading toward the inn.

A heavy silence accompanied them down Church Street and onto Lighted Way as Diane seemed to weigh her reply and Claire continued her mental browbeating for opening her mouth in the first place. In fact, they were approaching the last bend before Sleep Heavenly when Diane finally spoke, her tone one of understanding rather than the worry she tended to show when the subject of Ben came up in relation to Claire.

"I hope she's every bit as special and wonderful as I know you want for him, dear."

Relieved, Claire shifted her gaze from the road to the passenger seat. "I've been praying for so long that he would find someone who would treasure his kind heart, his amazing ability to listen, and that shy smile he gets that could power the entire town of Heavenly during an outage. Yet when Ruth first told me about this Rebecca the other day, I didn't get that burst of happy like I thought I would."

At the approach to the inn, she signaled right and pulled onto the shoulder in preparation for her turn. "At first, I was kind of upset with myself. I mean, despite your on-again, off-again worry regarding Ben and me, I really don't have any interest in that kind of a relationship with Ben. Yet there I was, sulking, and I couldn't figure out why. That is, until I was on my way home and I came across Bill." She swept her hand toward the windshield and its view of Sleep Heavenly. "He pretty much talked me off the ledge by saying it made sense for me to be apprehensive and maybe even a little worried. In fact, it was his suggestion that I try and find a way to meet her so I can see for myself that she's the right one for Ben."

Diane drew back. "*Bill?* As in *my* Bill?"

Pulling into her aunt's favorite spot beneath the maple tree, Claire shut down the engine and allowed herself a moment to relish the smile she felt racing across her face. "Yes, Aunt Diane, *your* Bill. He's a pretty incredible listener and a generally awesome guy. In case you're unaware of these things . . ."

Diane's cheeks flushed red. "Oh, I'm aware, dear. Very, very aware."

For the second time in as many steps, she bent down and picked Diane's car keys off Esther's driveway. It wasn't that she was particularly nervous, although there was some measure of that, for sure. It was more about the fog that had seemed to descend on her brain after the pit stop at the inn.

For starters, it was a workday. Yet, because of the funeral and the tea invitation with Esther, Annie was on her own from open until close. Then, there was the matter of Jakob. Yes, he'd been strong for Russ's daughter and grandchildren throughout the service, but beneath the stoic exterior was a man who was hurting over the loss of his friend and desperate for answers. And finally, there was the matter of Ben falling for someone she hadn't even known existed until that week . . .

"Perhaps you could just put those in your bag and then you would not have to worry about dropping them."

Wrapping her fingers around the key ring, she inventoried her surroundings until she found the face that fit the voice. Sure enough, Eli was watching her from just inside the fence line that kept his goats from straying into the driveway.

"Well, hello there, Eli, how are you?" She tossed the keys into her bag, repositioned the plate of cupcakes Aunt Diane had insisted she bring, and crossed the mouth of the driveway to her friend.

Eli gestured toward each one of his goats. "Giggles and the others are not feeling well. If they do not improve, I may have to put them down."

"How long have they been like this?" she asked, taking in the half-mast eyes and lack of energy that had them all sitting apart from one another, their heads lolled off to the side.

"Too long." Eli kicked at the empty metal trough with his boot. "That is the sound I heard last night. But I did not know it at the time. I thought maybe it was a noise Esther made when looking after the baby. When I did not hear it again, I closed my eyes."

"You heard a boot?"

"Perhaps they kicked it over to dump out the water, or maybe they just bumped into it with their boot when they filled it back up with alcohol."

She sucked in a breath as her gaze bounced between the empty trough and the clearly sick goats before moving, finally, back to Eli. "Alcohol? In the water trough?"

"Yah."

"But why?"

"I cannot understand why. It is not something I would have thought was fun when I was that age."

"That age?" she echoed, confused. "Wait. You mean, you know who did this?"

"I cannot know for sure . . ."

"But you have a guess, don't you?" she prodded.

Eli's attention lifted to the sky before settling back on Claire. "Yah. But it will do no good. John will not let me speak to him about it."

"Your neighbor?" She pointed down the driveway toward the farm across the street. At Eli's slow, almost begrudging nod, she returned her hand to the edge of the cup-cake plate. "Are you saying you think *John* did this?"

"No. But I think his eldest son did."

"That's the one on Rumspringa, isn't it? The one Esther was telling me about the other day?"

"Yah." Eli stroked the underside of his beard. "The boy has upset many people in our community. Esther thinks it will stop just as my fighting stopped, but he does not have someone like Dat or Benjamin to set him straight."

"What about John? I mean, surely he says something to the boy when he does things like *this*, right?" She nudged her chin at first Giggles, and then each of the other two goats.

"I cannot say, but I know he does not take well to others speaking of the things his son has done." Eli released his hold on his beard in favor of the metal rake resting against the fence post. "Esther thinks I should speak to the boy. She said it has not been long since I was on Rumspringa, too. I do not know if that will help, but it does not matter if John will not let anyone speak to the boy."

She watched him rake at the area sur-rounding the trough with more care than such a task would seem to demand, but when he suddenly stopped to retrieve a beer cap and a shard of dark glass, she understood. "Do you ever see this kid out and about? Working in the fields or walking along the road by himself like he was last night when you were on the way to the visitation? Maybe that would be your best chance to speak with him without John's interference."

"I will watch and I will see. Maybe you are right." He set the glass and the cap on the top of the fence post and continued raking, his movements growing more and more deliberate with each new shard he found. "I have taken enough of your time. Esther is in the kitchen with Rebecca and the baby. Esther made bread."

"Mmmm, I love Esther's bread."

Eli grinned. "Then perhaps you should hurry before it is all gone."

Claire returned his smile and then turned toward the house, her mind filling the gap between the fence and the front porch with images of a woman she was both anxious and hesitant to meet. When she reached the screen door, she paused her hand just shy of the trim on which she usually knocked. Inside, she could hear Esther moving about, her purposeful footsteps likely taking her between the counter and the kitchen with tea and cookies, or between the table and the handcrafted cradle Sarah napped in during the day. After a moment, she heard an unfamiliar voice — one so light and happy she felt her throat constrict. So many times, over the past year, she'd thought of Ben being alone in his house each evening . . .

Eating alone.

Sitting alone.

Climbing the stairs to his room alone.

And every time she did, her heart ached. Yet something about this new voice —

"Claire! I did not hear you knock." Esther breezed down the hallway, pushed open the screen door, and waved Claire inside, her hazel eyes dancing with their usual warmth if not also a measure of worry. "Rebecca is in the kitchen with Sarah. She is excited to meet you."

When Claire was safely inside, Esther closed the door and dropped her voice to a whisper. "Did it go okay this morning? With the funeral and my uncle?"

"As good as can be expected." Claire leaned in and kissed Esther's soft cheek. "And I'll make sure to let Jakob know you were asking about him."

"Thank you." Esther lifted the covering on the cupcake plate, peeked inside, and let loose the teensiest hint of a squeal just before she grabbed hold of Claire's arm and pulled her down the hall. "I think Rebecca likes my bread as much as you do!"

Shrugging, she followed her friend into the kitchen only to stop, midstep, as her gaze fell on the woman seated at the table with Sarah in one arm and a slice of Esther's bread in her opposite hand.

The woman, in turn, looked up at Claire and flashed an apologetic grin. "If I am to gain twenty pounds today, it will be because of Esther and this bread."

"I know the feeling well, I'm afraid." Claire crossed to the table and held out her hand. "I'm Claire. Claire Weatherly. And you must be Rebecca."

Rebecca set her slice of bread on the napkin in front of her and shook Claire's hand. "Yah. Esther and Ben have both told me so much about you, I feel as if we've already met."

At Esther's urging, Claire lowered herself onto the bench opposite Rebecca's and took a moment to soak in the face on the other side of the table — the soft green eyes bordered by long, dark lashes . . . the high cheekbones . . . the Cupid's bow lips that seemed at home stretched wide with a smile . . . and across the bridge of her narrow nose the faint dusting of freckles that hinted at a fun-loving personality . . .

"I'm sorry it's taken us this long to meet, Rebecca." And as the words left her mouth, she realized they were true. Not because of curiosity, but because the woman smiling back at her looked like someone she could call a friend. They hadn't exchanged more than a handful of words, yet everything in her gut was telling her Ben would be okay — *great,* even — with this woman by his side. "Where are you from again?"

"Clymer, New York."

"And you came to help Emma after Wayne's death?" she asked.

"Yah. I came to help with the children but I feel as if they have helped me, too."

She saw the woman's smile falter ever so slightly and rushed to ease the mood. "I heard about your mother and I am sorry. It must be a blessing to be close to your sister again."

"It is. Very much."

Esther took Sarah from Rebecca and carried her over to the cradle. When the baby was tucked in beneath the window, she returned to sit beside Claire. "Rebecca learned of Wayne's death from the paper I showed you the other day . . ."

"Yah. It is how many learn of their far-off kin. Deaths, births, weddings, illness . . . It is why less work happens on a paper day. Everyone stops to read the sections where they have kin." Rebecca shrugged, finished her slice of bread, and then splayed her hands at the rest of the loaf. "That is it. I must not eat any more."

Esther nodded. "It is how Eli's aunt learned of Sarah's birth. It is how Miriam Mast learned of Barley's failing health. It is why so many people from so far away came to Eli's and my wedding, and, later, to Wayne's funeral."

"I remember when I opened the paper the day I learned of Wayne's death," Rebecca said. "I was alone, on the porch, as I was most days since Mamm's death, and I was saving the day's paper to read at dinner-time."

Esther drew back. "You read at dinner?"

"Yah. It is less lonely that way without Mamm to talk to." Rebecca tried to smile but Claire could see it was an effort. "But that day I wanted company on the porch more, so I did not wait until dinner to read the notice from Heavenly. Two hours later, I was on the bus to come here — to be with Emma."

"Wow." Claire nibbled at her own still-warm slice of bread but her true interest at the moment was the conversation and yet another aspect of Amish culture she'd never really thought too deeply about until that moment. "I never really stopped to think about that. I guess I'm just so used to picking up the phone or firing off an e-mail whenever there is good or bad news to be shared."

"It is how people know when Ruth and Samuel Yoder are to be married. How they will know when Ben and Rebecca . . ." Esther's cheeks flushed with embarrassment as Rebecca's eyes snapped to hers, and Claire's snapped to Rebecca's. But instead of seeing confusion or perhaps even a little irritation, Claire saw only hope on her new friend's face — hope for someone to sit with on the front porch, to sit across from at the dinner table, to talk with and listen to . . .

And, just like that, she found herself sharing that very same hope. For Rebecca, and for Ben. Together.

CHAPTER 20

It was a solid fifteen minutes into Lighted Way's official *unofficial* lunch hour when Claire closed the door behind the last of the morning's customers and sank back against it. "I'm telling you, Annie, if I didn't know any better, I'd think it was either the middle of the summer or two weeks before Christmas with the nonstop traffic we've had in here so far today."

"Your autumn candles and Esther's dolls are all gone. So, too, are Martha's painted milk cans and that footstool Eli made." Annie scanned their surroundings and then, shaking her head, took off for the section devoted to home goods. "I do not know how a pile of place mats can get so messy all the time. I fan them out so people can see them all, and they always end up in a silly stack."

Claire watched the teenager fuss with the place mats and then made herself part company with the door. "When you're finished with that, let's take fifteen on the stools. I think we've more than earned it, don't you?"

"But there is much recording to do in the ledger," Annie protested.

"Which we'll do when our well-earned break is over." Claire crossed to the counter, pulled out the pair of stools she'd purchased back when Esther worked at the store, and flopped down on the cushioned top. "Oh . . . Yeah . . . Okay . . . This feels even better than I imagined when I was bagging up that last customer's purchases."

Annie's answering giggle guided her attention back toward the place mat display. "You should see your face right now, Claire. It is like it looks when Ruth brings over a warm chocolate chip cookie — only today there is no cookie."

"Right now, this stool is better than any cookie." She stopped, considered her words, and then waved a tired hand in the air. "Though that's not to say I'd turn my nose up at a cookie if one suddenly came through the door."

The giggle morphed into a full-fledged laugh as Annie — now finally satisfied with her place mat efforts — ventured across the store and around the counter to the shelf tasked with housing her lunch pail. "I made oatmeal cookies for Dat last night. Perhaps the one I packed for you will make *you* smile the way I had hoped they would do for Dat."

"Your dat didn't like the cookies?" Claire took the treat from her employee's out-stretched hand and then, without waiting for an answer, took a bite, her eyes rolling back in her head at the taste. "Oh, Annie . . . Wow!"

"It is just an oatmeal cookie. Like Mamm used to make."

Claire took a second and third bite and then stared down longingly at her empty hand. "No, I'm serious, Annie. I'm not a big oatmeal cookie lover and that was in-credible."

Annie's cheeks flushed at the praise. "Thank you, Claire. I am glad you enjoyed it. Here, take mine. I would rather eat the apple I packed."

She opened her mouth to argue but, instead, took the second cookie and popped half of it in her mouth. "There are times when you bake stuff like this that I have to wonder if you're making a colossal mistake working here, kiddo."

"I made a mistake?" Annie pulled her pail to her aproned front, her eyes wide. "I'm sorry. I will fix it . . . whatever it is."

Pausing, midchew, Claire shook off the girl's worry. "No, Annie, I didn't mean you made a mistake *here,* at the store. I just mean you made a mistake opting to *work* here instead of next door. With Ruth."

"With Ruth?" Annie echoed.

"Every treat you've ever made and brought in for me to try has been incredible. Truly."

"But they are things I just make from Mamm's favorite recipes."

"That doesn't matter. You still baked them, Annie. And they're still delicious."

Annie dropped her gaze to her boots. "I can't bake like Ruth bakes . . ."

"I disagree." Hooking a finger beneath the teen's chin, she gently lifted it until they were eye to eye. "But let's get back to what you said as you were handing me that first cookie. About your dat . . . Is everything okay at home? Are you two not having as much time together as you were?"

Slowly, Annie released her death grip on her lunch pail and set it on the counter, her fingers nervously plucking at the edges of its cloth cover. "No, Dat and I still have dinner together each night, and we still talk about our day, but I do not like to see him troubled. He works too hard to be troubled. It is why I told him of the things I did when

I first started my Rumspringa. So maybe he would see that it will be okay."

Claire patted the empty stool and waited until Annie abandoned her post at the counter and sat. "Surely your dat isn't worried about you any longer? You're wearing your Amish clothes, you work hard when you're here at the shop, you're sitting down to dinner with him every night, and you're talking. I don't see what the problem is unless you're keeping something from me?"

"It is not me he is worried about." Annie smoothed her dress around her legs with quick, jerky movements. "It is Amos."

She mentally ticked her way through the names of Annie's nieces and nephews but there wasn't an Amos among them, and there wasn't one of them that was more than eight years old. "I'm sorry, Annie, I don't know who Amos is. Is that one of your brother's children?"

"No. It is a boy in our district. Amos — Amos Bontrager. I have told you about him before. He lives with his mamm and dat on the farm across from —"

"Esther and Eli," Claire finished as the boy's name finally dropped into place in her memory bank. "Did Giggles and the others die?"

Annie's brows furrowed in confusion. "I

do not know someone named Giggles."

"Giggles is a goat. He belongs to Eli Miller."

"Did Amos do something to the goat?"

Claire shrugged. "Eli seems to think so."

"Dat does not need even more things to worry about with Amos," Annie mumbled.

"I don't understand. What does Amos have to do with . . ." A vague memory fired in some distant corner of her brain, making her sit up tall. "Wait. As the bishop, it is up to your dad to decide whether Amos is shunned or not, right?"

"Amos is on Rumspringa, so he will not be shunned. But Dat is being told stories by many people — stories of Amos getting into trouble with some English boys."

"What kind of trouble?"

"He was knocking down mailboxes with his English friends the other day. It brought the police."

"Is that who ran through the field? The Bontrager boy?" she asked while simultaneously flashing back to Jakob's office and the details he'd shared with her involving the call. "I guess that makes sense now. John Bontrager wasn't mad at Jakob, he was upset with his boy."

Annie shook her head. "That is why Dat is worried about Amos. Because John doesn't get upset with Amos for the things he does. John gets angry at those who speak of those things."

She drew back. "But why?"

"Dat does not know. John is a very . . ." Annie looked down at her hands and then back up at Claire, a familiar dullness from long ago muting her normal sparkle. "Dat says John is rigid. That he likes to do things his own way. But to me, he is very much like The Pest."

The Pest — aka Josiah Beiler, Annie's brother-in-law's father . . .

Closing her eyes against the memories of an encounter that haunted her until this day, she forced herself to breathe.

Breathe in . . .
Breathe out . . .
Breathe in . . .
Breathe —

"Claire?"

She forced her lashes apart to find Annie trying valiantly to keep from crying. Instinctively, she closed her hand over Annie's and squeezed. "I'm sorry, kiddo. I just . . . Well, we both need to remember we're okay now."

"I know. Dat tells me that same thing. Sometimes, when I am asleep, my dreams make me think that is not so."

Oh, how she knew those dreams well.

They came less frequently now than they had at the start, but they still came on occasion.

"Those are just dreams, Annie. Nightmares."

Annie tugged her hand out from under Claire's and stood. "I know. But . . . I am worried for Dat."

"Why?"

"Three times in the past few weeks, someone has come and spoken to Dat about Amos. One was Luke Hochstetler's dat. Amos and his English friends drove a car through two rows of corn! Another was about the sign he took down from Daniel Lapp's toy shop. For a week Daniel did not sell toys because there was no sign. And then last night, as we were finishing up dinner, the widow Graber stopped by to say she found Amos hiding behind her barn, spying on Miriam Mast."

Annie returned her untouched lunch pail to its proper shelf and then retrieved it again just as quickly. "Dat drove out to the Bontrager farm to talk to John and Amos while I was baking the oatmeal cookies. But John would not let him talk to Amos and told Dat to go home."

"But your dat is the bishop. I didn't know the Amish speak to a bishop like that."

"They don't." Annie pulled back the cloth cover, poked around inside the pail, and then pushed it aside. "He told Dat that Amos is *his* son and he will decide what is right and what is wrong."

Claire searched for something to say to ease the teen's clearly troubled heart, but she was at a loss for anything beyond the "wow" that kept looping its way past her lips every ten seconds or so.

"I tried to tell Dat that Amos will come around after Rumspringa, but Dat is afraid Amos will get hurt or be put in an English jail like The Pest if he does not stop the bad things he is doing now." Annie sank back onto the stool. "I do not like to see Dat worry, Claire."

"And, likewise, I don't like to see *you* worry, either. So let's give it a little more time. Maybe things will turn around for Amos like they did for you."

"I will try. But Amos does not have you, Claire. And he does not have my dat for a dat."

Claire wound her way between two parked cars and stepped onto the sidewalk, the foot traffic of earlier all but gone now that shops, like her own, were closed for the day. Up ahead and on the other side of the street, patrons still came and went from Heavenly Brews and Taste of Heaven(ly), but the bulk of the tourists that had kept her and Annie hopping throughout the day were back on their respective buses or enjoying a wider variety of dining options in one of the neighboring English towns.

There were different parts of the day's cycle she found appealing. She loved the brief window in each of her mornings when the inn's guests were still upstairs in their respective rooms and she and Diane were preparing breakfast together in the kitchen. Sure, there were times she wished she could sleep in as she might if she had her own place, but there was something calming and yet also motivating about starting her day humming along with her aunt. She also cherished the quiet times at the store for the opportunity they provided to get caught up on the books or to talk with Annie, as well as the busy, customer-filled moments that enabled her to worry a little less about finances. Dinner hour at the inn brought with it the opportunity to speak with guests from all over the country — learning about their hometowns while sharing tidbits about Heavenly. And the postdinner hour brought time to read and relax either on the porch swing or on her favorite couch in the parlor.

But her favorite time of any given day was just after she'd closed the shop, and the evening and all its possibilities were stretched out before her like a vast ocean.

Sometimes, when she had the night off from helping Diane at the inn, she'd lock the back door of the shop, slip the key in her pocket, and set off on foot into the Amish countryside, her destination merely as far as her feet could take her before the dwindling light of day demanded she head back. Other times, she'd take Diane's car and make her rounds out to Martha's and Esther's homes with earned money for their wares. But as much as she treasured both options, her very favorite way to spend a free evening was with Jakob.

It didn't matter if they went for a walk, sat across from each other at their favorite window-side table in Heavenly Brews, snuggled under a blanket in his apartment watching a movie, or swayed together on the inn's porch swing . . . If they were together, it was as if her happiness doubled.

Yanking open the front door of the police department, Claire stepped inside the building and headed straight for the desk and the balding fiftysomething manning it from the other side. "Hi, Curt, how are you?"

"Oh, hey, Claire," the dispatcher said,

looking up. "I'm good. You?"

"Good. Busy." She stopped at the desk and took in the wall of mailboxes behind Curt. Half of the dozen or so boxes boasted a temporary red placard she knew meant that particular officer or staff member was either out on the road or otherwise occupied outside the department's four walls. A quick glance at the box assigned to Jakob showed he was in. "Could you ring back to Jakob's office and ask if it would be okay for me to stop in and say hi?"

Curt flashed his infamous yet endearing lopsided grin. "I'm pretty sure we both know what his answer will be, but yeah, I'll check. He just got some tape he's been waiting for so I imagine he's watching that." Rolling his chair to the left, he picked up the station phone, pressed the number assigned to the detective's office, and held the receiver to his ear. "Hey, Jakob, I've got Claire out here at the front desk and she wants to know if she can pop back and — roger that."

He returned the phone back to its cradle and looked up at Claire. "I'll buzz you in."

"Thanks, Curt." She hurried over to the other side of the desk and, at the quick buzz that followed, pushed her way into the inner sanctum of the Heavenly Police Department. She followed the hall past the police break room, the file room, and the evidence room and then happily braced herself for the hug she knew was waiting on the other side of Jakob's open door.

Only there was no hug.

In fact, other than a fleeting smile timed with an even more fleeting glance as she stepped inside his office, there was little indication Curt had even alerted him to her presence. Instead, he beckoned her over to his chair and the small television screen that held the majority of his attention. "It took a little longer to get these tapes released to me, but I've got them now."

"Is that the footage from the night Russ was at Murphy's?" She dropped her purse on the chair she normally inhabited when visiting Jakob's office and circled around to his side of the desk.

"It is. The owner has different cameras wired into the bar area — one behind the till, one just inside the door, one angled to see the patrons seated at the bar, and one out in the dining area." He pointed at the screen. "I fast-forwarded through much of the till shots because that's not my focus at the moment. I watched the footage of the bar just long enough to ascertain that Tom Shaunessy did, in fact, spend some time sitting there. I also saw the moment Lauri's friend must have called to him because he goes from drinking and talking to someone sitting next to him, to glancing over his shoulder in the direction of the dining area, setting his beer on top of the bar, and then vacating his stool with what looked like an I'll-be-back type exchange with the bartender."

"Do you see him come back after a while?" she asked, perching on Jakob's armrest for its view of the screen.

"I don't know. I want to look at that *after* we see the encounter Lauri told us about. So I get a more accurate picture of the way — and the order — in which everything played out."

"Makes sense." She watched as he consulted a handwritten time notation on the notepad in front of him and then advanced the dining room footage currently on his screen accordingly. When the time stamp on the bottom right-hand corner of the screen was within a minute of where he wanted to be, he pressed play, sat back, and rested his chin on top of tented fingers.

There, on the screen, was a wide-angle shot of the handful of booths where people wishing to eat with friends or a significant other chose to sit. The camera was positioned to show one side of each booth. On the particular night in question, each seat they could see was occupied by one person when it was a couple, or as many as three people with a group. She scanned each seat she could see and then pointed to one with a man seated on the side facing the camera and talking animatedly with Lauri. "Is that Russ, there?" she asked.

"It is . . ." Jakob's chair creaked as he leaned forward. "Talking to Lauri, just like she said . . ."

They grew silent as the man Jakob looked to as a father figure chatted away, completely oblivious to the fact that his life would be over in a matter of hours. As the time inched forward to an exact match of the one noted in Jakob's book, a woman with long, dark hair, large hoop earrings, and a formfitting minidress stepped into view, appeared to say something in first Lauri's and then the bar's direction, and, like clockwork, Lauri turned, took a step toward the woman, and then said something to Russ across her shoulder. Russ, in turn, smiled and redeployed his own attention to the plate of previously untouched wings Claire could just make out on his table.

For a second or two, she simply watched Russ, his demeanor one of ease as he noshed on the first of what looked to be a dozen or more wings. Then she moved on to Lauri and a man she recognized from the near-constant coverage of his ill-fated mayoral run in Cedarville. Together, they leaned toward the dark-haired woman who, in turn, stood on one leg and moved her ankle in such a way so as to showcase the tattoo Claire couldn't quite make out. After a few seconds, the woman returned her foot to the ground, threw her hands up in obvious excitement, and kicked off an odd yet unmistakable shiver down Claire's spine. Before she could dissect it, though, movement at a nearby table pulled her attention back to a clearly agitated Russ and the nearly full plate of wings he was shoving to the side.

"He looks . . . I'm not sure," she murmured, matching Jakob's latest lean.

"That's Russ's high-alert face." Jakob reached forward, hit stop, and switched to the rewind button. When they reached the noted time once again, he hit play and grabbed his pen from its resting spot atop the open notepad. "Forget about Lauri and the others. Let's just watch Russ this time — you know, see when and how his expression first changes."

Again, they saw Russ talking animatedly

with Lauri. Then, they saw her start to walk away, say something to him over her shoulder, and saw him smiling as he turned his attention to his plate of wings. This time, however, instead of following Lauri over to her friend, she watched Russ as he ate the meat off his first wing, discarded the bone into an empty bowl, and reached for a second wing. He lifted it to his mouth, glanced off to his right, took a bite, chewed for a second or two, and then slowly lowered the largely uneaten wing until it was hovering above his plate. In a span of a few seconds, his brows lifted with curiosity, lowered with intrigue, and then disappeared from view completely as he let go of the wing, shoved the plate to the side, and then brought his right hand to first his chest and then his pants pockets in a patting motion. "He seems to be looking for something," she mused. "Maybe his phone or —"

"He's looking for his notebook. He kept a small one in his shirt pocket pretty much twenty-four/seven when he worked at the station. Wrote case stuff in it all the time." Jakob grew silent as, on the screen, Russ stopped patting, grabbed his phone from its resting spot next to the condiment basket on his table, hit a button, and casually held it in line with his table.

Claire felt her breath hitch. "He's taking a picture of something!"

Russ pressed a button they couldn't see from their vantage point and then slipped the phone into his back pocket. Seconds later, he tugged his wallet out, pulled a crisp bill from the billfold, tossed it onto the table, and, after yet another look to his right, slid out of his booth and all but ran out of the camera's view.

Silence hung between Claire and Jakob as they watched for a few more seconds, waiting to see if Russ would turn around and come back. When he didn't, Jakob switched to tape from a different camera — an exterior view. This time, when he advanced the picture, he did so to within a few seconds shy of the time Russ left. And, as expected, Russ came barreling out of the bar's front door and disappeared into the parking lot, his fingers moving across his phone's screen as if trying to enlarge something while also periodically looking up to make sure he didn't walk into anything.

"Whatever it was he took that picture of inside Murphy's certainly seemed to affect him," she mused.

"I agree." Jakob reached forward, hit stop on the parking lot tape, and then swapped it for the dining room tape once again. "But

I looked through his phone the other day and other than a cartoon character I didn't know and some sort of screen shot off his computer, there was nothing worthy of the angst we just saw. And he didn't make a call when he stepped outside, so I can't believe he thought there was any sort of immediate threat."

She considered his words as she massaged her temples. "Okay . . . So maybe we need to go back now and focus just on Tom the way we did with Russ."

"My thoughts, exactly." He advanced the footage to the moment Tom sidled up alongside Lauri and her friend and hit play. "We're watching for a glance toward Russ, any sort of odd movement that might have been picture-worthy — assuming that's what Russ was even snapping."

So they watched. They saw Tom embrace Lauri's friend . . . They saw him step back to accommodate the woman's raised leg . . . They saw him lean forward in tandem with Lauri for a closer look at the tattoo . . . They saw him point to the tattoo on the woman's opposite ankle as she lowered her leg back to the ground . . . When the woman threw her hands up in the air, Tom laughed.

In her peripheral vision, Claire saw Russ shove the plate of wings to the side but kept her attention trained on Tom. Tom, in turn, rolled up his shirt sleeve, pointed at a tattoo on his forearm, and then engaged Lauri's friend in some sort of animated discussion until Lauri disappeared and reappeared with a crisp bill in her hand. When she pointed toward Russ's now-empty table, Tom looked quickly, shrugged his shoulders, and then gestured back toward the bar. A few seconds later, Lauri disappeared into the kitchen, her friend wandered toward the billiard table they could just make out in a corner of the screen, and Tom ventured back to the bar.

Again, Jakob stopped the tape and swapped it for another — this time from the camera tasked with keeping an eye on the patrons bellied up to the bar. He advanced to the correct time frame, hit play, and sat back as, seconds later, Tom reclaimed his barstool, took a swig of his drink, and continued talking to the man beside him as if he hadn't missed a beat.

"If Tom saw Russ — and I'm not convinced he did based on everything we just saw — it didn't faze him." Jakob watched Tom interact with the other patrons at the bar for a few minutes and then shut the tape off, the disappointment he wore on his face a perfect match for his long, drawn-out exhale. "I feel like I'm right back at square one with this case. If Tom had seen Russ, if we'd seen even a grimace or a spasm of anger he managed to tamp down, I'd think maybe . . . Maybe the anger simmered while he continued to drink . . . Maybe he found out where Russ was staying while he was in the area or already knew where Callie lives, somehow . . . Maybe Russ heard someone outside and went out to investigate and it got out of hand . . .

"That is how it's been playing out in my head ever since we got verification that Tom was at Murphy's on Saturday night, too. But *this?"* He flicked his hand at the now-dark television screen. "This makes me think Tom had nothing to do with anything. That his being at the same watering hole as Russ on Saturday night was nothing short of a coincidence — a coincidence that meant absolutely nothing to anyone but me."

"And me," she reminded. Pushing off the armrest, she turned, perched herself on the edge of his desk, and book-ended his face with her hands. "Hey . . . Something caught Russ's attention in that bar. You and I both saw that just now on those tapes. Maybe this really doesn't have anything to do with Tom at all. Or maybe something Tom did

267

or said while talking to Lauri and her friend is what made Russ pull out his phone. Or since there wasn't anything picture-worthy on his phone, maybe it's something else entirely — something unrelated to the bar. I mean, those cameras can only show us what happened in that exact spot at that exact time. We don't know what happened afterward."

Jakob covered her hands with his and, after a quiet moment, gently lowered them to his lips for a brief kiss even as his attention traveled back toward the television. "Maybe I should watch the rest of the bar camera. See if something happens with Tom later in the evening."

"Such as?"

"I don't know. I guess I'm playing on what you said about Russ and that picture he took. Maybe Tom got a call an hour or so later that set him off . . . . Maybe another patron told him Russ was back in town and I'll see a reaction more in keeping with what I expected to see a few minutes ago."

She followed his eyes back to the screen and the button he was getting ready to push to start the intense viewing all over again. "Jakob, you've got to be exhausted after the funeral today. Why don't you put this on hold until tomorrow morning and we can go get dinner, or go for a walk, or watch some mindless television at your place, or even go back to the inn and sit outside on the porch swing. Just something to get you out of here for a little while so you can take a breath, clear your head, and get the sleep we both know you need in order to tackle this case the way you want to."

"The way I *need* to, Claire," he corrected. "Callie and her kids are devastated by what happened to Russ. And while finding his killer won't bring him back, at least it will enable them to mourn without all these unanswered questions muddying the water."

"I get that, Jakob, I really do. And I support you in that quest a hundred zillion percent. But *you're* grieving, too. That alone is exhausting even without adding all of this" — she hooked her thumb toward the TV — "to the mix, too. And even Superman needs to take a breath once in a while in order to be at his best."

Slowly, he lifted his chin to reveal a dullness to his eyes that didn't match the snippet of a smile she spotted near the right corner of his mouth. "Likening me to Superman is dirty pool, you know."

"I know." She reclaimed his hand and interlaced her fingers with his. "So will you? Take the rest of the evening off with me so you can recharge and refresh?"

He took her hand inside his own before releasing it to gesture at the TV. "Let me fast-forward through the bar footage to see if anything with Tom changes and then yeah . . . I'll give it a rest until morning. But only because that's what Superman would do."

CHAPTER 21

She could feel his disappointment just as surely as she could his hand inside her own as they left the police station and headed west. She wanted to say something, to offer some other possibility that could keep Tom Shaunessy on his radar, but she was at a loss. Nearly sixty minutes of fast-forwarding through footage of Tom in his spot at the bar yielded nothing worthy of a good story, let alone picking him up for questioning.

He'd talked to the man on his left . . .

He'd bought a round of drinks for the people sitting in his immediate vicinity . . .

He'd stepped away from the bar to use the restroom (as verified by a quick swap to the dining room tape) . . .

He'd tried to chat up a pair of women who stopped at the bar long enough to collect their drinks from the bartender . . .

And, shortly before eleven thirty, he'd polished off his last drink, shook hands with the people seated to his right and yet another newcomer on his left, and waved to the bartender without putting even so much as a buck on the bar for a tip . . .

He hadn't gotten any calls . . .

He hadn't checked any texts . . .

And he'd showed no signs of agitation at any point.

They — or, rather, *Jakob* — was officially back to square one with Russ's murder.

"I'm sorry that whole tape-watching thing just now turned out to be such a waste of time." With the help of his hand, she side-stepped an elevated brick in the center of the sidewalk, and then returned the favor as they approached Gussman's General Store. "I know it's frustrating."

Slipping his arm around her waist, they strolled past the driveway that would take them to the market's back parking lot and Jakob's apartment. "Frustrating? No doubt. But it was only a waste of time insofar as it didn't give me what I wanted. But I needed to look at that if for no other reason than to move that theory off to the side for a little while."

They followed the sidewalk until it ended and then continued into the Amish country-side, the sparsely pebbled road beneath their feet prompting an audible sigh from both of them. "Okay, and yeah . . . I needed to get out from behind that desk for a little while," he said. "Superman or not."

"I'm glad. I know I've always been one to walk when I need a break, but no walk I've ever taken clears my head and calms my heart quite the way this one does."

Farm after farm, they made their way west, the evening's sun beginning its slow, yet distinctive descent toward the horizon. Several times she started to ask what he was thinking but stopped herself each time with the memory of why she'd suggested the walk in the first place. When they reached the turnoff to Miller's Pond, they turned in sync with nary a word or a glance.

"Why do you think that is?" he finally asked as they walked under the canopy of trees that helped shield the picturesque spot from the curious eyes of passersby. "That walking out here, as opposed to anywhere else, clears your head the way you say?"

It was a question she, herself, had pondered many times. And while the answer she always came up with seemed to change, she did her best to finally nail it down for Jakob. "Well, in New York, there was always background noise — a siren, a horn, people, car brakes, construction, you name it. I think that stuff always being there makes it hard to completely declutter your brain."

"And the other side of Heavenly? What's different about your walks out there?"

"There's some of that same stuff I mentioned in New York, although to a much lesser degree. But when you pass a car over there, it's going somewhere — home, work, the store . . . all the places I need to go to, as well. But here, on the Amish side? It's tranquil."

"People work every bit as hard over here."

"Oh, there's no disputing that." She took a moment to gather her thoughts and feelings into a cohesive explanation and then quietly wriggled free of his arm. "But it's the *aura* around their work that somehow manages to be peaceful and calm. Likewise, it slows my heartbeat if I'm upset, and makes me smile even when I might have been sad or angry. But most of all, I think the slower pace out here makes *me* slow down, too. And when you slow down, you can process better . . . plan better . . . think better."

"I'd consider mounting an argument if I wasn't experiencing exactly what you're describing at this very minute." He bent down, sifted through the ground in pursuit of a flat rock, and, when he found it, led the way out of the grove of trees and over to the edge of the pond. "This was so normal to me growing up that I never stopped to notice how calm it was in comparison to other places. But it *is* different over here. And it really does have a calming effect, although I suspect being here *with you* is the biggest factor of all."

With a flick of his wrist, the rock skipped once, twice, three times across the water before disappearing amid a sea of rings rippling outward. She was just about to issue a challenge on who could skip more when a sound to their right drew her attention past the tree, and Jakob's hand upward in a wave.

"Miriam . . . Hi!" She stepped around the tree and over to the lanky Amish woman adjusting her boot atop a large rock. "We didn't realize anyone else was here. How's the foot?" Glancing at Jakob, she splayed her hand. "Miriam cut her foot on a piece of glass out here the other day."

Jakob pulled a face. "When I was a boy, the Amish were the only ones that ever used this pond. Walked around here with bare feet all the time — chasing frogs, skipping rocks, wading into the pond. But now, with the occasional Englisher — especially the teenagers — that come back here, I imagine there are probably a lot of cut feet these days."

With quick, efficient tugs, Miriam Mast laced up her boots and then slid off the rock and onto her feet. "Won't stop me from dipping my toes. Just means I need to keep better watch here, too."

Claire backed up a step so as not to block Miriam's view of Jakob and then swept her hand between them. "I'm not sure if you two have met, but Jakob, this is Miriam Mast — her husband is the new minister. Miriam, this is Esther's uncle — Jakob Fisher. *Detective* Jakob Fisher."

An odd expression crossed Miriam's face as she, too, stepped back. Only instead of doing it to include Jakob in the conversation as Claire had done, Miriam's was about initiating distance. So, too, was the fleeting nod she gave in lieu of actually returning Jakob's hello.

Turning to Claire, her pallor pale, Miriam grabbed a small backpack up off the rock and slung it over her left shoulder. "It is getting late. I must head home to cook supper for Elmer before he wonders where I've run off to."

"Oh . . . uh . . . sure." Claire snuck a quick peek at Jakob to see if he was bothered by the obvious slight, but his focus had moved to the grove of trees on the other side of the pond. "Is your foot okay enough to make that walk home?"

Miriam shrugged. "It's not like Elmer would come out of that field long enough to pick me up, anyway."

"I . . . I could drive you." She winced inwardly at the lack of sincerity in her voice, but after Miriam's attitude toward Jakob it was the best she could do . . .

"No, thank you. I'll take getting out any way I can get it." Then, with nothing more than a sidelong glance at Jakob, Miriam headed away from the pond, her limp beginning to show some signs of improvement.

When Claire was sure the minister's wife was gone, she wandered over to Jakob and threaded her arms around his neck. "Hey . . . I'm really, really sorry about that just now. I know you needed this time to relax and I guess I should have taken into account the very real possibility that we wouldn't be the only ones here. I just thought that with it being dinnertime and all, this place would be deserted like it is right at this minute."

"There's nothing for you to apologize for, Claire. This is the way things are for me with the Amish. Do I wish it could be different? Of course. I'd be crazy not to. But it's not a surprise." He lingered a kiss on her forehead for a few seconds and then lowered his lips to her ear. "As for the rest? The part about it being deserted right now? It's not."

She followed his gaze as it returned to the other side of the pond. Slowly, she scanned the water's edge, the picnic table off to the right and the wooded area beyond, only to come up empty. "I don't see —"

A snap, not unlike that of a branch or a stick, cut short her sentence and sent her focus back to Jakob as he, in turn, stepped closer to the edge of the pond. "Who's there?" he called.

Leaves crunched quickly and then nothing . . .

"Jakob?" she whispered. "Maybe we should just go. You've got to be getting hungry about now, anyway."

"I am, but . . ." He stepped closer, bobbing his head left and right. "Look, I know you're there. I can see the outline of your hat."

Claire came up behind him. "You can? Where?"

"Right there . . . By the maple tree on the right . . ." Pointing, he led her to the correct spot and the outline of what appeared to be an Amish male. When she nodded, he called out again. "Unless you're doing something in those trees you shouldn't be doing, you don't have anything to worry about —"

The figure stepped away from the protective shade of the tree and over to the pond's opposite shore, the day's remaining light offering a bit of clarity where moments before there had been none.

"I ain't doing nothing wrong." The Amish teen hooked his thumb inside his suspender strap and shrugged. "This pond is Amish. You're not."

Jakob's voice rose with his smile. "I'm pretty sure a pond can't be Amish any more than that rock to your left or that tree you were just hiding behind can be."

"I wasn't hiding," the boy protested. "I was just looking, is all."

"Looking at what?"

"The pond."

"And you needed to keep that secret because why?" Jakob asked.

"I didn't feel like talking to anyone, is all. Didn't want to have to answer questions *like these*."

"Questions I wouldn't have to ask if you weren't lurking behind a tree." Jakob watched the boy for a few moments and then bent down to retrieve two flat rocks. Displaying them on his palm, he held them out to Claire. "Pick your poison."

"Maybe we should just go," she whispered.

"Nope. I challenge you to a rock-skipping contest and I'm not leaving until we have it."

Hesitating, she glanced again at the teenager and then back at Jakob. "Are you sure?"

"Pick."

So she picked. "What's at stake?"

"Winner chooses dinner." He pointed at the rock. "Call your number."

Aware of the teenager still watching them from the other side of the pond, Claire shifted foot to foot. "Um . . . I don't know. Four, maybe?"

"Have you been engaging in some practice sessions I don't know about?" he asked, laughing.

"Maybe . . ."

His laugh morphed into a mischievous grin, dimples and all. "Okay, give it your best shot."

Closing her fingertips over the rock the way he'd taught her, she pulled her arm back, cocked her wrist, and let the rock sail across the top of the water.

One . . .

Two . . .

Three.

"Not four, but not too shabby, either," he said.

"Looked as good as what you threw earlier," the teen called out.

Together, Jakob and Claire looked across the pond. "So you were watching when we first walked up?"

"Maybe."

"And you were watching Miriam Mast just now?"

"What if I was? Ain't nothing wrong with watching."

She touched Jakob's upper arm, drawing his attention off the Amish teen and back onto her face. "Let's just go. Please?"

"It's fine," he murmured just loud enough for Claire to hear. Then, lifting his chin, he readied his own rock for battle. "There *is* something wrong with watching if the people being watched feel unsafe and want to file a report with the police."

"You gonna file one?" the teen challenged.

"I'm not the only one you were watching . . ."

The boy jutted his chin in their direction, his words and his gaze now aimed at Claire. "*You* gonna file one?"

"No." She turned back to Jakob to repeat her earlier suggestion of dinner but stopped as the teen folded his arms in defiance.

"It doesn't look like I have anything to worry about, does it?"

Jakob gave a half shrug. "Perhaps Miriam Mast would disagree."

The teen's laugh echoed across the pond. "I'm pretty sure she won't."

"Oh?" Jakob prodded. "What makes you so sure of —"

"Why don't you just throw the rock."

Jakob looked down at his hand, cocked his arm back, and, with a flick of his wrist, sent the rock hurling across the pond.

One . . .

Two . . .

Three . . .

Four . . .

As the rock sank into the water on what many might argue was an additional half skip, Jakob pulled a napkin from his pants pocket, wiped his hands, and smiled triumphantly down at Claire. "You good with pizza? I'm pretty sure I've got one in my freezer."

At her nod, he took her hand, walked forward about three steps, and then turned back to the teen. "Why don't you head on home, Amos. Best not to worry your mamm without reason."

The boy's answering gasp reached their side of the pond. "How do you know my name?" he demanded.

"Because that watching you were just doing?" Jakob called back. "That's *my job*. As is investigating the complaints that come in on things like letting your neighbors' cows loose, spray-painting graffiti on covered bridges, underage drinking, and poisoning goats."

Silence floated across the water only to be broken, several long seconds later, by the sound of the teen's footsteps running in the opposite direction.

CHAPTER 22

She balanced the bowl of popcorn between them and matched his sag against the back of the couch. "I didn't realize just how little sitting I've done today until just this moment."

"And I didn't realize how spent I was until just now, either." Jakob lifted his head enough to see into the bowl and pop a few pieces of popcorn into his mouth. "Thanks for being a good sport about the whole frozen-pizza-instead-of-going-out thing. It's just that our time together has been so harried and I don't really see that changing until I solve this case."

"Trust me, eating *anything* here with you is good enough for me."

He kissed the tip of her nose and then pointed at the bowl. "Eat some popcorn."

She took a piece, considered it, and then dropped it back into the bowl, uneaten. "Annie told me a little bit more about that young man from the pond. Seems he's been going a little crazy on his Rumspringa."

"That's an understatement." He scooped up a handful of the salty snack and deposited most of it into his mouth. When he was done chewing, he picked his feet up off the floor and extended his legs across the coffee table. "It's not how most spend their Rumspringa, but there's always one or two who do."

"Did you do any of that kind of stuff?" she asked. "Maybe not to that extreme, of course, but did you step out of line at all?"

His laugh was humorless. "You mean besides hanging around the police department? Uh . . . no. That was the extent of my" — he wiggled his fingers — "*experimentation* with the English world. I didn't drink, I didn't smoke, I didn't get ahold of a car and blare a radio so people could hear it two towns over. Nope, I just followed police cars around so I could watch them writing a ticket or taking a report, or, if I was really lucky, scored an invitation into the station, where I could listen to Russ or one of the other cops talking about catching a robbery suspect or breaking up a fight or whatever."

"If only Amos's parents could be so lucky," she mused as she finally helped herself to a piece of popcorn.

"I'm pretty sure my father would take issue with that statement."

Slapping a hand across her mouth, she bolted upright on the couch. "Oh, Jakob, I'm so sorry. I wasn't thinking. I . . ." She pinched her eyes closed, silently berating herself for being so dense.

"Don't." At the feel of his hand on her cheek, she opened her eyes. "There's nothing wrong with what you said. And I didn't mean to make that crack about my father to make you feel bad. The fact is, from the outside looking in, I was a pretty easy teenager. I didn't refuse responsibility, I sought it out on an ever grander scale. But that's from the perspective of the English world. From the perspective of the Amish, my fascination with the police was tolerated so long as it went away after Rumspringa. But it didn't. And, after a few years — which included baptism — I left the fold." He rested his head back against the couch. "You know all this. It's nothing new."

She did know. And it drove her crazy. But it wasn't a way of life she had a right to judge or dispute. Still, she reached for his hand and held it close. "Their loss is my gain."

This time, his answering laugh was more than just a noise, and she was glad. "It's good to see you smile like that, even if I know it can't last," she said.

"Hey . . . I know I've been preoccupied these last few days, Claire. But I need you to know that it's your text messages and our brief calls that are keeping me sane." He dropped his feet back to the floor and turned so he was facing her instead of the fireplace. "Having you with me at the funeral, and out at Murphy's? I'm not sure you can ever fully realize just how important that was to me, or how important *you* are to me."

She returned his kiss, breathing in his nearness, his warmth, and his love. When they parted, she ducked her head against his shoulder. "I feel the same way, Jakob."

"I'm glad." Wrapping his right arm around her, he reclaimed the popcorn bowl with his left. "So . . . Amos . . . If Annie is talking about him, I imagine her father is aware of this kid's antics?"

She accepted the piece of popcorn he brought to her mouth and then watched as he devoured another big handful. "Bishop Hershberger is apparently worried something will happen to Amos. That he'll get in the kind of trouble his father can't turn a blind eye toward."

"A valid concern if what I saw of John

Bontrager the night of the mailbox-bashing incident is any indication."

"Even more so, considering Amos was the boy you started to chase across that field."

He stared at her. "Are you serious?"

"Annie told me he ran."

"Wow. I could have locked those boys up that night." Jakob took another handful of popcorn but held off eating any more for a moment. "I suspect the bishop is worried about his safety at this point more than anything else."

"His safety?" Claire echoed.

"Sure. It doesn't happen often, thankfully, but there have been Amish teens killed while on Rumspringa — not all of them handle the freedom well, unfortunately."

She slid him a glance to see if, perhaps, he was thinking of Sadie Lehman and decided he was when he went on. "And sometimes, as you saw with Sadie Lehman's death last spring — or, rather, the discovery of her death last spring — they can get mixed up in things that can affect their lives or the lives of their loved ones forever."

At a loss for what to say, she simply snuggled against him and watched him eat, her thoughts revisiting memories she suspected she'd never forget. Jakob, too, grew silent until he leaned forward and set the empty popcorn bowl on the coffee table. "I really thought Tom Shaunessy was my guy. I really thought he'd seen Russ at Murphy's, was still fuming about losing the election, and railed against him as the reason for his loss."

"It still could have happened, Jakob. Just because we saw nothing on that tape doesn't mean it didn't happen."

"It's unlikely, though."

"But he was killed between two and four in the morning, right? And that tape you watched had Tom leaving around midnight. So he can't be ruled out completely. He still may have come to learn Russ was in town."

He massaged his temple for a few seconds and then dropped his hand back to his lap. "Maybe it really was just a random act — someone doing something they shouldn't have been doing outside Callie's house and Russ came outside."

She pushed off his chest and stood, the empty popcorn bowl a chore Jakob didn't need. "I suppose. But Heavenly isn't the type of town where people fall prey to acts of random violence.

"Every time something has happened, there's been a reason."

"True. But you saw Tom on that monitor . . . I don't think he even *noticed* Russ."

"Okay, but *Russ* noticed something." She carried the bowl into Jakob's kitchenette, placed it in the sink, and flipped on the water.

He followed. "Meaning what . . ." His voice petered out only to return bookended by a loud inhale. "The picture? It wasn't anything."

She squirted a little dish soap onto a sponge and used it to clean the salty residue from the bowl. "You saw him. One minute he was happily munching away on a wing, and the next he's pushing the plate away and almost frantically looking for his phone. At first, when we saw that, I assumed he was getting a call, but all he did was pull it out of his pocket to take whatever picture he took."

"And then he paid his check, left his food almost entirely uneaten, and took off into the parking lot like a shot," Jakob said, rubbing at his face.

"Is there a chance you missed a picture when you went through his phone?"

He shook his head. "All I saw was the kind of stuff you see on cops' phones. We're not always the most mature bunch. In fact, I'd lay good odds on the fact that cartoon character was going to be used to torture someone from his past."

290

"Could he have been trying to read a text he couldn't see and maybe *that's* why he held the phone the way he did on that tape?"

Again, Jakob shook his head. "I looked at those, too. The only ones from Saturday night were between him and Callie — with her asking him to come to the house and him saying he was too tired."

"It wasn't a call . . ." she said as much for herself as Jakob.

"No, but I checked that, too. There were three that night — his invite to me, a call to Murphy's an hour after he left, and then the call to me that I didn't notice until the next day. None of them lasted more than a minute."

She tried to keep her answering slump in check but if his own answering shrug-nod combination was any indication, she'd been unsuccessful.

"See? *This* is why I can't discount the possibility that he heard something, stepped outside, and surprised someone who didn't take kindly to being surprised."

She deposited the sponge next to the faucet, rinsed the bowl clean, and then, with the water off, dried it with a dishcloth. "I don't know how you were able to do that."

"Do what?"

"Go through his apartment looking for

clues while your heart was breaking the way it was."

"It was hard. Still is. Working a case that involves a friend is like nothing I've ever done before."

"Meaning?"

"Russ isn't just a victim to me, Claire. He's *Russ*. I *know* him. I know what he did in his spare time, I know what got him worked up, I know . . ." His words morphed into a groan as he slumped against the counter. "Maybe I shouldn't even be working this case. Maybe I'm too darn close to be objective."

"So step back. He can be Russ again when this is over."

"He can be Russ again when this is —" Jakob grabbed his phone, pressed a few buttons, and then held it to his ear, his eyes locked on hers. "Hey, Callie, it's Jakob. How are you holding up?"

She couldn't hear what the single mother was saying but she could tell he was torn between letting Callie speak and getting to the reason for his call. He nodded a few times, made a few understanding-type noises, closed his eyes as if in pain once or twice, and then mustered what sounded like a fortifying breath.

"No, nothing new to report on my end

292

yet, I'm afraid. But if it's okay, I'd like to get into the garage apartment again tonight. I could wait until tomorrow if you'd rather but . . . Thanks, Callie . . . Oh, hey, one last thing. Is his phone still in there or do you have it . . . No, no, I get it. I really do . . . How about everything else? I know we released the apartment, but have you moved anything or changed anything since Saturday night? . . . Yeah, okay, perfect. I'll do what I need to do and bring the key back to you in the morning . . . Thanks, Callie. Try to get some rest, okay?"

He pulled the phone from his ear and crossed to her spot beside the sink. "Look, I'm sorry about having to cut our evening short, but you're right. Something caught Russ's attention Saturday night. Those tapes we watched tonight proved that. And while it may have been nothing more than an image he wanted to share with one of his buddies, there's no denying the fact he seemed bothered. Add that to the fact he was murdered five or six hours later, and, well, it's *something,* Claire."

"I agree. Maybe you'll find nothing new, or maybe if you look at everything from a different perspective, you'll find something that'll get you moving in the right direction."

"I pray you're right." He pulled her in for a quick hug and then released her to grab his car keys off the wall hook. "Please extend my apologies to your aunt for not coming in when I drop you off. I'll make it right when things settle down."

She put the bowl away in the cabinet and trailed him to the door, her own thoughts rewinding to Russ's face as he looked up from the wing he was eating and —

"Jakob?"

He glanced back, one hand on the doorknob, the other wrapped around his key ring. "Yeah?"

"I'll understand if you say no, but if it's okay, I'd like to come along."

"You want to come to Russ's place with me?"

"If it's okay . . ."

A quick peek at his watch only served to intensify his surprise. "It's almost nine o'clock. Don't you want to go home and get some sleep?"

"I'd rather help you," she said. "If I wouldn't be in the way, of course."

"In the way? Are you kidding me?" He stepped back so she could pass and then pulled the door closed, his every move, his every step, indicative of an almost renewed sense of hope. "I wouldn't even be heading out there right now if it wasn't for this conversation. So yeah, absolutely. Let's go."

CHAPTER 23

Even though they'd never met, she'd heard so much about Russ Granger that it was hard *not* to picture him as Jakob described — on his back, eyes open, next to a series of mums his daughter had planted in anticipation of his visit, not far from the steps he'd descended before meeting his killer.

She looked from the spot Jakob indicated to Jakob, himself, and silently marveled at the way his voice remained steady as he talked her through the crime scene. He talked about the disturbed earth in and out of the woods not far from where Russ had bled to death . . . He talked about how that had him believing the killer had been on foot and possibly watching Callie's property from the protection of the trees . . . He talked about the position of the body and the fact that Russ had seen his killer . . . He talked about the manner of death and the more personal nature of a stabbing . . .

When it seemed he'd run through every-thing crime scene–related, he quietly knelt down next to the spot where his friend had lain and ran his hand along the earth, his eyes a curious mixture of pain and resolute-ness. "I can't tell you how many times these past few days I've wanted to pick up the phone and get his input on the case — *his* case."

Squatting down beside Jakob, she rubbed his back. "Maybe that's the answer here. You know how he thought, how he worked. Maybe, if you try to see this the way Russ would have . . . or the way he would have told you to do it . . . you'll figure it out."

"The thing is, whenever I'd out-and-out ask for his advice, he'd tell me I'd figure it out. And when I didn't ask, and I just shared the facts, he had this way of almost stepping back and walking himself through the case as I spoke." Jakob ran his hand across the earth one last time, stood, and wandered over to the exterior staircase that led to Callie's guest apartment above the garage. "I wish you could've heard what I'm talking about. It was like he was narrating a tour through a museum, only it was through whatever case I was working and he was giv-ing the talk based on the bits and pieces I shared. He'd narrate for a few seconds, stop and ask if he had it right or ask a pertinent question related to that particular leg of his verbal tour, and then move on. Made me see things in a slightly different way every single time. Which, if you think about it, is kind of fascinating seeing as how *his* tour was based on *my* case."

Jakob leaned against the side rail, fisting his hand at his mouth. "What I wouldn't give to have him narrating a tour through what happened here."

"Seems to me you just did the same thing for me." She motioned toward the spot where Russ had been found and then crossed to the stairs and Jakob. "You walked me through the scene and, when I asked a question, you answered it and then threw out some suppositions based on that. Like when you shared your theory that the killer came through the woods and I asked about the various points that can be accessed from this spot . . . You started throwing out roads where a car could have been parked . . . or someone could have been waiting . . . And you just jotted down a page of notes about houses the killer would have had to pass based on the various places he may have parked — notes that now give you a whole new list of people to talk to and find out what they may have seen or heard that night."

She guided his hand away from his mouth and held it tight. "Don't you see, Jakob? You're doing what Russ taught you. Right here. Tonight. With me. You're sharing details, I'm asking questions, and you're presenting theories as possible answers. It's like we've done in your office with the whiteboard a time or two. Russ *taught* you how to do this and it's what you were just doing a few seconds ago."

Wordlessly, he split his focus between her face, the spot where Russ had been found, and the sky, before settling completely on Claire. "You always have a way of pushing everything into focus, just like Russ did . . ."

"As you do for me, Jakob Fisher."

His brows furrowed in advance of the protest he started to mount but relaxed as his gaze traveled up the stairs to the hunter green door at the top. "We probably better move this along. I don't want to have you up all night again like I did earlier this week."

"I'm good. Really."

"Still, we should get started." Turning, he led the way up the wooden staircase and into the apartment.

Claire stopped just inside the door, her

gaze skirting the tiny sitting area to her left. An Amish-made quilt in varying shades of blue was folded neatly on the back of the love seat–sized sofa. Next to the sofa and positioned at an angle was a single armchair with an end table beside it. Atop the end table was a reading lamp, a set of coasters neatly kept in a wood holder, a small bowl of wrapped candy, and a paperback novel — a thriller, based on the chilling cover. An oval-shaped hook rug in blue and khaki covered the floor between the seating and the tabletop television.

In front of her was a small kitchenette that opened to the sitting area. The simple cabinetry was painted white and offset by a khaki-colored countertop. A single cushioned stool and a narrow overhang jutting out from behind the sink provided a place to eat in lieu of the two-person table that was covered, end to end, with manila file folders.

To her right was a small hallway she suspected led to a bedroom and a bathroom — a suspicion that was confirmed by the flick of Jakob's hand and the partially open door it directed her attention to.

"We know, from the fact that the bed was still made, that Russ hadn't yet gone to sleep. And, since there were no lights on in the bedroom, either, yet they were on out here, we are led to believe he was up and about. Or, at the very least, sitting at that table doing what he did."

"What he did?" she echoed.

"These" — he led the way over to the table and the manila folders scattered about — "are case files, Claire. Russ practically slept with a cop hat on his head. He was always going through these things looking to see what he could see."

She took in the pile to her right and the handwritten labels on several of the tabs. "Muncie, Indiana — Kidnapping . . . Wentz- ville, Missouri — fatal carjacking . . . Dothan, Alabama — missing teen . . ."

"It's like I told you, it didn't matter if it was a case here in Heavenly or on the other side of the country. If he got hold of the details via a BOLO or some other source, he had to read up on the case. He had a notebook where he'd draw out scenarios and jot notes. Sometimes, he'd even call the department handling the case and talk to the lead detective — posing theories and asking questions."

"And other departments were okay with this police chief from Heavenly, Pennsylva- nia, asking questions like that?" Claire asked.

Shrugging, Jakob picked up a folder marked with a town in Florida. "Sometimes yeah, sometimes no. Depended on the ego on the other end of the line. But Russ didn't do it to be obtrusive or arrogant. He did it because he had a genuine interest in figuring stuff out, and I think most of the detectives he talked to got that, you know?"

"Okay, but I've got a question . . . He just got here earlier that same day, right?" At Jakob's nod, she swept her hand toward the file folders. "How is all this stuff here when he lives in Florida?"

"He packed them in his briefcase and his clothes in his suitcase."

"But *all* of these?"

A slow, sad grin slipped across Jakob's face, sans dimples. "I'm not exaggerating when I say he never stopped. Though, considering his photographic memory, he probably didn't really need to bring them as most of them were filed away right here," he said, pointing at his temple. "Perp pictures, names, the towns and cities in which each particular incident occurred, you name it."

"Wow." She returned her attention to the pile on her right and, with his nod of permission, peeked at the folder in the center of the table — its various reports and pages spread outward like an open hand of cards — before spying the phone that had brought them to the garage apartment in the first place. "Is that his phone?"

"It is. Right where he left it, too." He liberated the phone from its spot beside the lone open file and nodded. "When there wasn't anything of note, I put it back where I found it. For Callie."

"Makes sense." She waited for him to hit the button near the bottom of the screen, and when he didn't, she cupped his face with her hand and rested her forehead against his. "I know how hard this is, but I also know how badly you want to solve this."

"You're right. On both counts." Inhaling sharply, he pulled back, kissed her forehead, and, with the tip of his index finger, illuminated the phone's welcome screen. A quick inspection of the half dozen or so icons on the main screen had him pressing a small button with a multicolored flower petal.

Claire pointed to the heading on the left side. "Camera roll should show us the last picture he took."

Jakob pressed it to reveal the final few rows of some 852 pictures — the last of which, as Jakob had said, appeared to be a screenshot rather than a photo. Tapping the image, he held the phone out for her to see. "It's a map. Of a place called Hutchinson, Kansas."

"I see that. Maybe he was planning a trip?"

"Maybe." Jakob studied the image for a few more moments and then returned back to the full camera roll and its thumbnail pictures. A scroll to the left showed that the image captured before the map of Kansas was yet another screenshot — this time of a Wikipedia entry on a cartoon character popular some two decades earlier. " 'Powerful Peg. Never, ever count her out.' "

Claire enlarged the image still further, scanned the article quickly, and then met his shrug with her own. "I don't know. Maybe he was a fan? Or maybe he was doing research for a Halloween costume? Callie has a daughter, doesn't she?"

"Yeah, Ava." Again he returned to the camera roll and scrolled left. "And here's a full-screen picture of this Powerful Peg character and — wait . . . That's skin!"

"Skin?"

"Yes, look." He pointed around the outer rim of the character. "That's skin!"

She leaned still closer to the phone. "You're right. Powerful Peg in this shot is a tattoo!"

"Hang on a second." Once again, he returned to the thumbnail page, clicked on the fourth-to-last picture, and, after barely more than a blink at the image of an airplane wing as seen from inside the aircraft, closed out of it in favor of the close-up shot of the tattoo. "Okay, so the time stamp on this thing coincides perfectly with what we saw going down on the camera footage the other night."

"May I?" she asked, pointing at the phone.

"Sure."

She backed out to the main photo menu, scrolled down, and clicked the album of recently deleted pictures. A quick scan turned up nothing to rival Jakob's words. "You're right."

"So what do we know about this shot?" Taking the phone back, Jakob stared down at Powerful Peg even as he began to answer his own question. "We know Lauri's friend was showing this tattoo to Lauri and Tom. We know that when Lauri first went off to speak to her friend, Russ was happy. He was eating wings . . . thinking his thoughts . . . enjoying his evening out . . . We also know, thanks to the video, that he looked over in Lauri's direction. Based on the facial expressions we saw when he looked, something bothered him. Something that made him push his food to the side, grab this" — he shook the phone — "out of his pocket, snap *this* exact picture, and then hightail it out the door without summoning Lauri over for a proper bill or to say good-bye."

"A shot we now know was of a tattoo on Lauri's friend's ankle," she added.

Spreading his fingers outward across the screen, he enlarged the picture for a closer look. "Something about this clearly upset him, but that alone doesn't make much sense. It's a tattoo . . . of a cartoon character who was popular — what? Twenty years ago?" He released the image to its normal dimensions and scrolled right, the screen-shot of the Wikipedia entry on Powerful Peg taking center stage once again. "So much for Russ being bored."

"Why do you say that?" she asked.

"The first time I saw this, I wrote it off. Figured it was some shot he'd taken out of a magazine or something for nostalgia or to send to another cop because of some inside joke or something. The fact he followed it up with a Wikipedia search didn't change that. But now, when you take into account it was this very character on a person's leg that had him ditching his dinner the way he did, it's pretty apparent this" — he shook the phone — "search was not random. He went looking for this."

"But why?"

"And *that* is our million-dollar question."

"Any chance what we saw on his face at Murphy's was more about recognition and familiarity than being upset?" she posed, only to wave off the question before it had time to gain momentum. "Actually, that's dumb. I didn't even know Russ and I could tell he was agitated."

Jakob moved back and forth between the two images — tattoo, screenshot . . . tattoo, screenshot . . . tattoo, screenshot — before scrolling too far to the right as evidenced by the reappearance of the Kansas state map. "And then there's this Hutchinson, Kansas, thing . . ."

Without waiting for a reply, he scrolled left again, hit select on both the tattoo shot and the screenshot of Powerful Peg's history, and sent them to himself via text. "Not sure what, if anything, this has to do with what happened to Russ, but I'll hang on to it just in case. That way Callie can do whatever she wants with her dad's phone."

Lowering herself to the chair Russ, himself, had sat on just days earlier, Claire took in the folders piled up to her left and her right and the lone open folder and its parade of contents in front of her. "Did your guys put these back like this when they were done? Or do you think Callie did this?"

"My guys didn't touch the table. Their focus was outside, at the actual crime scene. They dusted for prints, made an impression of a partial boot print we found coming out of the woods, and snapped pictures. I came in here with Callie so she could see if anything was missing and that's when we spotted her dad's phone lying right here. With her permission, I took a look at his call and text history from Saturday."

"And what about since then? Do you know if Callie put these here like this or were they already like this?"

"I picked a few of them up and thumbed through them, but they're just old cases from around the country that caught his attention. Typical Russ stuff."

She sat back, glancing between the table and Jakob as she did. "If this *wasn't* Russ, what would you think?"

Jakob set the phone on the table, his eyes narrowing on her face. "What do you mean, what would I think?"

Shrugging, she reached forward and tugged the open folder and its assorted reports and pictures closer. "I guess I'm just wondering about the moments leading up to whatever noise he might have heard that made him go outside in the first place."

"I think about that, too," Jakob said, his voice thick with emotion. "I think about whether he might still be here if he'd gone to sleep thirty minutes sooner instead of sitting here, at this table, playing cop."

She knew he was talking. Even registered some of what he was saying. But her primary focus at that moment was on the open folder and the series of faxed and photocopied reports fanned out across the centerfold. A glance at the name on the first of three suspect sheets yielded Margaret Mallory and a birthdate that, after some quick mental math, placed the woman at forty-five years of age.

"Okay, I'm guessing we should probably call it a night, yes?" Sighing, he ran his hand down the front of his friend's phone one last time. "We got what we came for, I've sent copies of both pertinent photos to my phone, and it's coming up on eleven o'clock. You're working at the shop tomorrow and I have a meeting with the chief about Russ's case — both of which will be a lot harder if we're short on sleep."

Jakob was right. Too many days without ample sleep was bound to catch up with them both. Besides, she wanted to get a peek at the inn's menu for the next day. If it wasn't too involved, maybe Aunt Diane and Bill could finally have a real date . . .

Swooping her hands inward, she gathered the loose reports into a neat pile only to drop them back down as her gaze fell on the folder's handwritten tab: *Hutchinson, Kansas — Bank robbery.*

CHAPTER 24

Jakob slipped his own phone into his pocket and reached for Russ's. "Callie said if we need any coffee or anything, it's in the pantry next to the oven."

"Did you tell her we found something?"

"No. I don't want to get her hopes up in case we haven't."

Claire looked from the last picture Russ took, to the folder in front of them, and then back at Jakob. "You don't find it interesting that the last picture he took was a screen-shot of a town in Kansas that matches the same folder he was looking at before he died?" she asked, nudging her chin in the direction of the folder.

"Considering who was doing the looking and the picture taking — not particularly, no. This was Russ . . . It's the way he was. There's probably tons of screenshots in this phone that correlate to one of the other files on this table or back at his house in Florida." Jakob pulled an empty chair next to Claire's and tugged the folder and its contents closer to the edge of the table. "He craved information the way most people crave food. In fact, in many ways, his obsession with old cases *was* his food. Heck, Callie told me in the car after the funeral that when she was little, instead of practicing her reading with regular books like her classmates did, she remembers sitting on her dad's lap, reading from case folders."

She didn't mean to laugh but the image created by Jakob's words was a bit comical. Especially when he followed them up with his own verbal take on a kindergarten-aged Callie going off to school proficient in words like *perp, mugshot,* and *apprehended.*

"He really was a workaholic, wasn't he?"

"You have no idea." Jakob looked again at the screenshot and its correlation to the handwritten folder tab, shaking his head ever so slightly as he did. "Most guys, when they retire, probably spend their days smoking cigars, watching old movies, puttering around in the garage, and driving their spouse nuts. But Russ? He spent his days trying to save the world in one way or another."

She closed her hand over his and squeezed. "I so wish I could have met him.

He sounds like such an amazing guy."

"He is . . . *was.*" Raking his hand through his hair, he let loose a tortured sigh. "Ugh!"

"No *ugh.* You were right the first time, Jakob. He *is* an amazing guy — an amazing guy who lives on right here" — she tapped his chest and then pointed upward at his head — "and here. For you, for Callie, for his grandchildren, for everyone who had the honor of calling him friend, and for me, too."

"You?"

"Sure. Because he was someone special to you."

He blinked against the emotion she saw building behind his eyes and, after a lingering kiss on her forehead, flipped open the bank robbery folder, moved aside a few papers, and froze.

"Jakob? Are you —"

"The tattoo!" He bolted upright in his chair and made a mad grab for Russ's phone. With several quick taps, thwarted only by a few fumbles, he pulled up the screenshot of the map and scrolled to the left, passing the description of Powerful Peg en route to the picture that had brought them out to Callie's apartment in the first place. When he reached the picture, he stopped, enlarged it with his fingers, and then swapped it for the third page of the report — a page that contained three black-and-white stills pulled from video footage. "It's the same picture, same scale, Claire!"

She, too, looked from the report to Russ's phone and back again, the realization that Jakob was right washing over her from head to toe. Before she could formulate her thoughts, let alone a response, though, he continued, his voice taking on an almost thunderous quality. "That's why he looked the way he did at Murphy's that last night! He saw this tattoo, recognized it as familiar, and came back here to see if he was right!"

"If he was, that would have to mean that this" — she sifted through the reports until she found the top sheet and the blonde woman who'd captured her attention not more than ten minutes earlier — "*Margaret Mallory* woman is one and the same as Lauri's friend."

"How did I miss this the other night?" he thundered.

"We hadn't seen the tapes yet, Jakob. Without that context, all of this was just normal Russ stuff."

"That's not an excuse. I should've looked at this" — he shook the phone with one hand and motioned toward the bank robbery reports with his other — "as *a cop,* not a buddy. If I had, then maybe I'd have been able to say what I wanted to say before Russ was lowered into the ground."

"Hindsight is always twenty-twenty, Jakob. For all of us."

Setting the phone down, he commandeered the sheet she'd uncovered and pored over every word on the page. When he reached the bottom, he ran his finger back up to the top. "Margaret Mallory goes by the nickname *Peg* — hence, the Powerful Peg tattoo on her left ankle. She's five foot four with dark brown eyes and blonde hair. The only significant identifying mark noted during the bank robbery was this particular tattoo.

"She was one of three, and the only female in the mix, who robbed the First Hutchinson Bank in Hutchinson, Kansas, fifteen years ago next month." He shuffled a few papers, moving a more detailed one about the crime in general to the top of the pile. "A bank guard — Derek Waters — was shot by one of the male suspects, Phillip Maxwell. A customer was hit over the head with the guard's stick by a second guy, a Ryan Westphal. Mallory is listed as the lookout, although she came into the bank early on during the process to give the other two the bags they'd apparently forgotten on the way in."

"Bags?" She craned her head around his arm to get a better view of the report Jakob was reading but gave up when he flipped to yet another page. "You mean as in the bags they used to put the money in after they stole it?"

He nodded.

"Kind of a big thing to forget, don't you think?"

Again he nodded. Only this time, he pointed her attention to a handwritten statement given by the only customer in the bank at the time of the robbery. She read aloud while he noiselessly tapped his fingers on the table. " 'In some ways you got the sense the robbery was planned. They knew the quietest time to hit. They knew which window overlooked the main road and how to position their bodies so as not to be seen by any potential passersby that might be on the sidewalk. And they rattled off the time it was taking in almost robotic fashion, like they were following a script of some sort. Yet the way they forgot the bags for the money and debated on whether the woman should stay and help or wait in the car made it seem like the whole thing was more of a whim, quite frankly.' " She looked up at

Jakob. "I can't imagine someone deciding to rob a bank on a *whim* . . ."

"You'd be surprised. Though, when they do, they're usually caught before they even make it out the door." He reached for the pile and, page by page, began to make his way through it, referring back to the sheet on Margaret Mallory again and again. "No, the ones who get away with it are usually the ones who spent years looking at it from different angles — escape routes, employee and customer patterns, viable plans for living off the grid after their escape, et cetera."

"And neither of the other two were caught, either?" she asked.

"Not at first, no." He stopped, read his way down the page he held, and then gave it a little shake. "But about five months after the robbery, the FBI tracked this Ryan Westphal to a beach in Santa Monica."

"And?"

"He grabbed a woman who was sunbathing next to him and held what he *claimed* was a gun to her back in the hopes the feds would let him go."

She pushed away the sudden urge for a bowl of popcorn and, instead, turned her chair just enough so as to afford a straight-on view of Jakob. "It wasn't a gun?"

"Nope."

"What was it, then?"

"A bottle of suntan lotion."

It took everything she had in her, as well as a silent reality check as to why they were looking at the reports in the first place, not to laugh. Still, she could feel her lips twitching with a smile. "A bottle of suntan lotion?"

"Seems the woman he was holding hostage knew it was a bottle of suntan lotion and proceeded to elbow him in the gut. The ensuing commotion led to a fairly easy arrest by FBI agents on the scene." Jakob flipped to a subsequent page and, after a moment or two of silent reading, continued. "Westphal, of course, lawyered up, promising to give up information on the other two, but before the feds could get any sort of deal fleshed out, he died in his cell of an apparent heart attack."

"Oh. Wow." She looked from Jakob to the stack of reports and back again. "So they got *nothing* from him before he died?"

Consulting the papers in his hand, he shrugged. "Nope, nothing."

"So what do we know about the one who killed the guard?"

Jakob exchanged his papers for the next packet — a packet that began with a black-and-white picture pulled from camera footage inside the bank and an accompanying description that described Phil Maxwell as approximately six feet tall with dark brown hair and brown eyes. His birthdate had him two years Margaret Mallory's senior. A few neighbors who lived on the same street as Maxwell referred to him as "trouble," a "good-for-nothing," and "the kind of guy everyone gives a wide berth." His police record included a few peace disturbance charges, a handful of fights, and several shoplifting incidents. His last known tie to Margaret Mallory was as her boyfriend.

" 'Sightings called into the FBI's most-wanted hotline had Margaret Mallory and Phil Maxwell together in a bar in Roanoke, Virginia . . . a billiard hall in Lansing, Michigan . . . and in the stands of a dog fight in Oklahoma City,' " she read over his shoulder. " 'The last reported sighting came in just a little over a year ago and had the pair walking along the side of the road just outside Adams County, Indiana —' "

"Amish country," he mused as he dropped Phil Maxwell's packet onto Margaret Mallory's and pushed them both into the center of the table. "So, did you get a good look at Lauri's friend on that tape from Murphy's? Because as much as I'd like to say I did, I was much more focused on watching Russ and Tom."

"Not really. I mean, I *saw* her, of course, but, like you, she wasn't my focus."

"I know what I'll be looking at after I drop you off at the inn." He pulled the reports to him again, perused the top page of each packet, and then neatened them all into one single pile for placement inside the waiting folder. "Maybe, with any luck, I'll be able to enlarge the frames she's in enough to see if I can pick out anything, feature-wise, that will identify her as Margaret Mallory."

She considered his words, comparing their face value with what they knew to be the case thus far. "Do you think Russ actually recognized her as Margaret Mallory? Or do you think he simply recognized the tattoo?"

"Based on the fact he only took a picture of the *tattoo,* my guess is it rang a bell in his head, but not one he could nail down on the spot. If he had, he never would have left the way he did."

"Meaning . . ."

He ran his finger across Russ's handwritten notation on the folder's tab and then tapped the cover. "Meaning, if he'd linked the tattoo to this case while he was sitting in his booth at Murphy's, the place would have been swarming with feds almost immediately. And if they couldn't be there to question Lauri's friend, he would have done it. No doubt."

"So maybe that's what happened." Claire stood and made her way over to the sitting room window and its view of the yard that had played host to Russ's final moments, as well as the wooded area Jakob believed was the entry and exit point for his mentor's killer. "Maybe he came back here, put it together, and somehow this woman beat him to the punch."

Abandoning his post at the table, Jakob joined her by the window. "But that doesn't make sense, either. If he didn't put it together until he was back here, how would this woman have known? How would — wait . . . I'm getting a call."

He reached into his pocket for his phone and glanced at the screen. "It's the station. I've gotta take this."

"Of course." Like clockwork, she stepped away from the window to afford him some privacy and wandered back to the table, her mind's eye placing Russ at the table — poring over the assorted reports from the Kansas bank robbery, periodically pausing to look up something on his phone, realizing he'd found one of the bank robbers . . .

Did he reach for his gun and run for the door, intending to drive back to Murphy's in the hope Lauri's friend was still there?

Did he reach for his phone to call the FBI or to tell Jakob he'd —

Grabbing Russ's phone from the table, she tapped her way into his recent call log, her gaze falling on the top two entries.

"Jakob!" She whirled around, phone in hand. "Russ's last call to you . . . The one you didn't notice until the next day . . ."

"Hey, Curt, can you hold on a second? Thanks . . ." Covering his phone with his hand, he turned his full attention on Claire. "What about it?"

"That whole Lake George fishing trip thing he said to you? Could that have been some sort of bet you two made with each other at some point? A bet that —"

Slowly, he lowered the phone to his chest, his mouth gaping open as he did. "Lake George . . . It's where he said we'd go when he solved the biggest of the big . . ."

"Well, I think a decades-old armed bank robbery would probably qualify, don't you?"

CHAPTER 25

Reaching past the dolls Annie had painstakingly posed in the front window, Claire flipped the shop's sign to OPEN and slumped against the edge of the wall. She'd tried to get some sleep after returning to the inn in the wee hours of the morning, but her efforts had proven futile with each passing hour.

A peek in the bathroom mirror upon arriving at the shop served only to underscore what she already knew — she looked as bad as she felt. Her only hope now was for customer traffic to be light. At least until Annie came in at eleven.

A vibration against the top of the counter beckoned her from her resting spot and over to the illuminated screen on the other side of the room. Two steps from her destination she lunged for her phone.

"Did you find something out?" she said by way of greeting.

"I spoke to the owner of Murphy's and he said he'd locate Lauri and have her give me a call."

Lacking the energy necessary to pull one of the two stools out from the overhang, she merely leaned against the counter's edge and closed her eyes. "Are you worried she'll give her friend a heads-up?"

"I didn't tell the owner what I wanted, just that I needed to speak with Lauri about a friend of mine." He rushed to stifle a yawn before continuing. "So? Did you get any sleep after I dropped you off at your aunt's place?"

She started to hem and haw, but gave up in short order. "I tried, but . . . no. How about you?"

"Not a wink."

"Is it like this for you all the time?" she asked.

"What? The not-being-able-to-sleep-because-my-brain-won't-shut-off thing?"

"Yes!"

"Pretty much, yeah. At least to some degree or another." A high-pitched squeak in the background let her know he'd leaned forward in his chair. Her mind conjured the accompanying image of him lowering his head to the top of his desk in much the same way she was contemplating the empty section of counter next to the register. "But we're also talking about a case involving Russ."

"I know."

"Is Annie on the schedule with you this morning?" he asked.

"She comes in at eleven."

"You have my key, Claire. Feel free to use my place for a nap if you think you can sneak away for an hour or so."

She managed a smile at the idea only to feel it slip away as the reason behind the day's scheduling choice reared its ugly head in her thoughts. "As tempting as that sounds, I've got a delivery coming in around lunchtime that needs to be unpacked and priced."

"Then I'll hope, for your sake, that Diane has something easy planned for dinner tonight so she can handle it alone while you get some sleep."

"There *is* something easy planned. Only we planned it that way so *I* can prepare it alone."

"You?"

Realizing her shrug couldn't be seen through a phone, she opted for actual words, instead. "Bill has been wanting to take her out on a date, so I offered tonight as a possibility."

"Maybe you can ask him to switch it to another day?"

"I can't. She's been so excited about this ever since I told her I would cover for her. And to top it off, when I suggested it, I told her I wouldn't accept any arguments to the contrary."

"But —"

"Jakob, I saw her dress for the evening hanging on the back of her closet door this morning as I went down the hall. I can't back out now."

His quiet yet lingering exhale made her wish she was snuggled up next to him rather than there in her shop, being propped up by the counter. "You're going to get sick, Claire."

"Said the pot to the kettle."

"Touché."

"You could come by if you want, you know. We could eat together in the kitchen after I've taken care of the guests. I'm sure there will be plenty to go around, there always is."

She could hear his tired grin in her ear. "Whatcha making?"

"Beef stew with homemade biscuits."

"Now you're talking . . . Oh, hey, can you hang on a second? Curt is buzzing me."

"Of course."

She made herself part company with the counter in favor of the clipboard and the list of delivery items expected that day. Some of the items would be set aside until it was time to start stocking shelves for the holidays. Other items would go up right away and —

"You still there?" Jakob asked, his tone suddenly void of anything resembling fatigue.

"Yes, I'm still here . . ."

"I've gotta go. Lauri is on line three, returning my call."

She was unpacking the third of five boxes when Annie stuck her head around the corner of the stockroom door with a cookie in one hand and a pretzel in the other. "I know it is not a phone call, but perhaps these will help?"

"I take it you've noticed me checking my phone?" At Annie's quick nod, she took the treats and lowered herself from a squat into a fully seated position next to the box. "Ahhh, yeah . . . This is good."

Annie's brow furrowed. "You have not even taken a bite yet."

She looked at the treats in her hand and then back at her teenage employee. "While I'm going to enjoy every bite of these —

and thank you for that, by the way — I was referring to the floor. I've been resisting the urge to sit knowing I might not be able to get up again if I did. But now that I'm here, it's worth the risk."

"If you could not get up, Claire, I would help you."

"I know that, Annie. It's just that I didn't get any sleep last night and it's really starting to catch up with me."

"Dat did not sleep much last night, either," Annie said, resting her cheek on the trim work. "I went down twice to see if he was okay. The first time, he sent me back to bed, saying I needed to get my sleep."

Claire nibbled her way around the outside of the cookie until the only thing left was the center. "And the second time?"

"He did not send me back to bed." Annie pushed off the doorframe and crossed to one of the two boxes Claire had yet to open. "I could go through this box until a customer comes if you'd like . . ."

Her whole body sagged in response. "Oh, Annie, that would be great. Thank you."

A few items into the carton, Annie resumed their conversation. "Another member of the community has complained about Amos Bontrager."

"Uh-oh. What has he done this time?"

"He is telling others he is going to get a tattoo."

Claire snapped her head up. "A *tattoo*? Do the Amish *get* tattoos?"

"Amos has not been baptized yet," Annie reminded across the top of her box.

"But even with that, do Amish kids your age really get tattoos?"

"*My* friends do not. Dat said *his* friends did not."

"Wow." She reached into her box for the last item and pushed the empty carton across the room toward the others. "Sounds like someone needs to talk to him."

"Dat has tried to speak with Amos about other things. So, too, has Eli Miller. But Amos says only that he is on Rumspringa."

"Maybe, if he speaks to his own dat, he'll opt not to do it."

Annie stilled her hand above her box and pulled a face. "I do not see John Bontrager as a talking dat."

"Actually, I don't really, either. I guess I was just hoping maybe he's different inside his home." She tugged the final box into striking range but stopped short of actually using the edge of her scissors to break the seal. "I know your dat is a busy man with his duties as bishop and your farm and you. But maybe Elmer could talk to Amos? He's a very nice man and he seems to really get a kick out of helping people."

"Yah. That is true."

Wedging the tip of the scissors against the taped seam, she pulled it toward her until the opening it created was big enough to reach inside. "Either way, hopefully this young man will get through this rebellious period as unscathed as possible. Preferably sooner rather than later, for people like your dat."

The jingle of bells from the front room alerted them to a customer and brought Annie to her feet. "I'll take care of it."

"Thanks, Annie. I should be done with this last box soon."

"Yah."

She watched the teenager exit the stockroom and then turned her own attention to the contents of the box. Item by item she compared the contents with her own copy of the order — three tabletop wreaths, three holiday napkin holders, four holiday —

"Claire?"

She placed a check next to *napkin rings* and then glanced back up at the stockroom door. "Yes, Annie . . ."

"Esther is here and she's asking to see you."

"Really? Perfect! Some Esther time is

exactly the energy boost I need." Dropping the pen onto the floor, she stretched her arms above her head and then gave the box a little shove. "Send her back, will you? I can finish this up while we're talking, or do it later after she leaves."

"Okay, but, Claire?"

Something about Annie's voice stopped her smile in its tracks. "Is something wrong?"

"I'm not sure, but Esther looks upset."

Using the partially empty box as leverage, she stood, her gaze meeting the teen's before traveling into the part of the shop she could see from her vantage point. "Is — is it the baby? Is she sick or something?"

"No. Sarah is sleeping in Esther's arms."

"Eli?"

"I don't think so. She mentioned needing to get the buggy back to him but did not say anything about him being sick."

"But you said she seems upset . . ."

"Yah."

She stepped to the side until she had a view of her Amish friend and the sleeping child nestled in the young woman's arms. The clues pointing to the accuracy of Annie's observation were all there — fidgeting fingers, nervous glances at seemingly nothing in particular, and a propensity for pacing that had her doubling back more than it had her actually getting anywhere. Oh yes, Esther was indeed upset or stressed about something.

"I'll take it from here, Annie. Thanks, kiddo."

CHAPTER 26

She settled herself on the shop's back stoop and watched as Esther, once again, glanced toward the window. "It's closed, Esther. I promise."

"You are sure?"

"Yes, I'm sure. Besides, assuming you're worried about Annie overhearing, you saw the two customers walking in as we were walking out . . . That means she's busy taking care of them." Claire wrapped her arms more snuggly around the baby she'd virtually swiped on sight and nudged her chin in the direction of the open stretch of concrete to her left. "Come. Sit. Tell me what's got you on edge like this."

Ignoring the invitation, Esther took three steps across the alley toward Shoo Fly Bake Shoppe and then reversed course three steps back, the rhythmic motion reigniting Claire's sleepiness. "I would not have told him how to find you when you are not here."

"Him? Him who?"

"The goat killer."

Confusion lapped at her exhaustion. "Esther, I'm trying to follow this, I really am. But I've been awake for coming up on thirty-two hours now and my ears don't seem to be connected to my brain the way they're supposed to be, so —"

She sat up so tall and so fast, Sarah stirred. When she was sure the baby was okay, she returned her focus to Esther. "You're talking about Amos Bontrager, aren't you?"

"Yah."

"Giggles died?" she asked.

Squeezing her eyes closed, Esther nodded.

"Oh, sweetie, I'm so sorry. I knew they were struggling the other day, but I didn't know they'd died."

"Eli didn't want to tell me, but I knew there was something wrong. I put Sarah in the cradle and was getting ready to go to the barn to ask him what was wrong when I heard them arguing."

"Them?"

"Eli and John."

Uh-oh . . .

"Esther? Did something happen?" She rushed to lower her voice as, once again, the baby stirred. "Did Eli lose his temper?"

Esther took off in the direction of Annie's tethered horse and buggy but changed course after only four or five steps. "He was not happy. He lost three goats because of that boy. Three good goats. When John found out, he came by. I do not know all of what was said. I heard only John's voice."

"Wait. Are you saying *John* was the one yelling?"

"Yah."

"But Eli's goats are the ones who were killed . . . by John's son. Why on earth would *John* be the one yelling?"

Esther, again, peeked at the window and, when it passed her inspection, she made her way back to Claire. "John is not a nice man. I know I should not speak such things, but it is the truth. I do not think that man knows how to smile. It is frown, frown, frown all the time. Eli says it is no surprise that Amos is the way he is, but I do not think that makes it okay."

"It doesn't, you're right. But maybe you're misconstruing what Eli is trying to say."

"I do not understand . . ."

"I don't think Eli is pointing to John as an excuse for Amos. I think he points to him as a way to understand the boy's behavior. That's all."

"That is because Eli knows only of goats. He does not know the rest."

Using her right hand as a shield for the sun, she studied her friend amid a growing unease. "Talk to me, Esther."

The young mother started to speak and then stopped in favor of yet another visual inspection of the still-closed window.

"Esther?"

After another beat or two of silence, Esther stepped still closer. "Yesterday, after you left, Rebecca and I were standing in the driveway, talking. Elmer was in the barn with Eli, and Miriam was asking about you."

"Miriam was asking about me?"

"And Jakob. They knew of the funeral and wanted to make sure you were okay." Esther's eyes darted back to the window. "I do not know how long we talked, but Rebecca is the one who heard it. Soon, Miriam and I heard it, too."

More than anything, she wanted to reach up, grab hold of Esther's hands, and shake the story out of her at something other than a snail's pace, but she resisted. Sarah had been startled enough in just the short time they'd been outside. Instead, Claire made sure the baby was snug, and then scooted forward on the step until she'd recaptured Esther's attention. "What did you hear?"

"He was in the bushes between the house and the English neighborhood . . . watching us."

A chill stirred at the base of her spine. "Amos was watching you?"

"Yah."

"How do you know? Did you see him?"

"Rebecca heard the rustling and quieted us with her hand. Soon, I heard it, too. At first, I thought it was one of the little boys who lives on the other side, chasing a ball. When there was no more noise, we started to speak again. But then there was more rustling. So I walked over to the trees and that is when he ran off."

"And you think he was just looking at you?"

"Yah."

Claire opened her mouth to pose other scenarios but closed it as her thoughts rewound to Miller's Pond and the exact moment she and Jakob realized they were being watched. By Amos. The fingers of unease moved farther up her spine. "And you didn't tell Eli?"

"I couldn't. Eli would get angry. I do not want him to get in trouble for such anger."

"But Esther, Amos shouldn't be doing the things he is doing!"

"Eli spoke to John about the goats. Others

in our community speak of the things that boy has done. But those are just goats and things. Eli would be angry to know he is watching me."

"And rightfully so!" she argued.

"But you know how Eli was before we were married — the trouble he got into for his temper."

"That was before. And that anger was different. He's fixed that . . . with your help."

"Anger is still anger, Claire, and I do not want Eli to be shunned."

She breathed it all in, her thoughts no longer hampered by lack of sleep. "Are you wanting *me* to tell him?"

Esther's face drained of all discernable color. "No! I do not want Eli to know! I do not want Bishop Hershberger to know, either! I just want you to be careful."

"Me?" she echoed, drawing back. "Why?"

"When John was yelling this morning, Eli told him that Amos must make amends for what he has done, that the boy needs to fill his time with other things. He spoke of the wood carving that Amos does and said he should show them to you . . . that perhaps you will want to sell them in the store. Eli thinks if Amos is busy with his hands, he will not have such time to do wrong."

"Okay . . ."

"Eli told John that Amos should stop by your aunt's inn if you are not at the shop!"

"That's okay," she said.

"No! It is not okay! If Amos came *here*" — Esther splayed her hands toward the shop — "there would be many people. There would be customers coming and going, Annie could be working, people would be walking by, and my uncle is across the street. But at the inn, if your aunt is busy and the guests are asleep, there would be no one to help if . . ." Esther's words trailed off in favor of a hard swallow and some rapid blinking.

She waited a beat and then, when Esther didn't continue, her own thoughts rushed to fill the void . . .

Esther was scared . . .

For Claire . . .

With one arm still cradling the baby, Claire reached her hand out to her friend. "Esther, I'm fine. I'm going to be fine."

"You do not know what is to be." Esther swiped at the set of tears that escaped down her cheeks. "Only God knows such things."

She watched until she could no longer see Esther and Sarah and then stepped back into the alley. Esther's concern for Claire's well-being had been touching, but also exhausting, and she wasn't entirely sure she'd been all that successful in abating it. Still, she appreciated the heads-up and made a mental note to share Amos's latest infraction with Jakob when they next spoke.

"Hello, Claire."

Fatigue gave way to joy as she turned back toward the alley and the tall, dark-haired Amish man she knew she'd find on the other end of the voice. Sure enough, not more than ten paces away, Benjamin Miller's ocean blue eyes greeted her with a sun-enhanced sparkle.

"Ben! I thought that was your buggy tethered just beyond Annie's, but I wasn't sure." Quickly, she closed the space between them to plant a kiss on his clean-shaven cheek. "It is so good to see you!"

"How is Jakob?" he asked.

She revved up to give the standard *He's fine* answer but swallowed it away as she considered the man on the other end of the question. Yes, Ben was Amish. Yes, Jakob was excommunicated for his decision to leave postbaptism. But somehow, despite that — and a strong childhood friendship that had soured in their teen years — the two had found patches of common ground over the past year. That common ground and their history together all but insured

Ben's question was borne on something very different from standard politeness . . .

"He's hanging in there. He's determined to find the person behind his friend's death and I think he's getting closer. That said, he was touched by your offer to help. I suspect he would have taken you up on it if he hadn't been operating on autopilot these past few days."

"I didn't think he would want my help. He has you." His focus shifted across her face. "That is why you look so tired, yah? You have been helping?"

"Yes."

Ben studied her for a few seconds and then, with a dip of his chin, led her own attention back to the road. "Rebecca spoke of the same thing when I stopped by Emma's farm this morning. I will speak to Amos and to John. There will be no more watching from trees, and he will not visit you at the inn to speak of his wood carvings. He will only come here, to the shop."

"You — you heard that? With Esther just now?"

"Yah."

It was hard not to grin at the obvious similarities between the man in front of her and the one likely pacing in his office across the street. Despite their attire and lifestyle, both sought to protect. "I wasn't worried about him coming to the inn, Ben . . ."

"He will come to the shop," he repeated.

She fell into step beside him as he turned and headed in the direction of his own tethered buggy. "I met her, you know. The other day . . . at Esther's."

His footfalls slowed but did not stop. Nor did he respond beyond the quick nod she was virtually certain she saw. Instead, he ran a gentle hand down his horse's neck and then moved the animal's water bucket to its resting spot behind his sister's bakery.

"I liked her, Ben. She was funny and sweet and kind. She was very gentle with Sarah. And" — Claire stopped, gathered her breath, and continued — "she spoke of you in a way that made me very, very happy. For her, and for you."

He returned to the horse and, with deft hands, untethered the animal in preparation for his departure. It wasn't until he was on the seat with the reins in his hands that he finally met her eye. Yet when he opened his mouth to speak, it was Annie's voice that filled the alleyway.

"Claire?"

She glanced toward the now-open window and the kapp-wearing girl peering out at her with unrestrained excitement. "Yes, Annie . . ."

"You will want to come inside now."

"Is everything okay?" she asked, stepping toward the window.

"Your call from Jakob! It has come!"

"He's on the phone now?"

"Yah."

Turning back to Ben, she hooked her thumb in the direction of Annie. "I need to take this. I've been waiting for his call all day."

"I understand." With the faintest flick of the reins, he brought his horse in line beside Claire. "What you said just now? About being happy for Rebecca and for me? That is how *I* feel. For you and for Jakob."

CHAPTER 27

"I know I should have argued with Aunt Diane more than I did about her and Bill postponing their date until tomorrow, but I've been dying to hear about your meeting with Lauri since your call."

Jakob pulled onto Lighted Way and headed west into Amish country. "I'm sorry I had to get off the phone within seconds of you picking up, but Curt had a situation come up that needed my immediate attention."

"Of course I understand." Claire settled back against the seat, the late-September air pleasant against her skin. "But I get to hear about it now, right?"

"Hear about what?" he teased.

"About Lauri and her friend. Who is she? Where does she live? Do you get the sense they're close? That maybe Lauri knows who she is?"

"The friend's name is Carla."

Claire sucked in a fast breath. "Carla —

yes! Now I remember . . ."

Jakob nodded. "Seems this Carla started coming in to Murphy's about seven or eight months ago. Doesn't come in often, but when she does, she likes to hang around the people Lauri refers to as regulars — the regular pool players, the regular bar patrons, and, of course, the staff."

"Interesting . . ."

"Trust me, it gets better." He slowed as they came up on a buggy but remained in line behind it, his focus clearly on the case he was building rather than the destination she'd requested yet hadn't fully explained. "She keeps an eye on the clock every time she comes in and never stays longer than ninety minutes — tops. Refers to it as her 'window of sanity' and . . . get this . . . 'his window of utter cluelessness.' "

"His window of utter — wait!" She sat upright so fast, the seat belt tightened in response. "You think she's referring to the one who killed the guard?"

"Phillip Maxwell. And yeah, could be. The few sightings that have been reported over the years always had them together. And you saw Russ's notes on the table last night. I suspect he thought it likely, as well."

She churned the possibility around in her thoughts for a few minutes and then moved on to her next question. "Do you get the sense Lauri knows anything?"

"I don't. She just answered my questions in much the same way she answered our questions the other night — matter-of-fact. She doesn't know where Carla lives, doesn't socialize with her beyond the occasional time at Murphy's. And even then, it's just snippets of conversation and other stuff here and there."

"Like showing off the new tattoo . . ."

"Exactly."

"So other than the name and a time frame of how long this woman has been in the area, Lauri didn't have a whole lot to offer?" Claire asked.

"You mean besides the proverbial smoking gun? No."

She stared at him. "Excuse me?"

"Remember that call Russ made to the bar an hour or so after he left?" At her nod, he continued, his voice rising with unrestrained excitement. "Seems he left a message for Lauri that she never got. And since he left it with Todd, who promptly wrote it down and forgot about it, the owner didn't know anything about it when I asked the other day."

"Okay . . ."

"Anyway, my reaching out to the owner to

speak to Lauri today, musta rung some bells in Todd's brain because he asked her if she ever followed up on the call from the guy who was asking about Carla. Only Russ referred to her as 'Lauri's friend with the ankle tattoo.' " He pulled onto the shoulder, shifted into park, and scrubbed a hand down his face. "When she said she never got the message, Todd told her he wrote it on a note and stuck it to his chair."

"Okay . . ."

"Lauri's boss has a landline phone at his desk."

"And . . ."

"Carla's cell phone was out of juice that Saturday night so she asked Lauri if she could use the office phone to call a cab."

Covering her mouth with her hand, her mind's eye filled in the details. Carla walking into the office . . . Carla seeing the note about Russ . . .

"When she came out, Carla started asking these seemingly random questions about different people who'd been in the bar when she first arrived. Lauri mentioned a few — including the 'super sweet retired cop who left the really big tip.' "

"So Carla knew she'd been seen!"

This time when Jakob lifted his hand, it was to fist it against the steering wheel.

"Carla knew she'd been seen," he repeated, his voice hoarse. "She asked Lauri where Russ was from and Lauri, in turn, mentioned that he was in town, staying at his daughter's house in Heavenly. Less than a few hours later, Russ was dead."

"Why didn't she tell us this the other night?"

"She didn't think it was anything other than normal conversation."

Claire rested a hand on first his shoulder and then his hand, the tension she felt there impossible to miss. "That's quite a smoking gun, Jakob. You're almost there . . ."

"It seems like I should be, doesn't it? But no one, including Lauri or her boss, seems to have a clue where Carla lives, or what she does, or *anything* about her other than she likes an old cartoon character named Powerful Peg."

"She had to have gotten the new tattoo somewhere . . ."

"On it." He hooked his thumb and her attention to the backseat and a picture of the tattoo sitting atop the very file Russ had pored over in the final hours of his life.

"And?"

"The tattoo artist works out of a storefront about a mile or two from here. Had never heard of the character when Carla asked him to put it on her ankle. But since she already had one on her left ankle, he took a picture of it and essentially copied it onto her right ankle. Carla was pleased with the result."

"That's it?"

"Pretty much, yeah. She paid in cash, so there's no paper trail. She arrived on foot, so there's no description of a car for us to work off. Said very little the guy can recall beyond some comment about it feeling good to be able to let her hair down." Turning his hand so their palms touched, he laced his fingers with hers and rasped an exhale. "Not much to go on, as you can see."

"Not much *yet,*" she countered. "But it's way more than you had this morning. Remember that."

"I'm trying. Either way, thanks for giving up your sleep, yet again, to help me. And for listening the way that you do."

"It's nothing you haven't done for me."

His smile stopped short of his amber-flecked eyes but still, it was something. "Should we continue on?"

"I feel kind of bad asking you to go with me to Esther's with everything that's coming together on this case right now."

"Don't. Russ always said that when you hit a wall, it's best to step away and regroup.

So that's what I'm doing."

He closed his hand over the gearshift and pulled back onto the finely graveled road. Farm by farm, they made their way toward his niece's home . . .

Hochstetler . . .

Kapp . . .

Hershberger —

"Oh, look, there's Annie's father and" — she pressed her face to the window and took in the six-foot-tall minister with the Eli-length beard — "Elmer Mast."

"That's the new minister, right?"

"Yes. He's a nice man. Likes to help everyone, according to what Annie says." Settling back in her seat, Claire did her best to ignore the wooded area that came next. Even now, some six months after her brush with death in those very same woods, she still felt her pulse quicken and her hands begin to sweat at the memory. Instead, she looked ahead to the mailbox she knew came next — Miller.

The farm where Ben resided along with his parents and sister. For now . . .

"I think Benjamin has finally found his special someone," she said, taking in the land her friend helped farm. "Her name is Rebecca and she's Emma Stutzman's sister. I met her after Russ's funeral service. Esther had us over."

"And? Does she pass?"

"Pass?" she asked, shooting a sidelong glance at the detective.

"I know you, and I know how Esther is about you. Therefore, I suspect Rebecca had no inkling the invitation was a setup." He met her side eye with a grin. "So, I repeat, does she pass? Or, to put it more bluntly, is she good enough for him?"

She could feel the warmth starting in her cheeks and spreading outward. Only it wasn't from embarrassment, like she would have expected. No, it was yet another reminder of just how well Jakob knew her, how well they truly fit with each other . . . Instinctively, she reached for his hand, the answering feel of his skin against hers quieting her heart. "I think she's *perfect* for him."

"Then I look forward to meeting her when things settle down a bit."

They continued on until they came to Bontrager's farm on the right, and Eli and Esther's farm on the left. Jakob slowed the car in anticipation of Eli's driveway but swept his gaze across Bontrager's fields. "So, do you think the oldest son has gotten into any trouble today?"

"You mean Amos?" At his nod, she, too, looked out over the same ground, shaking her head as she did. "With everything I've heard from both Annie and Esther, I think the likelihood he *hasn't* gotten into trouble is slim to none."

Checking his rearview mirror, he slowed the car to a snail's pace. "*Esther* has stories about this kid, too?"

"Enough that she sought me out at the store today just to warn me."

"Warn you? About what?" With one last scan of the Bontrager farm, Jakob turned left into Eli's driveway and immediately released a quiet, peaceful sigh. "I don't know what it is about this farm that calms me but . . . wow."

"Maybe it has something to do with knowing you're about to see your niece?"

"That doesn't hurt, for sure. But I've always felt this way about this farm. Even back before Eli purchased it."

She started to ask the obvious *why* question, but stopped as her mind filled in the answer. Harley Zook, the farm's former owner, had lived in the same house Esther and Eli lived in now. Only he'd lived there alone — his brother a victim of the very hate crime that had prompted Jakob to leave the community in order to pursue police work. Never married, Harley had had a special fondness for the cows he housed in his barn, giving them names like Mary and Molly. Harley had tried to farm, tried to make a go of the dairy business, but his passion had been working with his hands. Somehow, despite being Amish, Harley had felt it his mission in life to champion Jakob to anyone who would listen, and even those who wouldn't. It hadn't done any good and had surely angered many of his Amish brethren along the way, but it had meant the world to Jakob.

Giving his hand one last squeeze, she took advantage of the last few moments of alone time to give voice to her feelings. "That calm you feel on this farm? I suspect that's the same calm I feel every time I pick up the phone to hear your voice, every time I see your name on a text, every time you walk into the shop, every time I see your car heading up the driveway at the inn, and every time I round the corner into your office and see you standing there, waiting for me. It's the most beautiful, most perfect sense of peace and happiness I've ever felt."

He rolled to a stop and shifted the car into park. "That's good because that's exactly how I feel when I hear your voice, read your words, see you smiling at me from behind the counter at the shop, see you sitting on your aunt's swing waiting for me when I pull up, and when I feel your arms around my neck after a long and tiring day."

"Then we match, I see." She leaned across the console to collect his kiss and then wiped at the tears escaping the outer corners of her eyes. "I love you, Jakob Fisher."

"I love you, too, Claire." He kissed her again and then splayed his hand toward the windshield and the house beyond. "Why don't you go inside and see Esther while I stop out at the barn for a few minutes? I'd like to see if Eli will talk to me about that young man from the pond. Assuming, of course, he doesn't mind me asking about a neighbor."

"We're talking about Eli, remember? He'll talk to you. Besides, after the goat poisoning incident, I'm pretty sure he'll have something to say."

"Goat poisoning incident?"

Quickly she brought him up to speed on Esther's goat, Giggles, and the suspected culprit behind the incident. Jakob, for his part, listened, his jaw tightening in anger with each passing word. When she got to the part that had brought Esther to the shop, he looked toward the barn. "And Eli? Does he know this part about Amos lurking behind the trees, watching Esther, Rebecca, and Miriam?"

"No. Esther was worried it might reignite Eli's anger, but I don't agree. I think he's a calmer man now with Esther and Sarah."

"Best not to find out if we don't have to." Jakob opened the door, stepped onto the driveway, and waited for Claire to do the same. "I'll catch up with you in a few minutes, okay?"

Nodding, she headed up the porch steps, her fatigue lightening as she neared the screen door. Inside, she could smell fresh bread being baked and hear Esther chatting with her newborn daughter about the garden and the cows and the dinner she would soon be making. It was, in a word, idyllic, and for a moment she simply stood in place, soaking it all in. When her stomach began to rumble in response to the smell, she knocked on the door's frame.

Soon, Esther was at the door, her eyes wide. "Claire? Is — is everything okay? Did Amos come to the inn?"

"No, sweetie, he didn't. I just have some money that I forgot to give you when you stopped by the shop earlier." She reached into her purse and pulled out the semifull envelope. "See? It was a very good few days."

"You didn't have to come all this way to give it to me. You could have just given it to me another day," Esther protested. "*After* you've gotten some sleep."

"I know, but this way is more fun."

Esther looked from Claire to the envelope and back again as understanding dawned across her face. "I know I was upset earlier, Claire, but you *know* now. Jakob will make sure you are okay." The young mother paused as her gaze traveled past Claire to her uncle's car. "You drove Jakob's car?"

"No. Jakob is here. He's just in the barn hoping to talk with Eli." Esther's answering gasp sent her rushing to correct her mistake. "Not about what you told me, sweetie!"

Esther's body practically folded in on itself in relief, leaving Claire to open the door and step inside. "We had an experience with Amos that was similar to what you told me about earlier. Only we were out at the pond and he was watching from the other side, sheltered by trees. So Jakob just wants to get Eli's thoughts on the boy, I think."

"I tried many times to tell Eli and the others that Amos would stop, that he would settle down soon. But I was wrong." Esther summoned Claire to follow her into the kitchen and over to Sarah's cradle. "I hope *she* will not have such a Rumspringa when she is bigger."

Claire squatted down beside the baby and

simply stared at the perfect little features — Eli's cheeks, Esther's eye shape, and a chin that somehow seemed to be a little bit of both. "Sarah won't be like that because Eli is not like John. He is kind and patient and welcoming. And while I don't know Amos's mother, I know that you are the sweetest person I have ever met. Sarah is very blessed to have you and Eli as her — oh, wait! I forgot something in the car."

Kissing the pad of her index finger, Claire touched it to Sarah's head and then stood. "Esther, something came into the store today that I think will be adorable on Sarah. However, being as short of sleep as I am, I left it in the car. So if you give me three minutes, I'll be right back to hold that precious little baby, okay?"

"Yah."

She retraced her steps back down the hallway and pushed open the door, a flash of movement beside the car catching her by surprise. Steadying herself against the porch rail, she looked out to see a young man in Amish garb taking off down the driveway in a sprint. A second flash of movement from the area of the barn revealed itself to be Jakob as he, too, took off in the same direction.

CHAPTER 28

Claire and Esther were standing at the base of the porch steps when, no more than three minutes later, Jakob returned with a red-faced Amos Bontrager. Eli walked beside them, breathing heavily.

"Eli? Are you okay?" Esther quickly stepped toward her husband. "I did not know where you went when Claire shouted."

"Eli looped around the other side of the barn and helped stop our friend here." Jakob clapped a hand across the back of Amos's collar and turned the teenager so he was facing Eli. "Young man, perhaps you'd like to explain to Eli what you were doing on his property for the second time in as many days."

Amos lifted his gaze from his boots to first Eli, and then Jakob. "It is not the second time."

"He is right," Esther said, folding her arms across her chest. "It is not his *second* time on this property."

Eli looked a question at his wife. "It is *Amos* who killed my goats, Esther. That makes two times."

The teenager drew back, his eyes wide. "I didn't kill your goats! I just gave them something different to drink."

Eli clenched his hands at his sides. "A drink they were not to have!"

"They looked thirsty to me." Shrugging, Amos tried to wriggle free of Jakob's hand but Jakob held firm. "Hey . . . Let me go."

"I'm not sure how familiar you are with the law, young man, but if Eli here wants to press charges for the loss of his goats, I can put some handcuffs on you right now."

Esther slid a glance in her husband's direction and then stepped forward. "What about for someone who is on a property that does not belong to him — watching three women from behind a tree?"

"Did the women feel unsafe?" Jakob prodded.

"Yah."

"Then, sure, that could potentially be a charge, as well." Jakob leaned forward in an attempt to establish eye contact with the Amish teen, but the boy looked away. Still, Jakob kept on, his words clearly designed to strike fear in a boy largely unfamiliar with the ways of the English world. "And if even *one* of those women were someone he's watched before, a case might even be made for stalking."

Eli took hold of Esther's arm and turned her toward him, the anger he'd exhibited only seconds earlier now seemingly on pause. "What have you not told me, Esther?"

Shame sent Esther's gaze plummeting, but not for long. "Amos was here yesterday, too. Standing just behind that tree" — she pointed their collective attention to the natural border separating their property from the English housing development. "It was while I was speaking with Rebecca and Miriam. He did not speak, he did not tell us he was there. When I saw him, I called to him. But he ran away."

"Why didn't you tell me?" Eli asked as his gaze shifted back to Amos.

"It was too much after the goats. I was afraid you would get angry."

Before Eli could respond, or maybe even fully process what his wife was saying, Jakob released his grip on Amos's collar and gave him a shove in the direction of the car. Amos, in turn, lifted his chin with an air of defiance. "I haven't done anything wrong. I am on Rumspringa. I am allowed to do as the English do."

"I'm English and *I* don't feed alcohol to goats." Jakob motioned for Claire to come closer. "Claire, you're English. Do *you* feed alcohol to goats?"

"No."

"The goats were thirsty!" Amos argued.

"Did Eli invite you to his property and ask you to care for his goats?"

Amos pulled a face. "No."

"Then you were trespassing, young man. That's a charge."

"I didn't mean for them to die!"

"Hold that thought for a minute and let's move on, shall we? Did Esther and Miriam invite you to stand under a tree on Esther's property and listen in on their conversation? And, while we're on the subject of Miriam, did she invite you to spy on her out at the pond the other day? Because that could be a stalking charge. And that's on *top* of the mailboxes you knocked down with your buddies earlier in the week. *That's* destruction of property . . ."

"But I am on Rumspringa!"

"And that means, what, exactly? That you can break the law?"

"Yah."

"No, son, it doesn't. Quite frankly, the rest of the world doesn't care one iota about

361

your Rumspringa." Jakob reached into his pocket for his notebook and pen. "Now, you are going to stay right there while I check with Eli and his wife about the possibility of pressing charges."

Claire remained silent as Jakob turned his attention to Eli and Esther, her gaze riveted on Amos. Twice, the boy darted a nervous eye at the detective and his neighbors. Twice, he peeked into the backseat of Jakob's car.

Curious, she stepped closer. "There are a lot of people who want the best for you, Amos. Good people who are worried about the choices you are making and the repercussions they could have on your life."

"I do not ask them to worry."

"People who care about you don't need to be *asked* to worry. They just do." Again, he looked through the back window of Jakob's car, and again she was waiting when he stopped. "Rumspringa is for experimenting — wearing English clothes and listening to English music, not harming animals and making people feel unsafe."

"I can wear English clothes and listen to English music later . . . *after* Rumspringa."

"No, Amos, you can't," Jakob said, rejoining the conversation. "Not if you're baptized."

Amos leaned forward just enough to gain a clear view of both Jakob and Eli. "If I am quiet and find good hiding places, I can. But I will have better hiding places that no one will find."

"Hiding places for what?" Claire asked.

"English clothes when I am dressed as Amish, Amish clothes when I am dressed as English, and the music I will listen to when I go into the English world." Amos hooked his thumb toward the back door of the car. "But I wouldn't put that tattoo on *both* of my ankles. I would —"

Claire's answering gasp accompanied Jakob to the back window and its view of the report bearing Margaret Mallory's Powerful Peg tattoo. With barely a moment to breathe, let alone think, Jakob yanked open the back door, pulled out the sheet containing the image of the tattoo, and held it up in front of Amos. "Have you *seen* this tattoo on someone?"

"Yah."

"And it's on both ankles?" he barked.

"Yah. But one is new."

Without thinking, Claire grabbed the boy's arm and squeezed. "Who did you see it on, Amos? Tell us."

"The one who hides her clothes in a box under the big green bush near the pond.

The one who takes off her kapp and shakes her hair around. The one who does not look to see if there is glass around when she changes shoes. The one who was here talking to her" — he pointed at Esther — "and at the pond talking to *you.*"

"At the pond talking to . . ." The rest of her sentence faded away as Amos's words delivered up the new face of Margaret Mallory.

CHAPTER 29

Claire was waiting on the porch swing when she saw his sedan pull into the driveway, the sense of calm the sight brought rivaled only by anticipation of the news she'd been waiting to hear for the past twenty-four hours.

Yes, she knew Amos had led them to the minidress and hoop earrings they'd seen Lauri's friend wearing in the video footage from Murphy's. Claire had been standing right beside Jakob when he parted the branches of the very bush Amos had described . . .

Yes, she knew the FBI had been summoned. She'd seen their dark cars driving down Lighted Way en masse throughout the day . . .

Yes, she knew Amos was proud of himself for helping to finger a murder suspect. And yes, she knew he'd finally sat down with Eli and Bishop Hershberger for a heart-to-heart that had him apologizing for his actions and vowing to be better. Annie had shared that when she'd come in shortly before lunch, eyes wide, eager to hear more details from Claire . . .

Claire, in turn, had managed to deduce a few things on her own — pieces of the puzzle that had fallen into place as she'd stared at the ceiling above her bed, waiting for sleep that should have been easy but had proven otherwise.

Margaret Mallory's last known sighting had her in Adam's County, a largely Amish community in Indiana. Near as Claire could figure, Margaret must have seen the item in the *Budget* that spoke of Barley's illness and need for assistance in his final days. Taking a chance, the criminal came to Heavenly, invented the name *Miriam Mast,* and pretended to be the dying man's niece. Since Barley was in the final stages of what sounded like Alzheimer's or dementia anyway, it hadn't raised any eyebrows when he didn't know her. Margaret subsequently bided her time until Barley's death and then simply stayed on, living in a world no one ever thought to suspect.

The sound of Jakob's car door cut through her thoughts and she stood, her mouth stretching wide with what Aunt Diane had recently dubbed her *Jakob smile.* Crossing to the steps, she met him with the hug she'd been wanting to give him all day. For several moments neither spoke and that was okay. The intensity of his answering hug said what mattered most.

After a long while, he stepped back, laced his fingers inside hers, and led her back to the swing. When they were settled on the cushion and he'd found their favorite pace, he draped his arm across the back. "I just came from Callie's place."

"How is she?"

"Relieved, I guess. Knowing what happened and why has made it so she can focus solely on grieving her dad. It doesn't bring him back, unfortunately, but it'll hopefully pave the way to some healing. At least I hope it will . . . for both of us." His gaze skirted beyond hers toward the very countryside that had played host to his own childhood. "Margaret Mallory was living right here for almost nine months and I never knew. I passed her on the street. I said hello to her in the aisle of Gussman's about four months ago and she smiled and said hello back."

Slowly, he brought his eyes back to Claire's. "I remember being surprised that she spoke to me. But then I chalked it up to her not knowing my history and therefore not knowing I was under the ban."

"Whoa." She stopped the swing. "Are you trying to say you should have known who she was from the start?"

"Russ knew within minutes of her arriving at Murphy's."

"Because he saw her tattoo, Jakob! A tattoo that was hidden inside a boot when she was living her life as Miriam Mast."

"Yeah, but —"

"There are no buts." She captured his face in her hands and tilted her forehead to his. "They robbed *a bank,* Jakob. That means federal agents have been looking for them for years. And they didn't know she was here, in Heavenly, either."

"That's what Agent Adams said, too," he murmured.

"So listen to him. Please. And give yourself props for solving two crimes."

His head nodded against hers. "Yeah, he said that, too."

"I like this Agent Adams person."

His laugh was followed by a kiss on the tip of her nose. "Yeah, well, *I* like *you.* A lot."

"I'm glad." She sat back against the swing. "Now, tell me the rest."

"The rest?"

She made a face. "Ha, ha."

"Oh, you mean about the case?" he teased.

"No, I was really more concerned with what you had for lunch today."

"That's easy. Pizza." He stopped, lifted his chin, and sniffed. "And maybe, if I'm lucky, Diane will have enough of that beef stew I'm smelling that I'll get a bowl or two."

"Jakob . . ."

"I'm serious. Do you not smell that?"

She gave in to the eye roll his antics warranted. "Of course I smell it, I'm the one making it."

"Oh?"

"In light of everything that went on yesterday, Bill and Diane decided to go on their date this evening, instead."

"So my beef-stew-eating fate is in *your* hands?"

"You're darn straight it is. Which is why you better start talking, Detective."

He held up his hands in surrender. "Okay, okay . . . Well, for starters, it wasn't Margaret who killed Russ."

Toeing the ground, she halted their motion midswing. *"Phil Maxwell?"*

"Also known as Elmer Mast — yes."

"Elmer? But he was so . . . *nice.* So *genuine.*"

"Funny thing is, this place did that for him."

"I don't understand."

Jakob rose to his feet and wandered over to the front railing. "He came here with Miriam, looking for a place to hide. But as the days wore on, he realized he liked living a plain life. He liked the peace and the quiet. He liked the people. And he liked what it felt like to earn respect."

"Like having his name given as a potential minister?" she prodded.

"His face actually *glowed* when he spoke of that in his interrogation today. Seems our Elmer had something of an awful childhood. He spent years in the foster care system, moving from home to home until he was old enough to be on his own. And by the time he was, he felt so unloved, he lived his life that way. But living here, posing as Amish, he felt as if people saw him differently — like he had something to offer. Having his name given by multiple people for the minister spot really affected him. Said he was determined right then and there to prove himself worthy of their trust."

She splayed her hands in confusion. "By *murdering* someone?"

"When Miriam came home from Murphy's that night, she told Elmer they needed to pack up and get out. But he didn't want to go. He wanted to stay. He wanted to farm Barley's land, help his new friends, and live the kind of life he'd never had before. But to do that, he knew he had to get rid of Russ.

"Since Miriam had managed to get hold of that note about Russ's call without Lauri seeing it, Elmer knew he had to act fast. A quick search of the Internet on Miriam's phone led them to Callie's house. He was heading toward the main house when Russ must have heard something and came outside."

"The main house?" she echoed, midgasp. Jakob nodded.

"That's right. The main house."

"But that's where Callie and the kids were!"

"What happened that night could have been so much worse if Russ hadn't come outside when he did."

It was a lot to take in, a lot to imagine. Still, she was able to process enough to eke out a "wow."

"I know." Crossing back to the swing, Jakob held out his hand, pulled her to her feet, and wrapped her in his arms. "Russ was the ultimate cop until his last dying breath."

"Oh, Jakob, he'd be so very proud of you."

Jakob's breath felt warm as he lingered his kiss against her hair. "I'd like to believe that, I really would."

"Don't just believe it . . . *know* it."

ABOUT THE AUTHOR

Laura Bradford is the national bestselling author of the Amish Mystery series, including *A Churn for the Worse* and *Suspendered Sentence,* as well as the Emergency Dessert Squad Mystery series.